THE MOSCOW BRIEF

KJ KALIS

Published by:

BDM, LLC

ALSO BY K.J. KALIS:

New titles released regularly!

If you'd like to join my mailing list and be the first to get updates on new books and exclusive sales, giveaways and releases, click here!

I'll send you a prequel to the next series FREE!

OR

Visit my Amazon page to see a full list of current titles.

OR

Take a peek at my website to see a full list of available books.

www.kjkalis.com

1

"Easy, girl," Travis said, putting a hand on the mare's neck as he lifted her half-filled water bucket off of the hook on the wall of her stall. He slid the stall door closed behind him trying not to slosh water on his jeans as he carried it outside. Just beyond the last set of stalls, six other water buckets were waiting for him. In the Texas heat, the standing water became scummy and slimy in no time flat. It was one of his weekly chores to haul all the water buckets out of the stalls and take them outside, giving them a good scrub and replacing them with fresh water.

As Travis bent over to pick up the first bucket, swinging it off to the side and then tossing the water away onto the dry ground, he felt a drop of sweat roll down the side of his face, his arms burning from the heavy buckets. The fall had brought cooler temperatures to Texas, but the physical labor of working in the barn nearly always made him sweat. And the work never stopped. There were always chores to be done with the horses, feeding and medications to be doled out, horses that needed to see the vet, other ones that simply needed a good run in the pasture or some exercise under the saddle.

Travis walked back inside the barn after dumping all of the water buckets, turned on the spigot to the hose outside and grabbed a long scrub brush from the tack room that hung on the wall with some soap.

The physical labor of working in the barn somehow set his mind in order, the memories that chased him from his time in Delta Force settling down into an order that made sense as he worked. He picked up the spray nozzle and hosed out the interior of each one of the buckets, making sure to get the last bits of soap out of them, dragging his fingers along the inside to make sure there was no algae buildup left inside. Horses were expensive, and even more so if they got sick. His vet, Dr. Wiley, did what he could to help keep the costs down, but with the number of horses at Bishop Ranch, vet bills were an ugly reality.

Just as Travis finished hosing out the last bucket and refilling it with water, he saw a dust trail about a mile out from where he was standing outside the barn. He stopped for a second, adjusting the baseball hat on his head, narrowing his eyes as he stared off in the distance, his eyes locked on the driveway. The position of the barn and the house on the flat piece of land gave him several minutes of warning anytime someone approached. It was one of the reasons he'd bought the property in the first place. It gave him a tactical advantage, one that most people didn't bother to think about. But he did. Always.

Lugging two of the clean water buckets back into the barn, Travis took them into the stalls where they belonged and hung them back on the thick metal hooks that kept them in place, the horses nudging at him with their muzzles as he did as if offering a thank you for the clean water. Travis turned around, looking at one of the horses. He was a bay gelding, a purebred quarter horse with a dark brown coat and a white star on his forehead, and one white sock just above his right front hoof.

"You're welcome, Smokey," Travis muttered under his breath. He took a second to rub the horse's neck. "Looks like we have a visitor. I'll be back in a minute."

Latching Smokey's door closed, Travis walked quickly to the tack room, checking the window as he walked by. The dust trail from the driveway was getting closer. Passing the lines of saddles and bridles, he pushed open the door to the small ranch office at the back of the tack room. The office was spare with only a desk he'd salvaged from a flea market, a ladder-back chair, and a black, four-drawer filing cabinet in it. But it had two windows — one that faced out into the parking area and one that faced into the indoor arena. There was no one riding in the arena at the moment. He slid behind his desk, pulling a set of keys out of his pocket. He unlocked the top drawer and pulled out a pistol already loaded with nine-millimeter rounds in a holster. Separating the two parts, Travis clipped the holster to his side, checking the pistol to make sure it was loaded and ready to fire. He slid it into the holster and lifted the hem of his flannel shirt over the top of it to cover. Locking the drawer, he stuffed the keys into his pocket. He wasn't expecting any company, at least not today. From what he'd seen of the dust trail, whoever was driving didn't come to the ranch much, if at all. They were traveling too fast. Probably fast enough that they'd hit one or more of the potholes that hadn't been repaired on the driveway. Hopefully, that would slow them down a bit.

Travis walked out of the office, closing the door behind him. He stopped in the tack room for a moment, thinking. His eyes glanced over the saddles that were hung on wood pegs jutting out from the wall, the bridles on their hooks on the opposite wall, the reins looped over the top of each. Every saddle was covered by a saddle pad, the smell of damp leather and horse sweat never really leaving the barn. Three buckets of grooming tools -- brushes, hoof picks, and shedding blades -- were positioned next to the doorway. Travis considered getting in his truck and using the back driveway to leave, but by the speed of the car that was approaching, whoever was coming had already seen the truck out at the barn. There was no point in trying to avoid whoever it was. They were coming and likely knew his position already. Walking back down the aisle toward the half-scrubbed buckets of water, Travis straightened his shoulders and shook his head, tension filling his chest. He wasn't a fan of distractions, particularly ones that were uninvited. And that's exactly what this one felt like.

2

Travis had two more water buckets scrubbed and refilled by the time the car pulled up in front of the barn. Whoever had been driving it stopped at the house first, banging their fist on the door loud enough he could hear it where he was standing outside. There was no one at home to answer the door. The car started up with a rumble, leaving another dust cloud as they headed towards the stable. Travis heard the sound of hooves trotting on dry ground and glanced to his right. One of the horses was out in the corral nearby, getting some much-needed sunshine. He started trotting toward the back of the corral when he saw the oncoming car, spooked by the speed of their approach, "It's okay, Buddy," Travis called. The last thing he needed was one of the horses jumping the fence.

Travis kept working while the car parked. He glanced at it, but knew more about it than most people did about their own car without even looking. It was a newer brown sedan, American-made, four doors, Texas license plates with a green rental sticker in the lower left-hand corner of the windshield. The tires were newer, which told Travis the car didn't have much mileage on it. There was a single person inside; unless other people were hunkered down where he couldn't see them. But Travis guessed that wasn't the case, as he bent over to continue scrubbing the last two water buckets. If there were people hiding in the car, whoever was driving certainly wouldn't have approached the house and barn on the mile-long driveway leaving what looked like an obvious tornado of dust and grit behind them. Whoever was driving might as well have sent up a flare to let Travis know they were arriving. No, this wasn't an ambush, at least not in the way Travis thought of it.

Travis held the hose nozzle in his hand as he refilled the buckets, waiting for the person to get out of the car. His training was already two steps ahead of him. He switched the hose nozzle to his left hand, giving him the freedom to pull his pistol with his right if he needed to. Spraying someone with water was certainly a good distraction. It might buy him a half a second or so to draw his pistol and eliminate whatever threat had come in the sedan.

The door to the sedan creaked open. Travis saw a pair of tennis shoes under the edge of the car door, the blue denim cuffs resting on top. As the head and shoulders popped out of the vehicle Travis closed his eyes for a second and shook his head, "No," he called, loud enough for the person getting out of the car to hear him. "Whatever you've come here for, the answer is no."

"Now, is that a nice way to greet one of your oldest friends?" The man slammed the car door behind him.

"It is when you come out to my ranch uninvited. And you aren't one of my closest friends. Let's get that right." Travis grunted, bending over and picking up the two water buckets he'd just finished cleaning. He walked back into the barn leaving the man outside. "You can turn that rental car right around and go back the way you came, Gus. I'm not interested."

"But you haven't even heard what I have to say."

"I don't need to," Travis glanced over his shoulder. He lugged the water buckets down the aisle about halfway, leaving one outside of a door while he installed the other one in the stall of a gray mare. He gave her a little pat on the neck before stepping out and closing the door behind him. He did the same across the aisle.

"Come on, Travis. At least look at me. I traveled a long way to get here."

Gus had followed Travis down the aisle. Travis stopped to look at him. Gus had on what Travis called a city slicker outfit — an expensive-looking, white T-shirt with a navy sport coat over it, dark denim jeans, a matching belt with a gold buckle, and some sort of fancy black patent leather tennis shoes Travis was sure were all the rage. He wouldn't know. Gus had the same scraggly beard and clipped hair he'd had when Travis had seen him last, five years ago. It looked like he'd gone to one of those off-brand hair salons and they'd forgotten to cut half of it, but Travis knew better. Gus had probably spent a pretty penny to have the latest messy hairstyle. He looked like he was in good shape, probably still running every day. Gus was never that big, a good two or three inches shorter than Travis's six-foot-two frame, and definitely not as muscular. Gus was more the scrappy type. "All right, I've looked at you. You look fine. Now you can leave."

Travis took two steps, passing Gus, wanting to finish up delivering the last couple of water buckets into the stable before it was time to start riding the horses he had in training. Gus reached out and grabbed Travis's arm as he walked by. Travis whirled around, swinging his forearm up and knocking Gus's hand away. "Don't touch me," he hissed.

Gus held his hands up and took a step back, "Sorry. I forgot you are touchy like that. Not literally, though," Gus smirked.

Travis walked away, feeling the heat crawl up the back of his neck. He wasn't a touchy-feely person. Never had been.

He'd spent most of his childhood in foster care, ripped away from the house he knew when his mom died. His heart had broken that day and become shuttered off from the rest of him. His new foster family hadn't helped. The foster parents had been more interested in taking the money the government gave them and spending it on alcohol instead of the kids they were supposed to be fostering. Travis spent months trying to avoid nightly beatings when his foster dad, a man named Richard, got drunk. After eight months of it, Travis escaped from the foster home one night, taking what he had in a beat-up backpack and living on the streets until he could join the Army. He'd never seen or heard from his foster parents since. He was sure by now they were either dead or in jail. It didn't matter to him which one, only that they were out of his life.

Stepping out into the afternoon sunshine, Travis walked to the two remaining water buckets, running water in them. He could feel Gus's eyes on the back of his neck. "Listen, man. I'm sorry. Didn't mean to overstep. And I probably should've given you a call before I came out here."

Travis nodded, grabbing the last two water buckets, one in each hand, walking carefully down the concrete aisle trying not to spill any of the water, "Yeah, that would've been nice."

Gus smiled, "But then again, what's the fun in that? I know how much you love surprises."

Gus was acting like he was a lost kitten, following Travis, hoping for some scrap. Travis wasn't in the mood. "I don't like surprises. You know that."

"But even if I called you, you probably wouldn't have answered, and last I checked, your voicemail was full."

Travis didn't bother to respond. He took the last two water buckets into the stalls, hooking them back in place. He grabbed a red halter and a lead and walked to one of the stalls, flipping the metal latch open and stepping inside. "Come here, girl," he said to the chestnut mare inside. "I bet you'd like to go outside for a little while, huh?"

Travis slid the stall door open, leading the mare out into the aisle, her hooves making a clomping noise as she followed Travis down the concrete and outside. Travis glanced back at her. She had some sawdust on her back; like she'd been laying down in her freshly clean stall before he'd interrupted her nap. Gus jumped off to the side as they passed. Travis barely glanced at him. He was doing his best to ignore the fact that Gus was still in the barn being a pest.

Walking out into the sunshine, Travis led the mare past the wet patch of dirt where he'd been scrubbing the water buckets. He got to the fence, looking at the mare, "Whoa," he said. Opening the gate, he led the mare inside, turning her around to face him. He unclipped the throat latch of the halter and slipped it off over her ears. The big mare wheeled around on her hind legs and took off at a gallop, kicking her heels in a single buck before darting toward the gray gelding already in the corral.

As Travis closed the corral gate, he stood for a second, hanging the red halter and lead nearby so he could more easily collect the horses in an hour or so. They still had their evening exercise to do in the arena, but a little time outside in the sunshine helped to work the edge off of them before it was time for training.

Looking to his left, Travis saw Gus. His forearms were across the top rail of the fence, staring at the horses. "Those are some beautiful creatures. What are their names?"

The soft pedal approach. Travis almost called Gus out on his change in tactic. Gus tried barging in. That didn't work. He tried joking around. That also didn't work. Gus was on to his third option they'd been taught to build rapport, which was the soft pedal. He would try to get Travis talking, which would open the door to a conversation that would hopefully end up in

Travis doing whatever it was that Gus wanted him to do. Travis pressed his lips together. "The gray gelding, his name is Buddy. The other one — the chestnut mare — her name is Scarlett."

"Was that Kira's horse?" The words came out slowly; as if Gus was measuring each syllable.

Travis nodded. A flood of memories came back to him. Travis turned back toward the corral, watching Buddy and Scarlett trot together and then stop and touch noses, Scarlett squealing trying to get Buddy to join her in a game of running in circles around the corral. Buddy happily obliged, the two of them kicking up a ton of dust and dirt that would have to be brushed off of them later. It was good to let them be themselves for a while, Travis thought, wishing that Gus would do the same. "Yes. She was Kira's."

"How long has it been now?" Gus asked.

"Five years." A lump formed in Travis's throat. He hadn't heard Kira Pozreva's name in a long time. He bought the ranch just before she died. They'd had plans to get married in the backyard and then train and raise reining horses together. About a month before they were both due to leave the CIA, Kira had been sent on her final operation in Ecuador. She hadn't come back. Travis had kept the farm — it was his dream anyway — and raised the filly he'd bought for her as an early wedding present. Before she left on her mission, she'd given the filly the name Scarlett. She'd always loved the movie, "Gone with the Wind." Travis blinked, watching Scarlett in the corral, a memory surfacing of a night when Kira hadn't come back into the house after feeding the horses. He'd gone out at about ten o'clock wondering what was taking so long, only to find Kira curled up on a makeshift pile of saddle blankets in the corner of Scarlett's stall, the filly newly weaned from her mama. Kira was fast asleep next to the door. So was the filly, her nose nearly touching Kira's hand as they both slept.

Gus's voice broke through the onslaught of Travis's memories, "So, I hear you have a little side business going?"

Travis stared at the ground and blinked. He knew Gus well enough to know that at some point, Gus would tell him why he'd come the whole way out to the ranch. It wasn't a social call, not if Gus knew about his business. Whatever reason Gus had for visiting, Travis wasn't sure he was ready to hear about it yet. "You could say that."

"Skip tracing? What is that?"

Travis didn't bother turning towards Gus. He kept his eyes locked on the horses. The horses were his future. Gus was his past. He preferred to keep it that way. "It's like being a private investigator. Except I only look for things that have been lost. I don't go after bail jumpers or anything like that. I look for people and things that have skipped town and need to be found and brought back. It's pretty simple."

"Like what?"

Travis sighed. Gus's ploy to get him talking was working. "Well, a few weeks ago, I found a truckload of cattle that had been stolen a couple of counties over. The owner was grateful."

Gus raised his eyebrows and started to laugh, "Are you kidding me? That's how you're spending your time now? What do you do – stay out here watching the horses run around, clean water buckets, and then occasionally find a load of cattle or donkeys or mules or whatever? That's not very exciting, if you ask me."

Travis felt the blood run up the back of his neck. Everything in him wanted to ball up his fist and apply it to Gus's jaw and send the guy packing, but he knew Gus was trying to bait him. "It's quiet, peaceful. After the stuff I've done —"

"We've done..." Gus curled his lip.

Travis shot Gus a look, "We've done... I like it that way." Travis pushed himself away from the fence turning towards Gus, "Look, I have no idea why you are here. Personally, I don't care. I'm glad to know you're still upright and kicking, but it's time for you to go. I've got work to do." Travis turned and walked away, heading back toward the barn. He needed to start getting the first horse tacked up for training. His assistant would be arriving soon.

"You aren't the least bit curious why I'm here?" Gus called after him.

"Not really."

Travis was halfway back to the barn when he heard Gus's voice call to him, "Elena is missing."

Travis stopped where he was standing. His shoulders dropped and he looked at the ground for a second before turning around. He narrowed his eyes, "What did you say?"

Gus walked toward him, his hands stuffed in the pockets of his expensive jeans. "You heard me. I said, Elena is missing."

3

"You are kidding me," Travis grunted.

"No, I'm not," Gus protested.

In the background, Travis could see Buddy and Scarlett had calmed down. They were edging their muzzles out underneath the bottom rail of the fence to nibble at some wisps of grass that hadn't dried to a crisp. Travis didn't say anything else to Gus. He turned and kept walking toward the barn. There was a schedule to keep. If Gus wanted to talk, he'd have to keep up. Travis motioned with his hand for Gus to join him.

"Did you hear me?" Gus stopped just outside of the stall door that Travis had dodged into. Travis pulled a halter over the face and ears of the black gelding named Joker. He walked the horse out of the stall and passed Gus, putting him in the crossties, carefully clipping each side of the halter to the ropes at the side of the wall. "I heard you. I'm thinking."

"Thinking about what?"

"About the fact that you're kind of a jerk."

Gus laughed, "I know that already." His face became serious, "I wouldn't have come except she's gone, Travis. We can't find her."

Travis turned towards Gus as he brushed sawdust off of the horse's back before setting a saddle pad over the top of him, "And somehow you think a simple skip tracer from Texas is going to be able to find her?"

"Very funny. You know I wouldn't be here if I didn't think you could. And, you know her."

At least Gus was right about one thing. Travis had worked with Elena Lobranova for the last three years of his stint with the CIA after leaving the Army's Delta Force. He could see her in his mind as he went into the tack room and grabbed a saddle and a pad, swinging it up onto Joker's back. Elena was short and blonde. She had a gymnast's build, muscular for someone with her slight frame. She used to laugh that when she lived in Russia her parents wanted her to become the next Russian gymnastics star, maybe even an Olympian like Olga Korbut, but once she hit five foot two, no coach was interested in her. Too tall. Reaching down to tighten the girth on the saddle, a smile tugged at Travis's face. He remembered after an operation, Travis and Elena had found themselves standing in a field, not much different from the fields outside of his ranch. She'd been so excited it was over that she did a backflip in the air, surprising him. They both laughed, waiting for the helicopter to come and retrieve them. Travis looked back at Gus. "What happened?"

As the words came out of Travis's mouth, he heard a truck pull up out front. It was his assistant, Ellie. A second later, he saw the young woman walk into the barn, her jeans slung low on her hips with a wide leather belt and a big silver belt buckle holding them up, a T-shirt tucked into the waist with a flannel shirt over the top. She had her blonde hair in a ponytail with a baseball hat perched on top of her head. "Afternoon, Travis." Travis watched as she eyed up Gus. She didn't say anything to him.

"Want me to take Joker and get him warmed up?" Ellie said.

After slipping the bridle over Joker's ears, Travis handed the reins to Ellie. "Yeah. Work him through some small circles in both directions, especially to the left. He's not flexing in his back for his rollbacks and spins as well as I would like. I'll be in to take over in a few minutes and then you can get the next one saddled up."

"Roger that." Ellie led the black gelding away.

Gus raised his eyebrows, "Friendly."

"She doesn't know you."

"Well, she could have at least said hello."

Travis raised his eyebrows, "Like I said, she doesn't know you. She's like that."

"You mean she's like you." The words were meant to sting and they did. Travis remembered why he didn't like Gus. He turned, taking two steps forward, squaring off on the man, "Okay, Gus. You've wasted enough of my time. What's going on?"

"I told you. Elena is missing."

"What does that have to do with me? Why are you here? You go find her. She still works for the CIA, right?"

"Yes, but we've tried. She's disappeared without a trace."

"How long ago?"

Gus stared at the ground as if he felt guilty. "She went dark seventy-two hours ago. Completely off-the-grid. There's been no trace of her or any of her alternate identities anywhere. The guys at Langley are going nuts."

"And whose bright idea was it to come out here and bother me?"

"Mine, actually," Gus said, stuffing his hands in his pockets again. He glanced down the aisle toward the arena door and then back at Travis, "Listen, Travis. In all seriousness, I know you've got a good thing going here. It's not my goal to mess it up for you, but the reality is that we need to find Elena. And no matter how many resources the CIA has, you're the one that knows her the best. You can think like she does. If anybody can find her, it's going to be you."

Travis shrugged, "What if she doesn't want to be found?"

"That's not an option." Gus stared at the ground, shaking his head, his words firm.

"Why?"

"Because she's been working on a case and she's gotten intel about something that's been going on. Might be a possible invasion by Russia into the Georgian state, and soon. We need the intel that she's gathered."

"That sounds like a job for the DIA, not me." Travis knew the Defense Intelligence Agency was in charge of dealing with all of the incoming information on the intelligence side that informed the branches of the military, the President, and the Joint Chiefs, not to mention the National Security Agency and the CIA.

"Believe me, they're working on finding her too. The real reason I'm here is that I found out last night that the Russians have initiated a kill order on Elena."

Travis frowned, a shiver running up his spine. Russian hit squads were no joke. They were trained members of the KGB, now called the FSB or SVR, usually former special forces, much like him. But unlike him, they had no humanity and asked no questions. They were interested in dropping bodies assigned to them and that was it. "Are you kidding me?"

"I wish I was. We got the information from a reliable source in the Kremlin. Apparently whatever Elena has been able to dig up has rattled some cages in Moscow. They aren't happy with the leak. I imagine we will be hearing about some notable people committing suicide within the next week or so, but in the meantime, the problem is we don't know where Elena is or exactly what kind of information she has for that matter. Whatever it is, though, it's serious enough that the Kremlin has decided to act."

Travis sucked in a breath. He knew what Gus was referring to when he was talking about a rash of suicides. One of the KGB's favorite techniques for eliminating people was stealing them from their homes late at night and shooting them, then throwing them off a bridge. The local police knew to turn their heads when the body washed up on shore and quickly chalk it up as a suicide. There had been a rash of them during Travis's time with the CIA. He scratched the side of his face. "I don't know, Gus. I've been out of the game for a while."

"There's another issue. Given the fact Elena went dark, some people back at Langley are beginning to believe Elena is part of the problem, not the solution."

"Like she's a traitor?"

"Exactly."

4

———

"There's no way she's a traitor," Travis said, shaking his head.

Gus shrugged, "I know that. I'm only telling you what other people are telling me."

The way Gus said it made Travis wonder what Gus was really thinking. "You don't seriously believe she's switched sides, do you? I mean, this is Elena we are talking about, Gus. She's saved both of our hides on more than one occasion."

"Yeah, but things change." He looked at the ground for a second, "Listen, I don't want to get lost in the weeds on this. All I know is she's gone dark with some valuable information — information that both the CIA and the KGB want. That's put a target on her back. We've gotta try to bring her in before the Russians get to her. The clock is ticking. You know as well as I do the longer the KGB is on her trail, the better the odds are they're going to find her and kill her. Are you in or out?"

Travis pressed his lips together. If it was anyone else, it would be easy to walk away. He certainly wouldn't help because it was Gus asking. But it was Elena. He'd never seen any glimmer in her personality that told him she could become a traitor. Nothing. It was the farthest thing from his mind. He thought about her out on her own, running for her life. Where was she? Was she safe? It was no joke to have the KGB and the CIA hunting you at the same time. Whatever information she'd gone dark with must be valuable, maybe even more valuable than Gus had told him. Gus was known for his peddling of half-truths. It was possible Elena was injured or even already dead. A shiver ran down his spine, thinking of Elena's lifeless, bloody body dumped on the side of the road somewhere. In his entire career, Travis had never left anyone behind. It wasn't the time to start now.

Gus interrupted his thoughts, "Here's the thing, though. If you decide you're going to help track her, and you find her and bring her in, the CIA will make a nice donation to your farm here, or your ranch, or whatever you call it. We'll call it a fee for your skip tracing services. But it's Moscow rules."

Travis gave a short nod as the words sunk in. Moscow rules. The phrase meant the same thing to anyone who worked in the spy business — everyone is a potential threat no matter what side they were on.

Gus continued, "If you step off this property with the intention of going to find Elena then you will attract the attention of the KGB, or whatever they are calling themselves now, and anyone in the CIA who's been tasked with finding her. Heck, you'll probably end up on a kill list." Gus chuckled, "You can join me. I'm sure I'm already on it."

Travis shoved his hands in his pockets, staring at the ground. He kicked at a stray piece of straw with the toe of his boot and looked up, drawing a deep breath, smelling the hay and the sawdust and the sweet smell of the grain floating through the barn. He'd worked so hard to build a quiet life. With Gus showing up, it was like watching everything he'd built tumble to the ground, like a stack of canned goods clattering down on a grocery store floor. He could feel part of himself tumble with it. Gus was right. He could tell Gus to walk away and Gus probably would argue with him for another five or ten minutes and then he would. Travis would probably never see him again. And that was okay. Travis knew Gus showing up here wasn't out of the goodness of his heart. Gus wanted something. Gus always wanted something. It was one of the reasons he'd walked away from the CIA when he did. Travis was tired of trying to deal with everyone's agenda. He swallowed. No matter how he felt about Gus, the part that didn't sit well with him was knowing that Elena was on the run, needing help, with people from two powerful government agencies chasing her and not having anywhere to turn. The knot in his gut told him that turning his back on her wasn't a decision he could live with.

"I'm in."

5

E lena had tucked the short ends of her blonde hair under the Army officer's hat as she slung the backpack up over her shoulders. The hallways of Camp Swift were quiet. With most of the soldiers at dinner or done for the day, there were only a few left walking up the maze of beige painted passages through the base. Elena turned a corner, glancing up at a fluorescent light buzzing overhead as two privates passed her. They stopped and saluted. Elena saluted back awkwardly, not used to having that kind of attention. As soon as they passed, she ducked her head and moved quickly as she wove her way through the building, feeling the tightness of the pants across her hips and thighs. They were half a size too small for her, but it was what she could find in a hurry. She needed the uniform to acquire the last piece of intelligence for the brief, which was now safely loaded onto her laptop.

Stepping outside into the cool night air, she turned to her left as a military police vehicle stopped in front of the building, four armed officers running in the front door. They were there for her. She was sure of it. She swallowed, grateful for the fact that the sun had already gone down. How they had found out about the breach in the intelligence hub, she wasn't sure.

Elena walked as rapidly as she could without attracting attention, taking off the hat dodging behind the building, and sticking to the murky shadows. There was surveillance everywhere on the base. She had to get clear of it, and fast.

Hugging the side of the building, Elena ran to the parking lot. At the loading docks, she found a white van with its engine running, the driver was absent as he made a delivery to the building. She gingerly closed the back van doors and slipped inside, trying to move silently, throwing the van into gear and pulling away. Watching the rearview mirror, she saw a man run out wearing coveralls, waving and yelling at her and then pointing as if he was talking to someone else. "Shoot!" she muttered under her breath. All she needed was another minute and she would have gotten away clean. Not this time. Every single time someone saw her, the people chasing her closed the gap. She needed distance, and distance fast if she hoped to get away.

Stepping on the accelerator, Elena drove down the service road that led away from Camp Swift. Most people thought it was a small Army training facility, but it was much more than that. In the bowels of the building, she'd found a DCS-run intelligence hub that rivaled the one at Langley. Connecting to the Defense Clandestine Service servers, she was able to get the final piece of information she needed for the brief.

Trying not to get lost in her thoughts, Elena focused on the road. On the outskirts of the military installation, there was a small private airfield, not one the Army owned. From watching it for the last couple of days, she knew the Army used it on occasion, shuttling officers in and out of the base when their own landing strips were being used by fighter jets for practice. It was also the perfect cover for moving Agency assets in and out of the area, plus people and items the military might like to not have tracked so easily. She pressed on the accelerator a little harder, hearing the engine from the van rev. If the MPs had arrived at the building already, it wouldn't be long before they figured out she'd taken the delivery van. And then they'd be hot on her tail again.

Elena glanced at the backpack on the passenger seat, and then back at the road. She couldn't let the laptop fall into the wrong hands. Not if she had any choice about it. She knew she was risking everything, including her life and her career not going directly to the CIA, but what she'd found was a danger to the entire Western world. And, there were lingering questions in her mind about who she could trust. She swallowed. Fear nipped at her gut. She didn't have time to be afraid. She focused on the road in front of her, gripping the steering wheel tighter. The entrance to the airfield was just up ahead. She checked the rearview mirror, her eyes wide, scanning every angle she could find, her heart pounding in her chest. No headlights. That was good.

Taking the next right turn hard enough the van's tires squealed on the road, Elena jammed on the brakes and ditched the van just inside of the fence line for the airport. Hopefully leaving it a good distance away from the planes would keep anyone from following her, or at least buy her a few minutes while they searched it. Scooping up the backpack, she slung it over her shoulders and started running across the tarmac, headed for the buildings.

From her visit to the property the day before, she knew the airport had lax security, or at least more lax than it should have been given the proximity to the Army base. She managed to walk around for nearly an hour and a half looking at planes before anyone had even greeted her. That told her more than she needed to know. Coupled with the fact that there were no surveillance cameras anywhere in sight, told her that the little airport was being used for a lot more than only flying lessons.

Located so close to Camp Swift, it was a perfect transport point for CIA agents and diplomats who didn't want to be seen traveling to the base. She could only hope the gaps in security would hold out while she made her escape.

Running as fast as she could, Elena approached the buildings from the north side, hugging the fence line. Ahead of her, she could see the hangars, only one of the doors open, the yellow glow of the lights inside pouring out onto the ground in front. Sticking to the shadows as best she could, Elena sprinted to the front of the building as soon as she was parallel to the hangar.

By the time she got to the hangar, her chest was heaving. Even running the five miles she did every day wasn't enough to keep the adrenaline surge at bay. She broke down to a walk, checking behind her. She didn't see anyone following. In front of her, she saw a small dual-prop four-seater, a Beechcraft Baron, white, with a red stripe down the side. The sign on the outside of the hangar said Flatlands Air Instruction. From the looks of it, it was the perfect size plane for someone to learn how to fly in, or in this case, to try to escape.

Keeping the backpack on her, Elena ran to the front wheels under the fuselage, pulling out the blocks and tossing them off to the side. She didn't have time to go through a preflight checklist. Opening the side door, she ducked inside. "I sure hope this thing's got gas," she muttered under her breath. Pressing the button for the engine to start, she waited for a second, hearing the engines try to turn over, cough and then catch. "Let's go," she groaned, barely able to breathe.

As soon as she was sure the engines started, she glanced up. In the distance, out on the road, she saw the military police coming. A second vehicle had joined the first, their lights flashing. Elena shifted the propellers into gear, forcing the plane out of the hangar before it had properly warmed up. There wasn't time to wait. She felt a lurch as the plane started to roll forward and then reached for the seatbelt. She scanned the instruments. The plane had three-quarters of a tank of gas and the oil pressure looked good. At least that was something. As Elena pushed the throttle forward, trying to pick up speed and get to the runway, she felt her heart clench in her chest. Off in the distance, she could see one of the vehicles peel off and stop at the white van lights still flashing. The other one was careening toward her. Someone must have picked up on the fact that she wasn't exactly an Army captain after all while she was in the intelligence hub. It probably wasn't the uniform, though. She'd copied some classified files to her laptop, information no one was supposed to have access to without clearance. If she didn't get away, she was looking at spending a long time behind bars answering questions about why she stole them. But the laptop, and the information on it, was the only thing that could prove she wasn't a traitor. It was also the only thing that was keeping her alive. She swallowed. If she was caught, even though she was an active CIA agent, she wasn't sure she would be able to escape from the suspicions against her.

But she didn't have time to think about that now.

Giving the throttle another goose, the plane started to pick up speed as she turned it down the taxiway to the closest runway. She pulled on the headset, waiting for someone in the tower to radio her telling her she didn't have clearance to leave, but no one said a word. That was okay by her. She glanced in the distance. The lights were off in the control tower. With this small of an airport, it was probably only staffed during the day when flights were scheduled. This one definitely wasn't scheduled.

Checking out the window to her left, she saw the MPs – the Army's military police -- round the bend, the red and blue lights on the top of the vehicle reflecting on the pavement. They were gaining on the plane. She needed to get on the runway and accelerate before they were able to get in front of her. Pushing the throttle even more, Elena saw the props spin faster, so fast they became invisible. She cut across the taxiway and turned onto the strip, the MPs gaining ground. They were right on her tail. She turned, looking behind her. If she didn't get the plane in the air, they would be able to cut her off and she'd never be able to get away. Pressing the throttle forward as the plane gained speed, Elena pulled on the flaps, waiting for the plane to lift into the air, "Come on —!" she groaned, feeling that fuselage shudder underneath her. To her right, she saw the MPs accelerate, ready to make their move and cut her off. She had seconds to launch the plane into the air. Her heart pounded in her chest, a lump in her throat. "Come on, little plane. Let's go!" she yelled. She pulled back on the yoke, feeling the plane leap into the air just as the MPs tried to veer in front of her. Her heart in her chest, she glanced down as the lights receded into the background below her. If she had to guess, the rear landing gear probably missed their vehicle by just inches. Elena guided the plane straight up in a steep ascent away from the airport. Once she was about two miles out, she turned the plane, banking to the left. "Thank God," she said, leaning back in the seat, trying to catch her breath.

Realizing she'd made it, Elena checked her instruments. It was a short flight, less than an hour, to her next destination. She turned the plane due south toward the Mexican border. There was a small airstrip on the other side of the border that looked almost identical to the one she'd left She'd stashed a car there under one of her aliases. She was almost home free.

6

U ri Bazarov had been waiting for this moment for hours. He and his team had been watching Elena Lobranova for the last week, trailing her as she made her way into the United States through Mexico and ended up at Camp Swift southeast of Austin, Texas. They'd even managed to spend some time on the base itself, posing as a team of plumbers coming in to deal with some nasty sewage issues in the barracks. Luckily, one of the guys on his team, Sergey, had a father who was a plumber back in Russia. While they might not have actually fixed anything, at least they looked like they knew what they were doing.

The good news was they knew where Elena was. The bad news was they hadn't been close enough to get to her or the information she was carrying. During their briefing at FSB headquarters, formerly called the KGB before they'd been renamed in 1991, Uri's supervisor, a small, bald man with thick glasses named Antonovich, had told Uri there needed to be two outcomes from the mission — that Elena was dead and the laptop she had was recovered. Uri had gone to the briefing alone, getting the information and then taking it back to his team. What Uri didn't tell them was that failure was not an option. Antonovich told Uri in no uncertain terms that coming back without those two goals met would result in the most severe penalties. Uri knew what that meant. If he and his team couldn't get it done, there was no point in them ever setting foot on Russian soil again. And if the KGB got wind of the fact they weren't successful, even if they were able to disappear after their failure, their families would be punished. Uri remembered at the time looking at the ground but not saying anything as he heard Antonovich's words, realizing he was stuck. Taking the mission wasn't something he had a choice about. He couldn't refuse. He also didn't have a choice about the outcome if he hoped to survive. He needed to find Elena, kill her, and recover her laptop.

And now he was just about to meet his goal.

When Uri had discovered Elena spent time at the airport the day before, he realized it was likely she was scoping it out as a way to get away from Camp Swift with the final piece of information she had gotten. Antonovich had messaged Uri and told him there was a military intelligence hub at Camp Swift, one the Russians hadn't been able to penetrate. That left Uri with two options – catch Elena on the base or at the airport. He and his team had talked about trying to infiltrate the airport, but it was too small. There were too few people that worked there to stay anonymous. Seeing a team of four Russians moving together would be about as obvious as a blizzard in the middle of the desert. With the proximity to the Army base, it would only attract attention they didn't need. Uri also knew they couldn't spend too much time on the base even with their cover as plumbers. They'd had a tentative plan to intercept Elena on base until Sergey overheard some chatter walking through the mess hall about the military police getting a tip that someone was trying to steal classified files off their server late. The presence of additional security on the base was enough to force Uri and his team to scramble off base. Alexander had barely made it out, one of the MPs stopped to ask him a question. As much as Alexander tried, trying to hide his thick Russian accent was almost impossible. No, they wouldn't be able to intercept Elena on the base.

Given the information they had, Uri decided to take up a position on a low hillside above the airport. He and his team had gotten there late in the afternoon, as the sun was going down. After leaving the base, they'd found a van their contact had provided for them. It was identical to the one they were driving, except that it was stocked with guns, ammunition, cash, and supplies, including food, water, and camping gear. Their stockpiled van was parked behind them now, covered with camouflage netting so it couldn't be seen from the air. Choppers had been flying overhead for the last few hours. The Americans definitely knew something was going on, something within their own ranks. The buzz around Uri and his team reminded him of his time in the Russian Army during field exercises. It seemed the commanders were always sending them out somewhere to practice for a war that never happened. If they were able to stop Elena, maybe it finally would.

"There!" Sergey yelled from behind his binoculars. Uri squinted off in the distance, seeing a vehicle approaching down the service road to the airstrip faster than it should have been. He watched as it made a sharp right turn inside the fence and then stopped, a lone figure, no bigger than a black dot, darting out from the side of the vehicle. "That has to be her," Sergey said.

Uri looked behind him. "Alexander, get the weapon ready."

"Yes. It's ready."

Uri watched and waited, not taking his eyes off of the small speck in the distance that had to be Elena Lobranova. A tingle covered his skin. It was always exciting to finally acquire a target. This was the first time they had gotten this close to ending the nonsense with Elena and all the trouble she was causing for the motherland. He could feel the medal being pinned on his chest already, the pull of the smile across his face as he was told what a good job he had done protecting Russian interests.

But he didn't want to get ahead of himself.

Staring off in the distance, he waited, seeing Elena dart into the hangar where the dual prop plane had been stored. She'd eyed up the same plane the day before. If he had been trying to make an escape, it was exactly the plane he would have chosen, twin-engine, small, light, and fast. He shook his head.

Based on her profile, he knew she'd been raised until she was a teenager in Russia, had moved to the United States, had gone to college, and then had been recruited by the CIA based on her athletic ability and her knowledge of multiple languages. He pressed his lips together, still watching, his thoughts racing. How could she violate her homeland like that? Uri frowned. He had no problem with people moving to other countries, living their life peacefully, going about their day-to-day business and sticking to themselves. But it was something completely different to be raised in Russia then become a CIA agent. Hadn't the CIA had questions about her loyalty? He knew if he was running the CIA he would have. Once a Russian, always a Russian.

A moment later, he saw the little plane push its way out of the hangar. He was staring at it so intently he nearly missed seeing the MPs hot on Elena's trail. "Look!" Sergey said, pointing. Sergey was standing so close to Uri that he could feel the man's body heat behind him. He needed a shower.

Uri squinted off in the distance. One of the military police vehicles had stopped at the van Elena had ditched inside the airport's fence line. The other was beelining for the little plane that had just pulled out of the hangar. Uri held his breath, narrowing his eyes, trying to make out what was going on in the darkness. If the MPs were able to intercept Elena before she got off the ground, that would change the calculus of their mission radically. They'd pull her out of the fuselage and drag her away to a dark hole somewhere. On the other hand, if she was able to get the plane in the air, Uri might have a chance to complete his mission. It would all be decided in the next few seconds. "Come on, Elena. Get that thing off the ground," Uri mumbled.

The idea of Elena being locked up in a holding cell somewhere where it wouldn't be as easy to get to her would complicate matters. Uri's mind ran through the possibilities. They could show up there as members of the Russian delegation and demand to see her. Elena still held dual citizenship. During their so-called visit, Uri could certainly slip her some sort of poison. The KGB's research arm had become an expert at ways of dosing people with toxic substances without them ever knowing. They'd even pioneered the use of audio frequencies that caused debilitating headaches, ear pain, and memory loss a decade before. It had been used most effectively on American diplomats in Cuba, that was, until the large media networks in the United States got wind of it. Their covert tool wasn't so covert after that and the KGB had to regroup, going back to what they did best, murder by poison, and other more obvious ways, of course.

Uri didn't take his eye off the plane, watching as the MPs chased it down the airstrip. The plane shuddered as the MPs pulled next to it, gaining speed. If Elena didn't pull up on the stick and get the plane off the ground, the MPs would be able to cut her off, probably sending the plane tumbling across the runway as it shattered into a million pieces. Uri held his breath, waiting. As he saw the nose of the plane tug upward, he yelled, "Alexander, give it to me now!"

Alexander handed him the shoulder-fired missile launcher that was stowed in the back of the van as part of the weapons package. It was a MK 135, a multipurpose assault weapon used by the United States Army, similar to what they used in Russia. Uri adjusted the sight in front of his eye. Alexander had it primed and ready to go, the screen yellow waiting for target acquisition, the night vision enabled. "All you need to do is line it up and pull the trigger, sir," Alexander said in clipped words.

He knew that already, but Uri didn't say anything, watching as the plane darted off the ground and sped straight up into the air.

"What are you waiting for?" Sergey said. "Pull the trigger!"

"Not yet, not yet," Uri said, focusing on the targeting display in front of his eyes. He needed the plane carrying Elena to be far enough away from the airstrip that the wreckage didn't land on the property or anywhere near the Army base. Luckily, she was starting to circle toward the south. He tracked her movements with the weapon. As the plane banked, he rested his finger on the trigger, seeing the display light up green, the fuselage turning toward him.

"Uri!" Tereza called to him. "Now!"

"Three, two, one…" Uri pulled the trigger hearing the detonation first and then the hiss of the missile explode out of the wide barrel. As it left, he felt his entire body shudder, the force making him take a step back. He propped the weapon on the ground, waiting, watching. He wanted to glance at his team to see the looks on their faces, but he didn't want to miss what was about to happen.

Two seconds later, he saw a burst of red off in the distance, followed by a yellow haze and black smoke, the concussion of the miniature missile hitting the plane booming off the hillside a fraction of a second later. Uri watched as the plane dipped and rolled. It looked like part of the fuselage and one of the wings was still attached. The rest of it was raining down in pieces onto the ground below. An explosion like that could rain debris down over miles and miles. Uri smiled, hoping Elena had made peace with her maker before this mission, because based on how the plane looked, she wasn't long for the earth.

Uri glanced over his shoulder at Alexander who was watching through night vision enabled binoculars they'd found in the back of their van. "It's going down? Yes?" Uri said.

Alexander nodded, "Yes. Excellent shot, sir."

Uri grunted, "I made the shot even with that piece-of-junk American weapon." Uri looked down at the empty MK 153. "The Russian version is much better, just like everything." He looked at Alexander, narrowing his eyes, "Can you track the location?"

"Yes." Alexander had been an operations specialist in the Russian army. He had an uncanny way of understanding maps and locations, able to memorize a blueprint after looking at it for a few seconds. "I'll need to look at a map, but it looks about ten miles out. By the way it went down below the horizon line, I would guess it hit on a lower elevation than where we're standing."

"Excellent. The rest of you clean up the site and get everything back in the van. We need to get moving, but I can tell you right now, the threat is gone."

"Aren't we going to go to the crash site to confirm?" Tereza asked.

Uri narrowed his eyes. He didn't like to be questioned, especially not by new members of his team. Tereza should know better. "No. I don't really see any need to. Did you see what the missile did to the plane? There's no way Elena or the laptop could have survived it."

"But don't we want to be sure? I don't know about you, but I don't want to arrive back in Moscow to find out that Elena is still on the loose."

Uri paused for a moment, frowning. After seeing the way the plane went up in a fireball, he couldn't reasonably imagine Elena or anything she had with her would have survived the fall from that far up in the sky, not to mention the explosion and the fire. But, as much as Uri didn't want to admit it, Tereza had a point. "I suppose we could go take a look," he said reluctantly.

Alexander raised his eyebrows, "If we want to go, we should go quickly. Someone likely saw the fireball and the crash. The Americans will be all over it."

Uri looked back down at the tarmac below him. The MPs had disappeared, going back to the base before they ever saw the plane get blown out of the sky, or at least that was his hope. That was their loss, but perhaps it could be Uri's gain. It would alter their plans to leave the United States, but perhaps only by an hour or so if they were lucky. Uri did the calculations in his head. They had two cars stashed south of their location, parked in a lot of a bus terminal. Their contact had given him the coordinates. The plan was for them to drive the van to the parking lot, split the team in half and then drive into Mexico, getting on a plane and making their way back to Moscow. Checking the wreckage for Elena, or whatever was left of her, might change that plan – maybe ruin it altogether. Was it worth the risk? Uri thought for a moment and then relented. "All right. Let's do as Tereza suggests. Alexander, figure out where that plane went down. The rest of you pack up the site, make sure we don't leave anything behind and let's go take a look."

7

E lena saw the smokey trail from the incoming missile about a half a second before the impact. It was barely enough time for her to grip the stick and try to bank the plane away. Everything in her knew it was too late to avoid a collision and there was no time for fear to get a grip on her. There was a sudden blinding flash that forced Elena's eyes closed, the plane shuddering before Elena felt the plane fall underneath her, a passing intense heat from the explosion that felt like someone had opened the door to a blast furnace and then closed it just as quickly. She pulled up on the yoke, trying to right the plane, only to realize there was a hole in the back of the fuselage and the right wing was partially demolished. The right engine and propeller had disappeared somewhere in the Texas countryside.

Everything in her wanted to scream, her eyes wide as the ground accelerated toward her. She couldn't breathe. Out of pure instinct, she leaned back in the seat, frantically gripping the controls trying to bring the nose of the plummeting plane up, but it wasn't responding. There wasn't much left of it to respond and Elena had no idea what systems had been damaged in the blast. Glancing at the altimeter, the glass cracked from the impact, she realized she only had seconds left before she hit the ground. She had to somehow get the nose of the plane up to nearly level if she wanted to avoid a nosedive that would surely kill her in the impact.

In the few seconds she had, she knew if she didn't level the plane out, it would be over. Yelling at the top of her lungs, she pulled back with two hands, trying to get the yoke to respond. The ground was coming fast. She couldn't breathe. At the last second, the nose of the plane edged up just slightly, enough to give her a shot at putting the belly of the plane on the ground. Elena stared in front of her, unblinking, trying to see where she was going to end up. It was a flat piece of land, a shallow hillside to her left. She grabbed for the rotor control, trying to turn the plane away from the side of the hill, missing getting her hand on the control as the plane shuddered again. "No!" she yelled as what was left of the plane hit the ground.

8

There was no way for Elena to know how long she was unconscious. As she came to, the first thing she remembered was the acrid smell of electrical wires burning and a strange popping and crackling noise behind her. Her eyes were closed. She moved her body slowly. It felt like she was wading in gelatin until she felt a sharp pain in her right shoulder. She groaned, trying to open her eyes. As she did, her memory started to clear. Running from the base. The plane. The sleek vapor trail of a shoulder-fired missile a second before it impacted. The fight to get the plane on the ground. She sucked in a breath, her heart pounding as the memories formed a traffic jam in her head. She was alive, or at least she thought she was.

Reaching for the seatbelt, she said a silent prayer, thanking God that she'd taken a second to put on the shoulder harness as she left the hangar in a hurry, dodging the MPs at the plane at the airstrip outside of Camp Swift. If she hadn't, she knew her body would've ended up strewn somewhere out on the weeds in the field in front of her, ejected upon impact. Using her left hand, Elena flipped open the buckles, having to tug at them a little bit. The metal clasp popped away from her body with a little metallic jingle.

Her mind started to clear a little as her memories started to firm up. She struggled in her seat. Elena glanced left and right, still not moving. She put her left hand on her right shoulder. It was searing with pain. She had no idea if it was dislocated or if she'd broken her collarbone. All she knew was that it was excruciatingly painful. Elena wiggled her toes and moved her legs a little bit. Her lower body seemed to be in working order.

Elena pushed herself away from the seat, looking at the door to her left. The glass had blown out in the crash. She wriggled the latch to try to open it but it was jammed, the hinges mangled from the impact. Twisting to her left, she angled her body, using her feet to kick at the door until the flimsy metal popped open. She slid out of what was left of the plane and onto the ground, crawling away from the wreckage. Her breathing came in short pants, the adrenaline from everything that happened over the last hour catching up to her. She stopped, still on her hands and knees, and threw up. Wiping her mouth with the sleeve of the Army Captain's uniform she'd stolen, she sat on her knees in the grass with her eyes closed. She knew she couldn't stay there long. The crash hadn't been an accident. And whoever had shot at her would be coming to see if she was dead. And soon.

The laptop. Her mind flitted back to the black backpack she'd carried with her. Her life was only as good as the information she'd found in the brief. A surge of panic rose in her body, threatening to make her retch again. She swallowed, trying to take a deep breath, closing her eyes for a moment. Still on her hands and knees, Elena slumped down onto her hip, staring at the wreckage. Surprisingly, there was no fire. Whatever fuel had been left in the plane must have either burned up or dumped out during the crash. "At least that's one good thing," Elena mumbled.

Staring at the wreckage, Elena saw the right wing and propeller were gone. Where they were she had no idea. There was a hole in the roof of the plane, a giant cavern exposing the entire second row, plus more, to the outside. Somehow, the missile must have clipped the top of the fuselage before exploding rather than hitting it dead on. The control area was relatively undamaged. Elena sucked in a breath, realizing that banking the plane at the last second had probably saved her life. If she hadn't, it was likely the missile would have hit the plane dead on, shredding it in mid-air, leaving her nothing to try to land.

Not that the landing had been a ten out of ten, Elena thought, struggling to her feet. Keeping her right arm close to her body, she used her left hand to brush off the front of her pants. It was a reflex. Nothing more. She took a couple of hesitant steps forward. The ground seemed uneven. Whether it actually was or was her balance was off from the shock and the impact of the crash, she didn't know. She staggered forward a couple of steps, her vision blurry, putting her hand on the side of the plane near where she'd escaped the wreckage. She stared inside seeing how the seatbelts had flopped away from the seat as she'd crawled out. Swallowing, she realized the thick black nylon straps pinning her to the seat and a last-minute turn were probably the only things that saved her life. That, plus a little luck.

Leaning inside, Elena blinked. Her heart started to pound. Where was the backpack? She glanced at the hole in the top of the fuselage. It certainly could have gotten sucked out. She squeezed her eyes shut for a moment and then tried to focus on the fields around her, surrounded by darkness. There was no way she'd be able to find it if it wasn't on the plane. Another round of panic rose inside of her. The laptop was the only thing that could prove her innocence. If she didn't have it, she'd have no choice but to go on the run until she could recover the rest of the information, but the odds of her being able to go back and reconstruct what she'd found were nearly impossible. She leaned her hand on the side of the plane, bending over, trying to catch her breath. She felt her stomach contract as if she was going to throw up again, but she sucked in a breath through her nose, staving it off. Shock could do weird things to bodies. She'd seen it more than one time. There were CIA agents she knew who were completely fine during their missions, but promptly came home and hid in their houses refusing to talk to anyone for a month. Others got off the plane and fell to the ground, their body weak from the final letdown of adrenaline. Others had blood pressure that was so high all the CIA could do was meet them at their plane with an ambulance and transport them to the closest hospital. Many of those agents never returned to the field. Holding onto the plane, or what was left of it, Elena wondered if she was now in that camp.

Thinking about her future wasn't an option at that moment. Elena straightened up trying to ignore the pain in her shoulder. She glanced down at it, but couldn't tell what was wrong. At least it was still attached to her body. It could be fixed later. She took a step forward, looking through the fuselage the best she could and then glancing up at the hillside above. She'd wasted enough time. She needed to find the backpack and get out of there. It was an advantage that it was dark, but it wouldn't last long. Whoever had shot her down would come looking. Eventually, local law enforcement would come too. She didn't want to be around for either scenario. Feeling around in her pockets, Elena realized her phone was still buttoned in the jacket she was wearing. Using her left hand, she quickly opened the flap and pulled it out, fumbling to turn on the flashlight. It was a risk. Anyone who had seen the crash or who was tracking her would be able to see the faint light on the black field, but trying to search for the backpack any other way wasn't possible.

Holding the phone up with her left hand, Elena frantically

searched for her bag, shining the light on the ground under the edge of the fuselage. She turned, sticking the phone inside, pointing it at the passenger seat. That's where she'd seen it last. It wasn't there.

Grunting, she glanced over her shoulder. There was still no movement from anywhere around her. She held the light low against her leg, blocking its glow, and took a couple of steps toward the back of the plane where the gaping hole in the top of the fuselage was. The rest of the plane seemed to be empty. There was nothing left — not the emergency kits, not the cushions on the seats, not the toolbox that every plane carried. Nothing. Elena's chest tightened. She was about to turn away and start looking on the ground around the plane when the edge of the beam of light caught the glint of something silver pinned way back in the fuselage, near what was left of the tail section. The backpack. Somehow, it had gotten sucked off the passenger seat and made its way into the back corner of the plane. Elena turned off the flashlight, not willing to risk one more second of its light broadcasting her location out over the field. Waiting a second for her eyes to adjust, she used her left hand to brace herself against the edge of the shredded metal, careful not to touch it, knowing the torn metal would be as sharp as the finely ground edge of a knife. Stepping over into the fuselage with her left foot, she ducked down, crawling on her knees until she could reach the strap. She tugged on the laptop. For a moment, it didn't seem like the bag was going to come free, but then with a yank, she was able to get the backpack to come loose. Grunting, she pulled it toward her. What hadn't seemed like a heavy load when she got on the plane seemed like she was tugging on a boulder at the moment. Elena knew it was a cocktail of shock, adrenaline, and exhaustion. It didn't matter how heavy it seemed. She had the backpack. Glancing up at the sky again, listening, she knew she needed to go.

Stepping over the metal of the fuselage, she heard it give a little creak, the metal flexing underneath her weight. She shook her head. There was no doubt it was a miracle she'd survived. After the missile strike, the plane was nothing more than a shredded tin can.

Walking a few feet away from the fuselage, Elena stopped for a second. Gingerly, she inserted her right arm into the strap for the backpack leaning to her left to swing it around and pull it up onto her back. Even the slightest movement with her right shoulder sent searing pain through her body. She glanced around her, trying to make out anything she could see in the distance. As much as she'd like to get to the nearest town and get medical attention, that wasn't an option. She needed to stay concealed until she found someone she could trust.

Turning toward the plane one last time, she stared inside. In the darkness, she could barely make out the two front seats. She patted her pocket feeling for her cell phone, pulled it out of her pocket, and powered it down. It had encrypted cloaking technology that was supposed to prevent people from being able to track her location, but given the fact that someone had just shot a missile at the plane she was flying, it was clear she had no idea who she could trust.

There was one last thing. Elena sucked in a breath, pulling a hammered silver bracelet with colored stones out of her pocket, one she had been carrying since she'd found it. She scanned the ground, finding a rock near the plane. She draped it over the stone, leaving it behind. Walking away, she knew she had at least a chance that someone would find it. It was a message for the right person, but only one would know what it meant; if only she could get to him in time. And time was ticking.

9

Elena had hiked for about an hour, heading due south from the crash site, using the position of the moon to guide her. At least she was heading in the right direction, she thought, nearly tripping over another rock, her legs aching. The jarring motion sent another wave of pain through her body. Taking stock of where she was as best she could in the darkness, she stopped for a second, seeing a silhouette in the distance. She hadn't seen any roads or trucks or anything that resembled life on her hike away from the crash site. She was moving slowly, more slowly than she would have liked. At one point, she tried running, but the pain in her shoulder made it nearly impossible to grind along any faster than at a walk. "Slow progress is better than no progress at all," she mumbled to herself. She squinted at a nearly black silhouette that had emerged on the horizon. It looked like a single building in the middle of a field. Texas didn't have that many trees, or at least not as many she was used to seeing on her visits to Langley. The trees Texas did have seemed to be short and scrubby as though they were protecting themselves from the inevitable tornadoes or hurricanes that came across the landscape every year or so.

It was getting late. How late exactly, Elena wasn't sure. She wasn't willing to power up her phone in order to check, but by the position of the moon in the sky, she knew it was probably close to midnight. Fatigue washed over her as she stopped for a second, bending over and resting her left hand on her knee. It'd been a long day. The memories surged back as she started walking again. Questions rattled through her mind. Although she'd recovered the laptop, there was no way to know if it had been destroyed in the crash, the impact corrupting the hard drive. Her stomach tightened itself into a little knot. She glanced left and right. She needed a place to hide, a place to regroup. It looked like the silhouette in the distance was her best bet.

Elena walked for another ten or fifteen minutes toward the shape in the distance until she ran into a fence line. It extended out left and right as far as she could see, rough-hewn posts connected by two lines of wire. Elena searched to see if there was a spot she could get through without getting herself tangled. Looking at one of the posts, she realized it was rotten at the base. She gave it a kick with her foot and it flopped over with a dull thump, allowing her to step over it. Once across the fence line, she stopped, gazing up the hillside at the silhouette in front of her. She spotted a spire in the distance. Was the silhouette a church? From the little she knew about Texas, there were churches scattered all over the state. She swallowed, walking towards it, her hands clammy. There were no other buildings nearby.

It took another twenty-five minutes of hiking up a low grade to reach the church, or at least the outskirts of it. About a quarter-mile from the building, there was a stand of scrub trees. Elena stopped behind their stubby trunks and stared at the building, using them for cover in case anyone was watching. It was difficult to see in the darkness. The last thing she wanted to do was charge up to the building and find herself in the middle of someone's home. Not that anyone was living there, but many of the churches had parsonages — small apartments or homes nearby – for the families who served the church. With the number of guns in Texas, Elena knew she would be meeting the wrong end of a rifle or a shotgun if she snuck up on someone. Not that she could blame them. She was trespassing after all.

Still cradling her aching arm, she watched for a few minutes, realizing there were no lights and not even a vehicle she could see anywhere in sight. There was no way to circle around and check the front of the building without being spotted, but at least she could check three sides on her approach. She stepped out from behind the trees cautiously. Her mouth was dry. She needed water and food soon. Her body had taken a beating. While she might be moving on pure adrenaline at the moment, it wouldn't last for long. At some point, the inevitable crash would come. The only way to stave it off was by making sure she was hydrated.

But that would have to wait. The first thing she had to do was find shelter.

Feeling relatively confident the church was quiet for the moment, Elena walked toward it, her head on a swivel. She scanned the horizon, turning around several times to make sure she wasn't being followed from behind. Since the crash, she hadn't heard any helicopters overhead or heard any sirens. How it was possible that no one called in a missile strike on a small plane, she wasn't sure. Certainly, the fireball in the air had to let someone know something had gone awry. But given how small the plane was and the vast Texas countryside between Austin and the Camp Swift Army base, she could imagine that without an exact location it would be hard to determine where the plane had landed. At this point, even if her life depended on it, she wasn't sure she could go back and find the fuselage again and she had been the one flying it.

Her breath coming in short pants, Elena approached the building from the back, moving quickly, hunched over as she jogged toward it. She realized the spire going up in the air meant it was exactly what she thought – a church. There were no windows on the back. As she approached it, she looked up, seeing peeling white paint, flecks of it dusting the ground where it had gotten blown off the wooden siding. Looking up, she realized whoever was responsible for the church hadn't taken time to paint it, at least not recently. Darting around the side, she saw the only door near her was padlocked. That was a good sign for her, but probably not a good one for the local community. If she had to bet, the church was closed. Permanently. Sticking close to the side of the building, Elena made her way to the front. As soon as she got to the corner, she stopped. By the main doors, which were also padlocked, there was a thin driveway. She could barely make it out in the darkness, the gravel dotted with overgrown clumps of field grass, yellowed and dried out. At least the moonlight was giving her enough of a glow to see. There didn't appear to be any main roads nearby. It was almost as if the church had planted it in the middle of the field and then forgotten about it. She turned, glancing up at the front of the building. The only windows not boarded up were near the bottom of the steeple. Probably too high up to matter, Elena thought. "No one home," she muttered.

Walking back to the first door she'd spotted, she knew she'd need to break in in order to get some shelter for the night. She was too tired to go any further. Striding down the side of the building, she stopped when she got to the padlocked door, shrugging off her backpack, groaning in pain. Swinging the bag around in front of her, she opened the front pocket using her left hand, pulling out a small black pouch. Holding it against her body with her right forearm, she used her left to unzip it, pulling a few small tools out. Lock picks were more helpful than anyone ever imagined. They could be used to get into a building as they were meant to, or even stab someone if needed. Elena remembered one of her field instructors at "The Farm" — the name most of the CIA candidates called their training school, which was actually called Camp Peary — warning them, "If you have to abandon everything in your bag, the only thing you take is your lock pick set." He'd then given them an assignment to come up with one hundred different ways the tools could be used. Elena had come up with two hundred.

Today was one of those days she was glad she'd taken her instructors seriously.

It took her a little longer than usual to pick the lock on the side of the building, not that she was in any hurry. There wasn't anyone around, although she was anxious to get inside before she was spotted. Not being able to move her right arm was slowing her down significantly. After a few minutes of fumbling with the lock picks, she was finally able to move her injured shoulder into a position where she could use her left hand to get the padlock off. It gave a satisfying click as it let go. Elena glanced up at the peeling paint on the siding above her. Given the state of the building, it was lucky the lock had come undone at all. Holding it in her hand, she felt years of grime and dust attached to it. She tossed it into a patch of withered grass off to the side, the metal landing with a thump, as she picked up her backpack.

Elena leaned into the door. After a loud creak, the door gave way. She opened it enough that she could get inside and then, checking the darkness for movement following her, she closed the door. Pulling her cell phone out of her pocket, she flipped on the flashlight only long enough to get a glimpse of the interior of the church before turning it off.

Taking a few steps forward, all she could smell were years of dust in the building. She saw a few flecks of straw and twigs on the ground as if a bird had built a nest somewhere in the ceiling and the wind had knocked it down, scattering the materials all over the floor. In front of her were ten rows of pews. To the left, there was an elevated area with a wooden podium on it. That had to be the spot where the pastor had stood to give his message every Sunday when the church was in operation. She took a few steps forward and sat down on one of the pews, setting her backpack next to her. It was hard, the wood uncovered by any type of cushion at all. At that moment, she would have happily taken even a half-dry rotted piece of upholstery to rest on rather than sitting on the hard wood. Underneath her feet, she saw planked floors that looked like they had been old before the building had ever been built.

As Elena's eyes adjusted to the dim moonlight coming in from the windows above, she realized the building hadn't probably been used in at least a decade, if not longer. She sighed, "This'll have to do, at least for now." A tingle crawled down her spine, wondering if whoever had shot her down would come looking. Only time would tell.

Getting up from where she was seated, Elena stretched, taking stock of the aches and pains in her body. Other than her shoulder, she was okay. Spinning around her, narrowing her eyes in the darkness, she wanted to know more about the building. She wanted to see if there was a way she could climb up to look out the windows near the steeple to scan the land around her for anyone approaching. There had to be, didn't there? She looked up, wondering how any maintenance would be done that high up in the air without a ladder or staircase. Realizing the rungs might be dry rotted, Elena realized that would be a better thing to think about once the sun came up.

Elena walked back to the side door where she'd come in, cracking it open enough to glance out. There was no movement outside and barely any noise. The only thing she could hear was a few animals moving, probably field mice out scavenging for whatever they could find left of the dry grass.

Elena closed the door behind her, pushing on it gently, hoping it wouldn't creak again. It didn't disappoint. Given the fact she was miles out in the middle of nowhere, it probably didn't matter how much noise it made, but Elena shook her head. She didn't want to take any chances.

Going back to the pew where she'd set her backpack, Elena sat down again in the darkness, laying on her left side. She needed to get some rest.

At the moment she was safe, but there was no telling how long that would last.

10

It took Alexander an agonizing two-plus hours to find where the crash site was. "I'm sorry, Uri," Alexander kept muttering under his breath, after profusely apologizing for what felt like the tenth time. "It's this flatland," he grumbled. "There's no topography for me to get a grip on. It's just all flat. No landmarks to speak of. How do people live out here?" Uri shook his head. He knew Alexander was trying. But the fact of the matter was that if they didn't find the crash site soon, then Tereza's idea of looking for Elena would be a moot point. By then, it would likely be American officials scurrying all over the crash site. The only thing he could hope was that they were having as many problems finding it as he was. "Stop apologizing, Alexander. It makes you seem weak. Now, where is it?" Uri replied, the impatience evident in his voice.

"I don't know..." Alexander stammered and then looked up.

Uri saw the glimmer of recognition in his eyes as he glanced over to Alexander, who was sitting next to him in the front of the van. "Do you have something? Anything at all?"

"Yes, yes! Over there!" Alexander pointed to a small road. "I think if we go up there we'll be right above it."

Uri guided the van on what was not much more than a cow path that led up a shallow hill. At the top, he shut off the van, immediately dousing the headlights. The team got out, moving silently. He assumed they were as glad to get out of the van loaded with supplies as he was. It was cramped at best, but at least they had everything they needed from their American contact. The man was a lifesaver, even if he was American. His Russian wasn't half bad either.

Alexander was the first one out, darting away from the group and running toward the crest of the hill. Uri hiked behind him, not even breathing hard. Hills in Texas were nothing like the ones in the mountains of Russia. Alexander was right. Everything was flat in Texas.

"Over there," Alexander hissed, pointing down below them.

Uri stood next to Alexander, trying to see what he'd spotted. After a moment of letting his eyes adjust to the darkness, Uri could see the black remains of what looked to be a hunk of metal. "I can't be sure, but that looks like the main fuselage, doesn't it?"

Uri nodded, "It does, but there's only one way to be sure." Without saying anything else, Uri picked his way among the scrub grass on the rocks that peppered the hillside, climbing down ahead of the rest of his team. He didn't need to check on them. He knew they would all follow. Alexander would be right behind him followed by Tereza and then Sergey. Sergey always liked to bring up the rear, calling himself the rear guard. Uri knew it was his way to make himself feel important. Pitiful.

About halfway down the hillside, Uri could smell the smoldering wreck before he even got close. The noxious odor of charred electrical wires burning and melting metal hung in the air. He glanced out at the horizon. There were no emergency lights or helicopters approaching. That was good, at least for the moment. But if the helicopters came, they would be caught for sure. Four Russians with thick accents and a truck filled with weapons and supplies would require a lot of explaining. No, they needed to examine the crash site and get away as quickly as possible. Hopefully, it wouldn't take them more than a minute or two to find what they were looking for – Elena's dead, mangled body and her laptop. Uri swallowed, continuing down the hillside, sliding down the last few feet as the hill dropped off, a few rocks clattering off to the side as he went. He gave himself a push off the hillside and ran the last few feet toward the wreckage.

As he approached, he noticed the scent in the air hung thick, making his dark eyes water. If it had been light, he would've expected to see smoke coming off of the wreckage. But it was too dark. Making his way close to what was left of the plane, he reached under his jacket and pulled out a pistol, holding it in front of him. Elena Lobranova was smart and cunning. And if she was still alive, it wouldn't surprise him if she took a shot at him from somewhere nearby. He turned back to his team, putting a single finger up towards his mouth, telling them to be quiet, hoping they could see enough of his face in the moonlight to understand what he meant. If Elena was unconscious in the plane, the last thing he wanted to do was give her any notice that they had arrived.

The rest of the team held back and waited as Uri took a few steps forward. He walked carefully, hunched over, staying low to the ground, and looking toward the plane. Everything in him wanted to yell for Sergey to go back and get flashlights for them, but he knew in the broad, empty countryside that it would be like a beacon. Anyone who hadn't figured out where the plane crash was would know instantly. No, that wouldn't do. They'd have to operate under the cover of night. It was probably better anyway.

Taking two steps closer to the plane, Uri used his left hand to cover his face from the smoke, still holding onto his pistol with his right hand. The fumes smelled like burning oil and gas. Leaning towards the wreckage, Uri realized there was no movement, at least none he could see in the dark. "Get me some light over here," he hissed. From behind him, Tereza came close, the flashlight on her phone cutting through the darkness. "Give me that!" he said, yanking the phone from her hand. Directing the beam of light into the fuselage, or what was left of it, Uri half-smiled. The wreckage was smoldering from the damage. Much of it was still intact. That in itself was a shame. He would've felt more satisfied if the missile had shattered the plane into a million pieces in the middle of the sky, dropping Elena's traitorous body into a field somewhere in very small pieces, ending at least one phase of the mission. But based on the way the fuselage looked, that hadn't happened, unless of course she'd gotten sucked out of the massive hole in the back of the plane.

Uri scanned the remainder of the interior. There was nobody in the front, and no blood either. Pressing his lips together, he stepped further back, hoping to see a severed arm or leg or at least a pool or streak of blood, something he could take a picture of to send back to Moscow to prove to them that Elena was dead and that her information had gone with her. But directing the light into the plane, he saw it was clean. A knot tightened in his stomach. He looked over his shoulder "Start searching. She's not here. I don't see the laptop either."

Without saying anything, Sergey, Alexander, and Tereza fanned out, each of them staring at the ground, their bodies leaning forward. Uri saw the flashlights from their phones cutting through the darkness. Part of him wanted to tell them to shut them off, worried they would attract unwanted attention but he knew they were on the clock. They need to search efficiently and quickly and then escape into the darkness. Hopefully, the weak lights from the cell phones weren't so much that they would be detected from the air. Sergey was the first one to come back, his voice low and gravelly, "I didn't find anything. No body and no laptop."

A second later Alexander and Tereza joined Sergey and Uri. "I didn't find anything either," Tereza said, taking her phone back from Uri. "Do you think she survived the crash?"

Uri shook his head, "I have no idea. I certainly hope not. The biggest gift we have is that she could have been sucked out of the plane and smashed on some rocks somewhere in the middle of one of these fields. The only problem is that we still need a body to show to Moscow."

In the darkness, Uri saw Alexander wrinkle his nose, "If she got sucked out, it's going to be nearly impossible to find her body. The Kremlin would not be happy."

Uri tilted his head up to the sky. Part of him wanted to tell Alexander that Moscow was never happy. That's how they did business. Grumpy and angry was their brand and they were very good at it. Before he could say anything, he heard a noise over the horizon. "Turn off your flashlights," he barked. By the sound of it, there was a helicopter approaching. He glanced at his phone. A message had come in. Their contact told Uri they were needed elsewhere. "The crash site will have to wait. Maybe the Americans will do the work for us and find what we need. We gotta get outta here."

11

N TSB Investigator Patrick Mills was about ready to leave the office after filing a set of reports that were overdue to his boss when his cell phone rang. He groaned, looking at it, pressing send on his email. "If you're looking for the reports, I literally sent them to you a fraction of a second ago."

"Yes, I'm looking for the reports, but that's not why I'm calling," Doug Parsons said, sounding more whiney than usual.

"Well, I guess that's partially good news."

"Only if you like the idea of being out most of the night."

Patrick grunted. Night searches weren't his favorite. "Oh no. What happened?"

We got a report about a half-hour ago of an explosion over the skies southeast of Austin near Camp Swift Army base. I've already been in contact with the Army. They said they don't have any planes or helicopters missing. But by the number of reports we've gotten, something definitely happened."

Patrick frowned, standing up from his desk, balancing the phone on his shoulder. The Texas countryside was littered with small airstrips, some of them sanctioned by the NTSB and many of them not. Texas was the wild, wild west in a lot of ways and aeronautics was just one of them. He'd spent the first few years of his work with the NTSB trying to convince farmers who owned their own planes for crop dusting not to use their land for their own airstrips. After being not so politely ushered off more than one farm at the wrong end of a rifle, he discovered that was a futile exercise, one that the NTSB liked to send all of the junior investigators out on. "Any idea where the crash is?"

"Nope. And to be honest with you I can't even be sure that there was a crash. Could've been some people seeing something crazy in the air. Could have been a meteor, or some other weather phenomenon, like a short strike of lightning. The Army said they didn't have any planes leaving, but it could have easily been an afterburner from one of their jets and either the person I talked to doesn't have all the facts or they simply don't know."

Patrick raised his eyebrows, "You mean like the right hand doesn't know what the left hand is doing?"

Doug chuckled, "You could say something like that. You know how they are."

Patrick nodded. After being an NTSB investigator for the last ten years, he had spent plenty of his time at crash sites. His specialty was aviation, but the NTSB covered all sorts of public transportation nightmares, including train derailments, bus accidents, and even once in a while helping out the Coast Guard when they needed an extra hand. The last time he'd been on a marine case, a tanker had gotten beached in low tide. It had been a mess, a whole alphabet's worth of agencies trying to solve the problem and fighting for jurisdiction. "So, I'm assuming you're sending me out on a wild goose chase for the evening?"

"Kinda looks that way. I've got a helicopter en route. Should be there in the next fifteen minutes. We got some basic coordinates from the phone calls we've received, but nothing firm."

Patrick's mind started to race. If what everyone had seen was a jet afterburner, then there was nothing to find. The jet would be long gone. If on the other hand, a small plane had gone down, it could have ended up anywhere. And, depending on the damage, pieces of the fuselage could be scattered over a ten-mile radius as the plane made its descent. In the dark, it would be like finding a needle in a haystack. Dawn might not make it considerably better. "I'll take care of it. I'll keep you posted from the helicopter," Patrick said.

"Thanks. Radio if you need anything or if you happen to find a crash. I have a feeling this one is nothing. You'll probably be back in a few hours after a fun helicopter tour of the Texas countryside."

"I hope you're right."

12

Twenty minutes later, Patrick slid into the cockpit of an NTSB helicopter. As promised, Doug had texted the pilot the relative coordinates of the phone calls they'd gotten. As Patrick secured his harness, he gave a nod to Buddy Driscoll, the pilot. He and Buddy had worked together for the last five years. Buddy was an Army veteran and had flown chopper missions overseas. After retiring, he got the itch to fly again but didn't want to reenlist. That's when Doug, Travis's boss, had found Buddy and brought him into the NTSB. If there was anyone Patrick wanted to be out searching the Texas hillsides with, it was Buddy. He was a great pilot and a good guy. "What's going on, man?" Patrick said, slipping on the headset and adjusting it over his ear.

"Not a whole heck of a lot. I was about to start in on my eighth beer of the night when I got the call."

Patrick snapped his head towards Buddy. He spotted the wide grin across the man's face, framed by a wide mustache that seemed to take up the entirety of his face. Alcohol was a no-no for pilots that were on call, but Buddy liked to joke around. "Yeah, I can see you're looking really impaired. Maybe we should call in one of the relief pilots?"

"And miss the opportunity to go night flying? Never. How've you been?"

Patrick blinked for a second, grabbing the harness attached to the helicopter's seat, double-checking it was secure before they took off. Flying with Buddy wasn't like flying commercial. There were no reminders to put your tray table in the upright position. Buddy had been a combat pilot and flew that way, his thick hands controlling the stick like no one else Patrick had seen. Satisfied he was strapped in, Patrick looked at Buddy. He hadn't seen Buddy in a couple of months, not since the last time they'd had to go out to try to find a plane that went down. After a four-hour search, they never did find it. That happened sometimes. "All right. Things are busy at work. Got rid of the girlfriend since the last time I saw you."

Buddy raised his eyebrows as he flipped a few switches on the instrument panel. "Really? This one wanted to get married, too?"

Patrick glared at Buddy, then cracked a smile. "Yeah. I guess. I'm too busy with work to settle down."

"People still don't know how to drive?" Buddy flipped a few switches on the panel in front of him, his small eyes narrowing.

"Not so much. But then again, we'd both be out of a job if they did."

"True enough." He glanced over at Patrick. "Ready to go?"

"Yep. Let's get this party started."

With a short nod, Buddy grabbed the yoke of the helicopter. Patrick could hear the beating of the blades overhead intensify until their individual turning sounded like nothing more than a single thrum in the background. The earphones did a good job of blocking the sound, but they did nothing to mask the heavy vibration in his body. Patrick felt the initial thrust as the helicopter lifted off the ground and then felt it ease forward as

Buddy took it off the pad behind the NTSB offices. At least that was one good thing, Patrick thought. Having a helicopter accessible would make the search easier than trying to traverse the Texas countryside in a Jeep or an ATV. A ground search would be pretty much useless in the dark.

Once they were in the air, Patrick glanced over at Buddy. "So, where did we get the reports from?"

"Slightly south of Camp Swift."

Patrick nodded. He knew there was a small Army base there used for training purposes, or at least that's what he'd been told. With the military, no one ever knew exactly what was going on. Buddy's voice interrupted his thoughts, "I've put the coordinates into the GPS. But you know as well as I do that where people call from and where the crash site is..."

"Are two different things."

Patrick and Buddy rode in alternate states of silence and mindless chit-chat as Buddy started the grid search pattern programmed into the helicopter's advanced onboard search and detection systems. The Coast Guard had pioneered the use of grid searches, particularly when looking for missing sailors thrown off sinking fishing vessels in the frigid waters of the Bering Sea. They created sophisticated technology that would take an area, break it down into sections and then assign different search groups to work each section, taking into consideration tides and wave patterns as well as possible drift. The Coast Guard had become expert at finding sailors floating in the water in gumby suits or in bright orange lifeboats, employing helicopters, reconnaissance planes, and large cutter vessels on the rough seas off the Alaskan coast. The NTSB had adopted much of the same procedures in a rare moment of interagency cooperation. The only difference was, in this case, it was just Patrick and Buddy out searching. Patrick knew they could call in for planes and trucks, but it probably didn't make any sense to do that until the morning, at least for the trucks.

The helicopter had a four-hour range before needing to be refueled. They'd stick it out for that long and then regroup.

After an hour or so of searching, Patrick looked at Buddy, "You think we're going to find anything?"

"Heck if I know," Buddy shrugged. "You know, I'm only here to fly the bird. Whatever happens after that is up to you."

Patrick looked over the side of the helicopter, scanning the ground. The searchlight hadn't shown anything at all except a few startled cows out in the field. His eyes were getting tired from staring, especially after spending the day working on reports for Doug.

Ten minutes later, as Buddy made the turn onto a new section of the grid pattern, he mumbled, "Whoa."

Patrick straightened up in his seat, "What's whoa? What do you see?"

Buddy hovered the helicopter in a single spot, stopping their forward progress, "Take a look at that," he said, nodding his head toward the beam of light.

Patrick leaned toward the front windows of the helicopter, trying to see what had gotten Buddy's attention. Caught in the beam of light looked to be a single seat from a small plane laying on its side, the striped upholstery still attached to the frame.

"That look like a plane seat to you?" Buddy said, backing the helicopter away so they could get a better look.

Patrick nodded. "Yeah. Can you put a pin in that location? Let's scan the area."

"You want me to put it down here so you can walk around?"

Patrick thought for a second and then looked at Buddy, "No, not unless we see something more. All this tells us at this point is that we have a seat in the middle of a cow field. We're looking for something bigger than that. But I gotta know where this is so we can retrieve it for the report."

"Pin entered," Buddy said, touching the onboard navigation. The tracking system that the helicopter used for the grid search had the ability to mark individual spots where items had been found. Patrick pulled his phone out of his pocket and opened up the NTSB app that coordinated with the grid search software. He connected to the system and entered a note saying they'd found a seat at that location. Not every investigator took the time to take notes, which was a problem. It was one thing to mark the location, but another to remember what was there. Cleanup was that much more difficult if they didn't know which pieces of debris were in which locations. If Patrick had learned one thing in his ten years as an NTSB investigator it was that details always mattered. They could be the difference between solving a crash and never getting the answers they needed.

Leaning forward in his seat, Patrick looked at Buddy, "Now we're rolling the dice. We can go any direction from here and we might find something or we might find nothing."

"You've got that right. Which way do you want to head?"

Patrick stared at the navigation screen in front of him while the helicopter hovered. Looking at the way the seat landed wasn't of any help. It wasn't as if it had a flare attached pointing in the direction of the rest of the debris. A seat or a toolbox or body — anything launched out of a plane from hundreds of feet up in the air, or even thousands, could drift and twist and turn riding on swirling wind currents before it finally landed. All they knew at this point was that one piece of evidence had been found. Something had happened. What exactly, they didn't know yet. And in order to get any kind of indication of the flight path, they'd have to find a second piece of debris. A prickle of excitement ran up Patrick's spine. They'd found one needle in the haystack, but they needed two in order to play connect the dots.

Patrick sighed. "As much as I'd like to be able to easily solve this, I have no idea. What do you think?" he said, looking at Buddy.

Buddy shrugged. "We might as well stay on the same grid pattern. Even if we don't find something, at least we know this section will have been covered. It becomes a process of elimination then."

"Sounds good."

Almost another half hour later, Patrick spotted the second needle in the haystack. "Hey!" he said, reaching for Buddy's arm and grabbing it. He pointed over his shoulder, "Take a look at that. You see something orange out there?"

Buddy looked, the glow of his face illuminated only by the lights of the controls in the helicopter's cockpit, "Sure do. Something orange?"

"That's what I'm seeing."

"Glad to know my eyes aren't going," Buddy said, nosing the helicopter toward the orange spot. Hovering overhead, Patrick used the onboard cameras to record what they saw and enlarge it. "Toolkit. You know, the kind that has the flares and emergency supplies built-in."

Buddy nodded, "Yeah. I'm not a plane guy, but if I remember correctly, they use those on a lot of the small, twin-prop models. They're lighter in weight than the kind of stuff they put on the bigger jets."

Patrick nodded. With small planes, everything came down to weight, from the overall heft of the plane itself, to the people, the cargo, fuel, and any luggage they had onboard. That's why most small planes crashed. It was either they were overloaded and didn't have the thrust to maintain their flight or there was some mechanical issue because of not being maintained correctly. Patrick pressed his lips together and shook his head, "If people only knew how fragile little planes were, they'd never get on one. Never." Patrick paused, "Okay, let's put a pin in this one too. I'll mark it in the notes. Can you extrapolate a flight path from this?" Patrick said, typing into his phone again.

"Yeah, maybe," Buddy nodded. "With two points, it's likely to be one direction or the other, but no promises. You want to go north or south first?"

"Recommendation?"

"Well, given the fact we've been out here for a while, starting south gets us closer to the refueling pad. We can go south for the next five miles or so and then if we don't find anything we can head back, refuel, and then I'll take you back up again and we can go north."

Patrick nodded, "Sounds good. Let's do that."

Buddy swung the helicopter around, heading south, the onboard computers calculating the likely direction of the flight path as they flew. It wasn't an exact science, that was for sure. Debris could scatter to either side of a flight path, so even after finding two points, there was no guarantee they were any closer to figuring out where the actual crash site was. Their odds improved dramatically if they could find one or two more items. Patrick stretched his shoulders as they flew. It'd been a long day. But it was the job. At least they knew there was something going on and it wasn't nothing. He sent a quick text to Doug, "Found debris. Nothing on the crash site yet. Will keep you posted."

Buddy guided the helicopter slowly over the area, the searchlights scanning the ground in an automated pattern. They flew for another twenty minutes or so and didn't find anything. Patrick frowned, looking at Buddy, "Don't you think we should have found something else by now?"

"Your guess is as good as mine," Buddy mumbled. He pointed at the screen, "The problem is if the toolbox and the seat were ejected at the same time, they could've landed far apart, but on the wide side of the debris field, and not on a single line."

Patrick understood what Buddy was saying. His stomach tightened with frustration. Debris was unpredictable.

"Do we need to go back and refuel yet?" Patrick was feeling impatient. He knew they'd need to get fuel for the helicopter. He also knew that neither he nor Buddy was going home until they found something.

"Not yet. We've got a few more minutes. Let's keep looking in this direction and then we'll regroup at the refueling point."

Patrick nodded.

It wasn't more than thirty seconds later when Buddy said, "I think we just found the Holy Grail, Indiana Jones."

For a second, Patrick didn't know if Buddy was being serious or not. He glanced at him, his eyebrows raised. Buddy looked back at him, pointing, "Over there, dude. You see what I see?"

Narrowing his eyes, Patrick nodded, "That looks like a Holy Grail to me."

13

A fter a brief conversation between the two of them, followed by sending a brief text to Doug, Patrick held onto the harness as Buddy veered the helicopter to the side of the crash site, putting the helicopter down with only the slightest bump. Buddy glanced at Patrick, "I'll stay on board while you take a first look. I'll send the coordinates over to headquarters and have them get the locals moving."

"Perfect," Patrick said, taking the headset off and hanging it on the hook behind his seat. He unlatched the harness, dropping the thick black webbing to the side, and opened the door.

Sliding out, he landed with two feet squarely on the ground, grabbed a flashlight from the mount next to his seat, and closed the helicopter door behind him, leaning over, avoiding the rotors overhead. Even with their slow movement and the fact they were a good ten feet above his head, the wind was still intense.

Taking off at a jog, Patrick ran towards the site he and Buddy had spotted from the air. The white metal of what was left of the plane glimmered in the darkness, or at least the part of the plane he could see. With the fuselage still intact, it was entirely possible there was someone on board. His first job was to figure out if they needed medical attention or the coroner.

Slowing down as he got close to the scene, he could smell smoke. It didn't look to be an active fire, the odor was a result of some of the wiring in the remaining engine smoldering after impact. He stopped for a second, his eyes scanning the plane. "NTSB, anyone here?" he yelled as loud as he could above the noise of the helicopter humming behind him. It was entirely possible that when the plane came down if someone had survived, they had crawled away from the scene. They could be anywhere by now.

Patrick stopped and listened for a second. There was no reply. He took a few more steps forward and yelled again, "NTSB! Investigator Patrick Mills. Anyone here? Do you require medical assistance?"

Still no reply. Picking his way over the rough ground to the fuselage, Patrick started at the tail end, working his way forward, scanning the ground. There was a smattering of chunks of metal, screws, and bolts littering the area near the plane where it had ground to a halt after falling out of the sky. He made his way to the cockpit, noticing the right engine and wing were both gone. He made a mental note they would have to try to find those parts, but that wouldn't happen until the morning.

As he got to the front of the plane, he was surprised at what good shape it was in. If he hadn't already seen the back of it, he would have assumed the plane itself was fine. He used a flashlight to light up the interior. There was no one there. No bodies. Part of him breathed a sigh of relief. He'd seen his fair share of mangled tissue in his job. Not having to see more, or at least avoiding it for the moment, seemed like a blessing.

Patrick looked up, scanning the hillside, and using the flashlight to search the area. "NTSB! Anybody here? Can you hear me?" He walked around the front of the plane, panning his flashlight on the ground, looking for any signs of life. There weren't any.

A second later, Buddy hopped out of the helicopter's cockpit and wandered over to the debris. "What the –?" he said, his hands on the hips of his flight suit.

Patrick stopped and turned, frowning. "What is it?" He'd been so busy trying to find the pilot that he hadn't really looked in detail at the fuselage, other than to notice that the cockpit was still in pretty good condition.

Buddy shook his head and pointed a thick finger at the hole torn through the top of the plane, "I haven't seen anything like this since I got back from the Middle East."

"What do you mean?"

Buddy raised his eyebrows, "Dude, that looks like a missile strike to me."

Patrick shook his head, staring at the plane. Slightly above the junction where the fuselage met the wings, there was a gaping hole in the top of the plane in the shape of a half-circle. The edges were charred and black. The entire right engine and the majority of the right wing were gone. The left engine and wing were intact. Patrick pressed his lips together, running his hand over the metal. It was cool. The left engine and wing were probably what had allowed the pilot to get the plane on the ground. Patrick directed his flashlight back at the pilot's seat. No blood and no body. As he looked inside, he coughed, the smoldering fuselage sending fumes into the air. The harnesses were still attached to the frame. If the pilot had taken the time to strap themselves in before they took off, then there should be a body in that seat, unless the person had been able to get out. If they hadn't used the harness, they could be anywhere in the Texas countryside, dazed, confused, and injured, or even picked up by a good Samaritan. Patrick stared at the fuselage. That still didn't explain Buddy's comment, though.

Patrick's mouth went dry. "Are you kidding?" Patrick's mind

reeled. Surely Buddy was making another one of his jokes. He stared at his pilot, waiting for him to start to laugh with another one of his gotcha moments.

"I wish I was." Buddy took a couple of steps closer to the plane and pointed to the black edge of the fuselage. "See how the burn marks are only right around the edge? And see how it makes a jagged half circle?"

Patrick nodded, a knot tying up his stomach, the muscles in the back of his neck tightening. A missile strike on US soil was no joke. This was no mechanical failure, that was for sure.

"My guess? Whoever was flying this plane saw the trail of the missile coming at them and banked towards it. It looks like the missile clipped the top of the plane as they were banking left. The missile took out the right wing and the right engine. That maneuver probably saved the pilot's life. Whoever was flying this plane had some serious training. Probably military or something similar."

Patrick shook his head. He wasn't inclined to argue with Buddy, not with all of his experience. "But the problem is, there's no pilot."

14

Once Buddy called in the coordinates to NTSB headquarters, it didn't take too long for the local fire department and police departments to roll their rescue crews. As soon as they arrived, Patrick sent Buddy off with the helicopter to refuel and take a break from flying. Patrick would do the initial search of the scene with the locals and then bring in the rest of the NTSB crew the next morning to bag, tag, and remove the debris.

Luckily, the local fire department was well prepared for disasters. Within a half-hour of finding the scene, not only had the local fire department arrived complete with lights and sirens, but they brought portable lights and a generator with them, somehow managing to get the equipment down what was barely a road nearby and then across the field. "We always keep these in the truck because of tornadoes," the white helmeted captain said to Patrick. He'd introduced himself as Fred Velasquez. Patrick hadn't met him before, but then again, plane crashes weren't exactly a regular, everyday thing the same way a car crash or a cat getting lost in a tree was. Patrick nodded, "I'm glad you guys have these with you. Can you leave them here overnight?"

Captain Velasquez nodded, "Yeah. My guys have taken care of the electrical fire. Wasn't anything big. Mostly smoke. Can't promise how stable the fuselage is if you want to go inside, but at least it's sitting flat on the ground. Local PD will stay with you and secure the scene until you're ready to release it. They'll leave two guys here with cruisers in case you need a ride into town for anything."

By his calculations, Patrick figured he was about twenty miles from his office. Having a ride ready to go would be helpful. He was sure Doug would come out in the morning, but for now, the scene was all his. "Thanks. Did you guys have any luck finding a body?"

Captain Velasquez shook his head, "Naw. We scoured the hillside and looked around the fuselage at a radius of about five hundred yards. Nothing. Maybe your pilot made it out alive?"

"If he did, he's the luckiest person in the world."

"Oh, by the way," Velasquez said, pulling something out of his pocket. "One of the guys brought this over to me a minute ago. He found it on a rock right near the fuselage. Looks like it had been set there."

As Patrick opened his hand, Velasquez dropped a silver bracelet with multicolored stones in it, blue and red and green turquoise. Patrick frowned. "Where did he find this?"

Velasquez looked over his shoulder, and yelled, "Marcos? Over here."

A black helmeted firefighter trotted over to the captain, glancing between him and Patrick. "Sir?"

"I handed off that bracelet you found to the NTSB investigator. Where did you find it? Can you show him?"

Marcos gave a curt nod, glancing at Patrick, "Yes, sir. Right this way."

Patrick followed Marcos, the bright lights from the generators casting sharp shadows as they walked away from Velasquez. There was a boulder about ten feet from the crash site. Marcos pointed to it. "Over there, sir. It was draped on top of the stone." He frowned. "I thought it was strange, so I took a picture." From out of his pocket, Marcos pulled his phone, opening it up and showing the image to Patrick.

Patrick cocked his head to the side as he looked at it. He put the bracelet back down on the rock trying to match the same angle and position. "Like this? Is this how you found it?"

Marcos nodded, "Yes, exactly. I thought it was weird; like it was a message or something. You don't think it fell out of the plane that way do you?"

Patrick looked up at the sky and then back at the plane, the broken fuselage looking black and tired. He shook his head, "No, Marcos, I don't think it did."

15

"Man, all of this ranch work is exhausting," Gus grumbled, stretching as he stood up from the dusty bench on the edge of the indoor arena where he'd been perched while he watched Travis ride. Unfortunately, as hard as Travis worked to ignore Gus, he had refused to leave. He brushed off his hands as Travis handed off the last horse he'd trained for the night to Ellie to cool down and put away. Gus grimaced, pointing at the empty arena. "You do this every single day?"

Travis nodded, "Except for Sundays. Horses need a day to rest, but there are still chores to do."

Gus shook his head, "I can't imagine." He glanced toward the driveway, "I'm getting hungry. When do we eat? Shouldn't there be a chuckwagon pulling up at any minute?"

Travis narrowed his eyes, adjusting the baseball cap on his head, ignoring Gus. He knew Gus was just trying to be funny, but somehow it came out demeaning and sarcastic. Gus didn't agree with Travis's decision to leave the CIA, but it wasn't up to him, and Travis had never asked his opinion.

Travis walked down the concrete aisle between the two

rows of stalls, checking on the horses one last time, while Ellie was taking the saddle off his last ride. The steam was coming off the horse's back from underneath the saddle, the horse's nostrils flared as his heart rate came down from the last run down the arena. The gelding had offered a perfect sliding stop, the horse's thick back haunches locking into place and sliding along while his front legs allowed his body to move forward. He'd thrown up a wake of dust and dirt that collected in a cloud and hung in the air. Part of him hoped Gus choked on the dust. Travis shrugged to himself.

Travis turned to look at Gus after glancing at Ellie. "There's no chuckwagon," he said matter-of-factly.

Gus shrugged and nodded, "Okay, well then how about if we take a ride into town and I'll buy you dinner."

Travis knitted his eyebrows together, "You're buying? This is a first."

Gus held up his hands, "I know, don't get your chaps in a twist. There's a new sheriff in town."

Travis shook his head. Gus's cowboy jokes were starting to wear thin, "I'm not wearing chaps."

Gus chuckled, "Yeah, but I bet you look darn good in them. Let's go."

Gus insisted on driving back into Austin, complaining about the restaurants near the ranch. Where Bishop Ranch was located outside of Burton off of the 290, there weren't too many, or at least any that Gus had found suitable. Gus had checked himself into a hotel on the outskirts of Austin, about an hour away. "Mind if we head back in that direction? I've got a couple of things I want to check on and something I want to show you," he said, his voice suddenly serious.

Travis shrugged, wondering what the change in attitude was about, but not wanting to make a big deal about it. Gus was the kind that the more rope you gave him, the more he took. "Yeah, that'll work. I don't have anything going."

"Not even with that cute girl that came in?" Gus grinned.

"Ellie? No. She works for me. That's it."

"Keeping things simple since Kira, huh?"

The words stung. Of all people, Gus should have known how painful it was for Travis when Kira died. They'd never found her body. A car bomb had taken her out, shredding the sedan she'd been in and two more cars nearby. There was nothing left to find. She'd been awarded a Distinguished Intelligence Medal of Service in a solemn ceremony at Langley attended only by the people in their group at the time – he and Gus, Elena, and a couple of other people plus the Director of the CIA and one of the assistants. Kira's name wasn't engraved on any wall or her name on any plaque. There was no record of her life or the work that she'd done except what was sealed in her CIA files. The star installed on the wall was simply another silver star embedded in the white marble in the lobby, anonymous exactly like the others.

Not acknowledging Gus's comment, Travis glanced out the window as Gus drove them to Austin. That's what his life was like now. Anonymous. And things had been going fine until Gus showed up that afternoon.

Travis glanced back at Gus, who had one hand on the steering wheel and the other hand on the sill of the driver's side door, tapping his fingers. He was humming along to some song that Travis couldn't recognize, a pop song. Travis looked back out the window, not saying anything, noticing the buildings were starting to appear in closer proximity to one another. They were getting closer to Austin. His stomach rumbled. Usually by now, he was back in his house, heating a can of soup or making himself a sandwich after a long day in the barn. The physical work had helped him sort through the memories in his head, many of them ones he didn't want to remember.

Travis frowned. Gus's arrival in his fancy jeans and sports coat had upended everything in his mind, particularly the carefully constructed layers of distance he put between himself and his memories.

Looking at Gus now, all Travis could think of was Elena. A lump formed in his throat. If even half of what Gus had said was true, Elena was out there, somewhere, alone and in trouble.

Being in trouble in CIA terms was a very different situation than getting school detention, getting pulled over for speeding, or even getting deployed as part of the military to a hot zone somewhere in the world. In each one of those cases, there was a prescribed path forward. A person would serve their detention, pay their fine, or spend their time in the Middle East, like he had, and then come home, hopefully in some similar form to the way they'd left.

With the CIA, it was completely different. An agent out on their own and in trouble likely had no one they could turn to. No backup, very likely no plan, and even fewer resources. Even though Travis hadn't eaten all day, he suddenly lost his appetite. Part of him wished that it had been him out on his own, not Elena. Questions rose inside of him like logs stacked on one another, each one building off the one before. He chewed his lip. If Gus had come to him to trace Elena there were only two possibilities — Gus really didn't know where Elena was and needed to find her, or Gus had something else entirely planned. Travis hated to think that way, but unfortunately, he'd been the recipient of one too many of Gus's ill-fated plans in the past, plans that had sounded fully formed with all of the expectations and outcomes outlined, only to get halfway through and feel like he'd been thrown into a whirling dervish, not sure which way was up.

But that was Gus. And for some reason, the CIA kept him around.

"Where are we going to eat?" Travis said as they pulled off of the freeway.

Gus didn't answer for a second, but at least Travis recognized the area. They were southeast of Austin proper, in one of the suburbs. He couldn't remember the exact name. He knew he'd been there a few times going to a specialty saddlery store to pick up some custom leather work he needed, but that had been several years before. He hadn't been back since, preferring to stay close to home.

"I'm staying at the hotel on the other side of the park. Pretty nice place." Gus scratched his beard. "We'll grab something and then we can talk now that you're done playing cowboy for the day."

Travis bristled. Nothing about what he did with the horses at Bishop Ranch involved playing. He had paying customers who wanted their horses trained and ready for the spring reining circuit. He'd had some good luck in the few years before, attending the horse shows in a couple of the surrounding states, but he needed a big win in order to get his name on the map with some of the most pronounced in the industry like Tom McCutcheon, Andrea Fappani and Matt Mills.

"Sure. Whatever you want, Gus." It probably sounded to Gus like Travis was acquiescing. Part of him was. Gus was like a hangover in a lot of respects. He just had to let it play out and then it would leave.

After pausing at three stop lights, Gus pulled into the hotel parking lot. The sun had been down for a while, the last couple of horses Travis exercised plus the drive into Austin taking up a good chunk of the evening. The crowds outside had thinned out, although there was still a pretty good group of people in the park despite the darkness. Café lights had been strung in the green space across the way from the hotel and a couple of food trucks had pulled up, setting up tables and chairs. The smell of garlic and chorizo floated through the air, making Travis's mouth water.

As they got out of the car, Gus stopped, frowning, staring at his phone. Travis looked at him, "What is it?"

Gus shook his head, "A local news report just popped up on my phone. A small plane went down somewhere outside Austin."

"Everybody okay?"

Gus shrugged, "Doesn't say. Probably some teenagers borrowing Daddy's crop-dusting plane for a joyride."

"I hope you're right."

16

Gus jumped out of the rental car and charged across the street without a word. Travis followed. "Let's try over there," Gus pointed.

Travis followed, "I thought you said you were buying dinner."

"I am. See the food trucks?"

"I didn't realize dinner from a food truck counted," Travis grumbled. Sitting down on a soft chair with a cold beer and a juicy hamburger in front of him would have been better than following Gus to a food truck. Gus's presence was beginning to wear thin. He could feel himself becoming grouchier by the moment. Gus hadn't even offered to let him run into the house and change his clothes. He still smelled like a combination of horse sweat and dirt from the barn. Part of him was hoping the rush to get to Austin would help Gus hurry up the process — give Travis whatever information he wanted to pass along and then leave him alone to do his job. The memory of Elena's face settled in the back of his mind. If she needed to be found, then it would probably be better if Gus stopped messing around with finding dinner and just got on with it.

But that was Gus. Wasting time was one of his specialties.

Following Gus to the park across the street from the hotel, Travis sighed. Gus looked a lot more like the mayor than a guest. He held his head high, waving at people and smiling as he trotted across the street; like he was having the time of his life. Travis strode along behind him, his dust-covered cowboy boots looking a lot more appropriate than Gus's shiny designer tennis shoes.

Over in the park, the smell of garlic and frying meat got even stronger. Travis's stomach rumbled again, his hunger taking precedent over the fact that he was with Gus or that he was concerned about Elena.

Two food trucks had pulled up head to tail in the park near the grass, their vending windows open, an upbeat guitar melody pouring out from inside of one of them. "I got these tacos last night when I got in. So good! Have you ever had them?"

Travis shook his head, staring at the brightly painted food truck. "Can't say I have." The side read, "Tommy's Tacos and Modern Mexican," in bright yellow looping lettering. Scanning the crowd, there were a few tables of people sitting and eating, the rustle of paper being crinkled as people finished their meals, the hum of conversation and laughter in the background floating over the music. Travis's gut tightened. He hadn't seen that many people in one place since his last horse show and that had been a few months. Travis followed Gus as he made his way to the window. "I'll have two of the pork belly tacos and one with carnitas." He glanced back at Travis and winked, "And whatever my friend wants here." Gus leaned toward the dark-haired woman standing in the window, "it's my turn to buy tonight."

As Travis looked at the woman, he realized her eyebrows were raised. Whether it was in surprise or disgust, Travis wasn't exactly sure. "I'll have the same." Travis nodded to the woman. "Thank you."

"No problem," the woman said, giving Gus the total for their order.

Travis stepped away while Gus was paying. The truck next to Tommy's Tacos and Modern Mexican was selling ice cream. A little girl with bright blonde hair and two pigtails stepped away from the window, carrying a double-decker ice cream cone that seemed almost taller than she was. The smile on her face stretched from ear to ear. There was something about the girl that looked like Kira, maybe the arc to her nose or the flat spot at the bottom of her chin. Travis wondered if the child looked like one of the kids they would've had together. Travis pivoted away, pushing the memory from his thoughts.

"Travis! Over here," Gus yelled. As Travis looked back, he saw Gus with a tray full of food, walking toward a wooden picnic table with two benches that had just opened up. Taking a couple of steps, Travis glanced over his shoulder, looking for the little girl with her ice cream cone to see where she went, but she was gone. Travis turned towards Gus, following him, stepping over the worn wooden bench and easing himself down onto it, settling himself in. Gus already had half a taco shoved in his mouth, talking as he chewed. "These are so good. Do you guys eat like this in Texas all the time? Man, I'd be five hundred pounds if I lived down here. Maybe it's better that I'm in DC. You know, all the salad eaters."

Travis shook his head, not sure exactly what to say. He picked up one of the tacos and took a bite out of it, the combination of the garlicky pork belly and the sweetness of the corn salsa filling his mouth. The fact that he was so hungry made it taste even better. Gus was right, these were good tacos. Too bad they were an hour from the ranch.

The two men ate in silence for a minute. Gus plowed through his tacos like a man that hadn't eaten meat in a decade or more. As Gus pushed the paper tray away from him, he looked at Travis, "All right, well now that we're here, I guess I can fill in some of the blanks for you about Elena."

Travis picked up his napkin and wiped his mouth, "That would be nice. I mean the tacos are good and all, but it'd be helpful to know exactly what I'm looking for."

Gus leaned forward slightly, "As I said, Elena went dark seventy-two hours ago. She was somewhere in this area."

Travis chewed his taco and stared at Gus, "And that's how you ended up in my backyard?"

"That, and I wanted to see you," Gus grinned. "Had to see if you've lost any of your edge."

Travis raised his eyebrows ignoring the comment. "Okay, so you think Elena's in this area. Why?"

"Her last call to the office tracks from Texas, though it was so quick, we couldn't get an actual location on it."

"Texas is a big state. You can't track her phone?"

"No. Since you left the agency, we've gone to new technology that cloaks the locations of the phone unless the user enables it. Either Elena turned it off right after that, or she ditched her phone. Either way, we haven't had a signal from her in a while, longer than I'm comfortable with."

Travis took another bite of his taco and looked down at the worn wood of the table. Someone had scratched initials and a heart into the surface. He stared at it for a second, then started to think. Not being able to reach a CIA agent wasn't all that unusual in the scope of things. There were plenty of times when he was active that he'd shut off his phone or dumped it, then gone into a local store and purchased a burner. They were all taught exactly how and when and why to do that during their training. The question was why had Elena?

Gus took a sip of his drink, a slurping noise coming from the straw. "Anyway, so Elena has been tracking some problems we're looking at out of the Eastern Bloc."

"What part of the Eastern Bloc?" Travis frowned, ignoring the slurping. In CIA language, the Eastern Bloc could represent anything from a tiny country like Moldova to the entirety of Russia with all of its complex history, politics, and agendas. He pressed his lips together. It was just like Gus to be vague.

"I think Russia, but I can't be sure. As I said, our communication with her hasn't been that good."

Travis blinked. Russia and then Texas. How did this even fit together? And why was Elena operating on US soil? If she'd gone dark, it would make more sense for her to be outside of the territorial United States boundaries. Technically, the CIA was not permitted to operate inside of the US borders, although it happened more than people knew. Something didn't seem right.

"And you think she's still alive?"

Gus shrugged, "Honestly, I have no idea." He looked down for a second, fiddling with his napkin. "All I know is..."

Travis looked up wondering why Gus hadn't finished his sentence in time to see a red dot appear on the front of Gus's white shirt. Travis's eyes went wide as he dove for the ground, yelling, "Gun!"

By the time the words came out of his mouth, a crimson stain spread across Gus's chest, the crack of a rifle shot bouncing off of the buildings surrounding the park. People screamed as they heard the noise, scattering away from the picnic tables and the food trucks. Travis crawled towards Gus. His body had slumped onto the table. A few more shots rang out, whizzing overhead. Travis, his heart pounding in his chest, reached up and fumbled through Gus's sports coat pockets, pulling out his hotel room key phone, wallet, and rental car key. There wasn't any point in trying to offer aid to Gus or checking his pulse. The shot had been center mass. From his time in Delta Force, Travis knew no one could survive that.

Glancing over his shoulder from his position under the

table, Travis knew he had to get to cover. He put his hand on the grip of his gun but didn't pull it. From the direction of the noise, he could tell the shots were coming from one end of the park. It was too far to fire back without risking shooting a civilian. His only hope was to get away. He scrambled for the nearest food truck. As he ran behind it, he glanced inside to see the three women who had served them tacos just a few minutes before, cowering on the ground. "Stay down," he yelled. Behind the safety of the taco truck, Travis stopped for one second, plastering his body up against the back of it, the cool of the metal soaking through his shirt. His mind was reeling. What just happened? At that moment, there was no way to tell if it was a random attack, like the mass shootings in Las Vegas, or if it was an assassination attempt specifically designed for Gus. Travis didn't have time to try to figure it out.

Hearing the crack of rifle fire in the distance and more screams, Travis started to move. Even further out than that, he heard the howl of sirens. The last thing he wanted to do was get caught up in the middle of a police investigation. He shook his head, licking his lips. His mouth was dry from the surge of adrenaline in his system. He needed to get away from the park, and now. "Why did I let Gus drive?" he mumbled, making his way along the back of the taco truck. As he got to the edge, he looked between the two trucks. There was still an occasional shot here and there, but he didn't see any other bodies on the ground. He spotted an older man slumped nearby, holding a bleeding wound on his upper arm, but Gus looked like he was the only casualty.

Darting off into the darkness, under what he hoped was enough cover from the trees, Travis bolted to the opposite end of the park. He stopped about halfway across the lawn, dodging behind a stand of trees, listening, his heart pounding in his chest. He took a deep breath then, trying to regain his composure. He'd been in combat before. This was nothing new, except for the fact that he had no idea who was shooting at him, or why. "War is a lot less complicated," he mumbled, trying to catch his breath. "At least you have some idea who is shooting at you." Checking over his shoulder, Travis had the distinct impression someone was watching him. He couldn't shake the feeling, but he didn't have time to give it much more than a passing thought.

Taking off at a quick walk, Travis emerged at the opposite end of the park as he saw two police cars, lit up with their red and blue lights, racing toward the scene. Gus had been trying to tell him something about Elena before he'd been shot, but what? Out of his pocket, he pulled the hotel key card for Gus's room. Gus hadn't been able to tell him anything before he died, but maybe something in his room would.

17

The howl of the incoming emergency vehicles only got louder as Travis crossed the street at the other side of the park, Travis walked on the closest side street around a bank that was closed for the night and then headed north, toward the hotel, which was directly across the street from the ongoing chaos in the park. It would be a reasonable guess that the local law enforcement would be so focused on the incident they wouldn't have much concern about a single guy walking empty-handed toward the back entrance of the hotel. Hotel guests did that all the time, especially those who were close to a shooting and were seeking shelter. It took him another three minutes to navigate behind the string of buildings and circle back toward the hotel.

Pushing his way into the lobby from the back entrance, Travis could see a line of people standing behind the plate glass windows that spanned the front of the hotel, their backs turned toward him, staring at the park, the murmur of their voices echoing off the walls. Someone was crying. He paused and shook his head ever so slightly. Part of him wanted to tell them that if the shooter was still active, a thin pane of glass would do absolutely nothing to protect them. They all needed to seek cover. But he didn't have time and it wasn't his business. He needed to get to Gus's hotel room and figure out what was going on and disappear. If the attack on Gus had, in fact, been a hit, that didn't bode well for Elena. She'd already been dark for seventy-two hours. Was whoever was going after her also going after Gus? Was there a target on Travis's back now?

Travis turned away from the mass of people plastered to the glass windows and strode toward the stairwell. The fewer people that saw him in the building, the better.

Grabbing the metal handrail in the stairwell, Travis took the steps two at a time, noting the scrawled handwriting on the paper key card that said room 301. He stopped a few feet below each landing, scanning above him and below, listening, his training kicking in. Landings between floors were the perfect place to get shot. The faster he moved through them the better. It took him less than another minute to scale the next two flights, pushing the doorway open on the third floor, a sign with a big black number three posted on a placard right next to the steel door.

Emerging out into the hallway, Travis stopped for a second, getting his bearings. The hotel seemed to be newly remodeled, the faint smell of fresh carpet and paint hanging in the air. Low light poured out of wall sconces that were mounted every few feet down the hallway, the thick carpet on the floor muffling his footsteps as he walked forward. Travis's mouth hung open slightly as he sucked in as much air as he could get. He wasn't exactly out of breath, but was still feeling the effects of running through the park and seeing Gus die in front of him. He needed his mind clear. He pushed the thoughts of the blood on Gus's shirt away. There'd be time to think about what happened to Gus later, but right now he needed answers.

Getting to the door for room 301, Travis slid the key card into the lock, seeing the light on the door turn green. He heard a slight beep as the lock popped open. Resting his hand on the knob, he realized his palms were sweating as he put his hand on the butt of his gun. He twisted the knob slowly, pushing the door open inch by inch, listening for any movement inside. There wasn't any.

Slipping into the room and closing the door behind him, Travis moved silently along the short hallway into the main area of the hotel room. It was clear.

Leaving the lights off, Travis strode over to the windows, which had a direct view of the park. He quickly tugged the curtains closed, using the thick fabric to mask the fact that he was in Gus's room from any peering eyes. With the curtains drawn, he flipped on the closest lamp. As he scanned the room, he realized he wasn't the first one to visit. The drawers were open, clothes were strewn across the bed, a suitcase laying upside down at the edge of the mattress nearly teetering off onto the floor. The closet door was open as well. Travis walked over to the safe, noting that it was open and empty. A small desk in the corner revealed a charging cable with nothing attached to it. "They even got your computer," he muttered under his breath.

The damage to Gus's room told one story and one story alone — Gus was the target of the incident at the park. Nothing about it was random, not by a long shot. And while Travis had bought himself a little bit of time by pulling Gus's ID out of his pockets, eventually, the local police would figure out who Gus was and that he was staying in the hotel. Travis needed to do his search of the room, find what he could, and get out, especially before whoever had come looking before Travis decided to come back.

Making his way to the desk, Travis used the edge of his flannel shirt as a glove to pull the drawer open. There was nothing inside, save a customized thin notepad with only a few sheets left on it, the name of the hotel emblazoned on the top for the guest to use. Travis stared at the empty cable. There had definitely been a computer there, but unless it was in Gus's car, it was gone. Someone had gotten to it before Travis.

Walking over to the dresser, the drawers scattered on the floor, Travis knelt down, looking inside. If whoever had trashed Gus's room was looking for things hidden either behind or underneath the drawers, they were looking for something specific. What, Travis had no idea. He spun around, putting his hands on his hips. He felt like there was a giant stopwatch on the wall in front of him ticking down, the room getting smaller and smaller the more time he spent in it, the walls shrinking toward him. His chest tightened, feeling like at any second there would be pounding on the door, the FBI or the police on the other side of it wondering what he was doing in there. That wasn't an explanation he was prepared to make.

He needed to think; and think quickly. Gus was smarter than taping something to the underside of a drawer or putting it in the hotel safe. That was bush league level espionage, the stuff of children's books. Gus would never do that. If there was anything on his computer, it was heavily encrypted and would probably destroy itself if it sensed any attack from inbound decryption software. That was standard with the CIA these days. Travis frowned. Where would Gus put information someplace that no one would ever look?

Turning on his heel, Travis went into the bathroom. Save for the single white towel hung on a hook near the door, it looked like the bathroom had been relatively undisturbed, as if whoever had tossed the room had completely forgotten to look in the bathroom. "Your mistake might be my gain," Travis mumbled under his breath, looking around. He pulled the shower curtain to the side, seeing a couple of bottles of the hotel shampoo in the shower along with a thin bar of soap. Gus mentioned he'd gotten in the night before. It would make sense that he would have showered in the morning before coming out to the ranch. Just thinking about the shower made Travis feel even more gritty than he already did; layers of sweat and dust from his work around the ranch, plus the adrenaline and sweat caking on his skin from running away from the shooting. His eyes scanned the space. On the counter next to the mirror there was a toiletry kit. "Bingo."

Picking it up and zipping it closed, Travis walked back into the bedroom area, sticking his head inside of the closet. On the wall was a white plastic drawstring bag emblazoned with the name of the hotel on it. He pulled it open and dropped Gus's toiletry kit inside. It would look a lot more normal if Travis was walking out of the hotel with one of their own bags rather than something stuffed under his flannel shirt.

It was time to go.

Going into the bathroom again, he picked up a white washcloth and carefully wiped down the light switches, turning them off as he went. He wiped the inside and outside handles of the room and stuffed the washcloth in his pocket.

Striding down the hallway, Travis went back the way he came in, pushing open the stairwell door and running down the three flights of steps, emerging at the back of the hotel lobby. He glanced to his right. The crowd near the windows had thinned a little, but there were still far too many people there for his fancy. It didn't matter, though. Maybe it would work to his advantage. They'd all be focused on the park while he made his way away from the scene.

The automatic doors at the back of the hotel whooshed open and he stepped out into the warm night air, the humidity immediately sticking to his skin. He could hear the low thrum of chatter, the whine of an ambulance siren in the distance as he walked to the parking lot, pulling Gus's keys for the rental car out of his pocket. He hit the fob, slid inside and closed the door, setting the plastic bag with the toiletry kit on the seat next to him. He started the car, feeling the automatic air conditioning kick on, the cool blowing on his face making him realize how hot and sweaty he really was.

"Gus, you son of a —." Travis stopped in mid-sentence, feeling heat rise to his cheeks, "What did you get me into this time?"

18

U ri and his team had driven directly from the crash site into Austin after Uri spotted the message on his phone from their contact. It was time for phase two, but the trip to the crash site had put them out of position. Uri pounded the wheel of the van several times as they sped down the freeway, swearing in almost indecipherable Russian. Everyone in the van knew exactly what he was saying even if they couldn't make the words out. Assignments like theirs never went according to plan and seemed to require immediate adjustments in strategy and tactics, something that infuriated Uri to his core. He liked sticking to a single plan. He liked order. Nothing about the mission they were on seemed to be following either of those precepts.

He glanced in the rearview mirror, gritting his square jaw and narrowing his almond-shaped eyes with the thick black eyebrows. He caught Sergey's eye. "Get your equipment together. We won't have long once we get there, especially now that we aren't where we should be." He sent a glowering glare through the rearview mirror to Tereza who didn't meet his eyes.

From behind him, he could hear the plastic latch on the

case for the Ruger Creedmoor rifle case open, the parts to the long-range barrel snapping together behind him. Their target package in the US included more than just Elena Lobranova.

THIRTY-FIVE MINUTES LATER, watching the scatter of people in the park running like a flock of chickens scared by the tractor at his grandfather's Russian dacha, their bodies darting this way and that, some of them quivering and hiding underneath picnic tables, Uri smiled. Their target was down. "Excellent shot, as usual, Sergey," he mumbled in Russian, looking over the scene with a pair of binoculars pressed up to his eyes. "For good measure, let a few more rounds fly over their heads. Let's create a little chaos. It'll make it easier to get away."

Scanning the crowd as Sergey fired the rifle six or seven more times, Uri scanned the crowd. The figure sitting with their target had immediately hit the ground at the first crack of the rifle. From the way the man moved, Uri could tell he had some sort of training, but whether he was law enforcement or military, he couldn't quite tell.

Uri trained the binoculars on the spot where he'd last seen the man near the food trucks. He watched as a shadow passed behind the trucks into the open park. He caught a glimpse of the man's face in the binoculars. Pulling the optics away from his face his stomach knotted, his eyes wide. Pressing his lips together, Uri pressed the optics back up to his face and trained the binoculars on the spot where he'd seen the man last, but he was gone. On foot, he couldn't have gotten far. Uri scanned the area, listening to Sergey pull the trigger of the 6.5-millimeter chambered rifle a couple more times for good measure, the explosions from the barrel almost as loud as cracks of thunder. Uri gave him a nod. It was time to go.

Uri scanned the crowd and then began to work his way outward. He picked up the figure as he exited the park at the other end, probably a good five hundred yards from where Uri was sitting. He pressed the capture button on the binoculars. The high-tech version their contact had left them had the ability to record what was being seen through the optics for playback later. Very helpful. As the man walked under a streetlight, he turned his face toward Uri. Another long string of Russian vulgarities came out of his lips in a hiss. "Travis Bishop," Uri said with a sense of finality. "I honestly never thought I would see you again."

Into the microphone attached to the comms at his wrist, Uri barked for the team to bring the van around. "We need to move." He kept his eye on Bishop for as long as he could until Travis disappeared behind a wide swath of buildings.

Alexander slammed on the brakes with a screech, stopping the red van at the back entrance of the office building Uri had chosen as their perch for the assault on the park. It'd been a split-second decision once they saw their target, but one that had worked well. Traveling down the back staircase, Uri and Sergey emerged outside of the building as Alexander pulled up. Uri slid into the front passenger side, slamming the door. He did a quick calculation in his head and pointed toward the hotel. That was the last direction Travis Bishop had been moving. The question was, could they pick up his tail? Uri licked his lips. Ending Bishop would be a bonus as far as Moscow was concerned. Travis Bishop wasn't on their current target list, but he was someone that Uri had been longing to see dead for what felt like eons.

"God's fortunes are upon us," Uri stared at Alexander as the red van pulled away. "We might be able to make this more of a success than Moscow ever imagined."

19

Travis glanced at the white plastic bag sitting on the passenger seat of Gus's rental car as he sped out of Austin. He noticed a few faint smudges of Gus's blood on his hands as he gripped the steering wheel. He reached up, adjusting the brim of his baseball cap. His hands were shaking. How had a normal day at the stable turned into a mass casualty event? His mouth felt dry, the coating of Texas dust in his mouth seemingly stuck to each one of his teeth and his tongue. He swallowed as best he could as the memories of what he'd just experienced filtered through his mind like individual fragments of broken glass. It was impossible at that moment to put together the whole.

Travis had distanced himself about two miles from the hotel, wanting to escape the scene as fast as possible, and was about to swing the sedan onto the freeway when he saw a set of headlights approaching fast from behind. He narrowed his eyes, watching them in the rearview mirror.

The enormous green signs for the freeway were up ahead, leaning over the road. He glanced in the mirror again. The headlights were still there, about a quarter-mile back. If he got on the freeway and someone was following him, it would be nearly impossible to evade them. The side roads would be a better bet. Travis swallowed, gripping the steering wheel tighter. It might take him longer to get back to the ranch, but he couldn't be too careful, not after what happened to Gus.

Taking freeways was not one of Travis's favorite pastimes, so he'd mastered the network of narrow grit-covered roads between Austin and Burton. There weren't many, but there were enough that he could get himself back to the ranch. Turning right onto State Highway 23, he began to head southeast, still checking the rearview mirror. He pressed his lips together, staring at the road ahead of him, wondering if he was just being paranoid. Gus had been in the city for less than twenty-four hours and now he was dead. Were the same people following Travis? Was there some link to the work they did for the CIA?

Travis sucked in a deep breath, trying to release the last of the butterflies out of his stomach. He glanced in the rearview mirror again. The same set of headlights was still behind him. As they passed under one of the last streetlights as he left Austin, Travis could see it was a red van. Both front seats were occupied.

Seeing the van still there, Travis grunted, "All right, you want to play, let's play." He set his jaw and leaned back into the stiff upholstery of the rental car. He pressed on the accelerator, pushing the sedan past the speed limit. He waited for ten seconds, counting slowly in his head, waiting to see if there would be any reaction from the vehicle behind him. If there wasn't, then it was unlikely he was being followed. If it reacted, that might mean something entirely different.

Travis watched. For a moment, the van lagged behind, enough that Travis felt like he was imagining things, then he saw it suddenly lurch forward, as though the driver suddenly noticed that Travis had gotten some distance on him.

There was no doubt about it, he was being followed. Travis glanced in the rearview mirror and the side mirrors, a bead of sweat forming on his upper lip. On the nearly straight path of Route 23, there weren't many options to evade the van and the people inside of it. Not a curve, not a valley, not a hillside. As his mind searched for a solution, all he could think of was the crimson red stain seeping through Gus's shirt. It had to be the same people. And if anything Gus had said to him was true, they were probably Russians, chasing Elena, assuming Travis knew where she was. The only problem was he had no idea where Elena was or what she was up to or how she'd managed to draw the ire of a foreign government. He felt the muscles in the back of his neck tighten as though someone had put a helmet on his head that was two sizes too tight. His thoughts whirled in his mind like the rush of wind from a tornado coming off the plains. He stepped on the accelerator even harder, pushing the sedan across the dusty roads.

A bitter taste filled his mouth. He licked his lips and slammed the steering wheel with his open palm, the combination of metal and plastic giving a satisfying thud, anger filling him as the sedan careened down the rapidly narrowing road. His heart tightened in his chest as the crimson van bore down on him. Up ahead, Travis knew there was a single turn off onto a dirt road he'd explored a few months back. If he was able to make the turn fast enough, the van would likely speed out of the way, not being able to match him.

Checking the rearview mirror once again, Travis sucked in a deep breath. He eased off on the accelerator a little, enough to let the van get right up on his tail. They'd need to be close in order for his plan to work. He rested his hand on the emergency brake, tightening his grip, and then put more pressure onto the accelerator, urging the van to stay close. "Come on," he growled under his breath. He needed the van to stay on his rear bumper. The closer the better. The road he was looking for was small and went off at a sharp angle from Route 23. He had only one shot. His breath became shallow as he glanced between the road ahead of him and his rearview mirror. The lights from the van grew larger, washing over the trunk of his car and creeping into the back seat like an uninvited guest. Travis narrowed his eyes. The road he was thinking of was barely marked, only a small green sign with white lettering and a series of numbers on it, the markings of a remote county road.

Travis checked the speedometer and then touched the gas, adding a bit more pressure and a bit more speed. He saw the familiar landmarks whip by him as two vehicles raced along together, so close their bumpers were nearly locked, only a few feet keeping them apart. Travis blinked. He saw a large oak tree, an abandoned log cabin...

"There!" Travis yelled, spinning the wheel wildly to the right and pulling up on the emergency brake at the same time. He felt the back end of the car fishtail as the front tried to gain purchase on the dirt road, the gravel and clay sliding underneath him, spraying out from underneath the tires. As the back of the car slid Travis jammed the emergency brake back into place, releasing the rear wheels and stomping on the gas. The car lurched down the road, Travis sucking in a deep breath, realizing the van had kept going, unable to make the turn at that speed. Travis flicked off the headlights, plunging the sedan into the darkness, and slowed down. He felt the adrenaline pouring into his system, his heart pounding in his chest, his breath ragged. He'd gotten away, at least for the moment.

Slowing the sedan down to a crawl, Travis squinted into the darkness. He needed to make it down the road at least a couple more miles before it would be safe to turn the headlights on again. Every few seconds, he checked the rearview mirror. There was nothing there. No van. No other cars. He ran through the scenario again. Would his trackers be able to find the road? Even if they did, Travis had a head start on them.

Confident he'd lost the tail at least for the moment, Travis stared forward, concentrating on the road.

The murky darkness of the Texas night covered everything around him. The sky was clear, the stars above him bright. He passed up a farm on the left, a few lights on inside of the front room, and then the open fields next to it, the wheat already cut down and bailed, enormous rounds scattered all over the acreage, wrapped in white plastic-like giant marshmallows that glinted against the moonlight.

As Travis regained his composure, his breath steadying, his mind was flooded with questions. He glanced at the plastic bag on the seat. It had rolled to its side as he made the sharp turn onto the dirt road. There was no doubt the van had followed him out of town, but who? Was it something harmless, like some kids seeing if they could put the scare into a random car, or was it someone who picked up Gus's rental car and was coming after him? Travis swallowed, the image of Gus's face as the projectile entered his chest seared into his memory. It was another in a long line of bodies Travis had seen. He shook his head, blinking. He was supposed to be past all of this. He'd walked away from the military and the CIA, closed the door, never to return. He'd had enough. That part of his life had ended five years ago. All he wanted to do was take care of his horses and be left alone, and here he was, driving down a side road in the middle of Texas with his headlights off trying to avoid being found by who were likely the same people tracking Elena and murdering Gus.

Travis gritted his teeth together and focused on the road for the next hour, checking his rearview mirror every few seconds. Confident he wasn't being tailed, he pulled off the side of the road after traveling nearly ten miles, pulling his cell phone out of his pocket. He checked his location. In his head, he imagined he was about five miles out from his ranch. The last thing he wanted to do was lead whoever had been chasing him back in that direction. And they would be looking for Gus's rental car, that was a fact. Whether they were actually looking for Travis in it, or not, Travis didn't know.

Barely able to get a signal, Travis's phone confirmed exactly what he expected. He was a little over five miles from the ranch. He glanced around him and then put the car into gear again driving another hundred yards or so. He pulled it into a turnoff that seemed to lead to nowhere, probably a path onto hunting acreage, he imagined.

Shutting off the car, Travis popped the trunk, looking in the back, wondering if Gus had left anything else in the vehicle. The yellow glow from the interior light flipped on. There was nothing inside, save for an emergency bag left by the rental agency. Travis frowned, unzipping it. Inside, he found a red emergency flare. He pulled it out and stuffed it in his back pants pocket. He patted the carpet in the back and lifted it up, looking underneath. Gus hadn't hidden anything in the back either. Walking around the far side of the car, Travis opened the door and pulled the white bag out, going through the glove box. Nothing. Checking his pockets, he realized he still had Gus's phone, wallet, and hotel key with him as well as his pistol, still in the holster on his side. He flipped the hotel key on the driver's seat. He wouldn't need that anymore. He shrugged off his flannel shirt and tore a strip off the bottom of it, about four inches wide and about a foot long. He repeated the procedure, knotting the two of them in the middle to make a long strip. Going to the side of the car, he flipped open the fuel door, jamming the fabric inside of the hole, using the end of the flare as a ramrod. Leaving the flare by the side of the car, Travis searched the interior one more time, making sure he hadn't forgotten anything.

Picking up the flare from the ground and lighting it, he touched the flame to the edge of the flannel that was dangling out of the fuel door and picked up the white bag, hiking in the direction of the ranch.

By the time he'd made it about fifty yards down the road, he heard a deafening boom, the rain of glass and metal dropping on the ground like the sudden deluge of a spring storm. The explosion was over as fast as it happened. He glanced over his shoulder to see the glow of the vehicle's carcass on fire behind him as he walked into the darkness.

20

"Did you deliver the package?" the voice said on the other line in broken Russian.

"Yes. We just did."

"Good. I'm on my way to Washington."

Uri had only been on the phone with their contact, a man he knew by the codename Stinger, for the last few minutes, trying to understand him through his thick American accent. After losing Travis on one of the country roads, Uri told Alexander to turn the van around and head back. They had time to find Travis, but they needed to drop Tereza off at the airport first. She was traveling to Washington DC to meet up with Stinger. At that moment, none of them knew who Stinger was. They only knew him as the benefactor who provided the financial and supply support while they were in the United States. A smile crept across Uri's face. "I wanted to thank you for the van full of toys."

"I'm glad you've enjoyed them. The party you threw at the park was highly successful."

Uri nodded, encouraged that Stinger agreed. "Yes. Quite so.

I think we put on a good show. By the way, while we were there, we spotted Bishop."

Stinger was quiet on the other end of the line, "Really? I'm imagining you'll take care of that, correct?"

"Of course. We will see where he leads us."

"Good."

21

The hike back to the ranch from the dirt road where Travis had ditched the car wasn't necessarily unpleasant, Travis decided as he crossed onto the mile-long driveway that led to his ranch house. It'd been a long time since he'd been stranded in the middle of nowhere. In fact, the last time was when he and Elena had been in Croatia. The meeting they were scheduled to have with an arms dealer in the little village north of Rijeka had gone wrong. Travis had gotten shot and somehow, Elena had managed to get him out of the firefight and patch him up well enough for him to get home. He still had the scar on the right side of his chest that only hurt when he moved too many hay bales at one time. She'd saved his life. It wasn't the only time.

As much as Travis would have liked to stay hidden as he walked the long driveway to his house, there wasn't any cover to be had, only the darkness and a long line of fences that flanked the paddocks gracing the front of his ranch. There were no trees or scrub brush to hide his walk without adding several miles to the hike. And while the walk hadn't been unpleasant, his mood had slumped as he thought through what had happened. He wanted to be home. The quiet and the darkness had given his body a chance to relax after the excitement of the shooting in the park, scouring Gus's hotel room, and the chase back to the ranch.

And now, he was only filled with one emotion. Anger.

The same litany had run through his mind about a thousand times since he left the burning car behind him. He'd been having a perfectly peaceful day and then Gus arrived.

Gus.

Why did every single issue in his life start with the three-letter word Gus? Part of him wanted to feel sad that Gus was dead, but he had brought more problems to Travis's life than anything else. Travis shook his head and kicked at a rock that was in front of his boot. It tottered away from him and landed next to one of the fence posts with a clunk. He glanced up, looking at the lay of the land in front of him. On both sides of the driveway were large open paddocks where he could leave the horses loose to run and play when they weren't being trained. Watching them run was one of his favorite things to do on a Sunday morning from his porch. Just beyond the paddocks, at the end of the driveway, he could see the farmhouse, a log cabin that had come with the property, looming larger with every step. He'd spent the last few years renovating it section by section. He looked at the ground again. It was supposed to have been a project for him and Kira, but she was long gone.

Glancing up again to see how far he'd made it, he could see the barn far off to his left, the stretch of the long white building illuminated by a single floodlight in the front shining up at the sign he'd ordered from town that read Bishop Ranch. He checked the time on his cell phone. It was nearly four a.m. At least he was almost home.

Another ten minutes of walking got him to his front door. Instead of going through the front entrance, Travis walked around the garage to the back door, using the keypad he'd installed to get inside. It gave a little beep and a hum as he pressed the code. Stepping inside the dark garage, he pulled the door firmly closed behind him hearing the lock click into place. He walked past the two vehicles he had in the garage — a navy blue Jeep he'd bought a few years before and his pickup truck. Going to the back door, he keyed in another code, a different one from the one on the exterior door, and waited as the lock popped open. After juggling keys for too long, he decided that a higher-tech version of locks might be for him.

Stepping inside the house, Travis kicked off his dirt-covered boots inside the door, glad to finally get them off. Hiking for miles in cowboy boots wasn't ideal, but it had worked. At least they were well broken in.

Stopping for a second to straighten them on the mat, he realized he'd had them on for nearly a full day. He wrinkled his nose. They smelled like it too. Flipping on the light in the kitchen above the island, he emptied his pockets. Gus's cell phone and wallet, Travis's cell phone and his wallet, plus the white bag filled with Gus's toiletry kit all lined up on the slab of brown marled granite. Travis stared at the refrigerator for a second and then turned on his heel and walked into the bedroom, flipping on the light. The red and black Navajo blanket resting on the king-size bed was tucked in neatly, just the way he'd left it the day before when he'd headed off to the barn. It was hard to believe it had been almost twenty-four hours.

Travis turned to his right, pushing open the bathroom door and flipping on the light and the exhaust fan, the hum starting immediately from the ceiling. Starting the shower, Travis stripped off his dirty horse sweat and dust-filled clothes and left them in a pile on the floor, stepping under the hot water. He stood there for a long time, letting the hot water run over him, his mind thinking about nothing in particular. He scrubbed every inch of his body, the same way he used to when he returned from a mission. It was a transition of sorts for him, a return to normal life.

Stepping out of the shower and wrapping a towel around his waist, Travis picked up the pile of clothes, not realizing how much dirt and stink he'd brought into the house. He padded down the hallway and tossed them in the washing machine, and started it up. Going back into the bedroom, he slipped on a fresh pair of jeans and a T-shirt, threading a leather belt through the loops and tightening it closed. In the bathroom, he combed his hair and brushed his teeth. Leaning into the mirror, his head tipped to the side, he rubbed his chin. He needed a shave but wasn't in the mood. Hanging the towel up near the shower, he turned and flipped the light off.

As he walked back to the kitchen, traveling the planked wooden floors in his bare feet, he eyed up the line of trinkets he'd recovered from his night away from the ranch suspiciously. Turning away from them, he filled up the carafe for the coffee pot and added grounds from a strong dark roast, pulling out a stool and sitting down, waiting for the coffee to brew. He crossed his arms across his chest, staring at the items lined up in front of him, not moving. If anyone had been watching him, he was sure they would think the items on the counter were staring back. In a way, Travis realized, they were. He was attempting to figure out what they were telling him. That was a question he didn't have an answer for yet.

Two minutes later, Travis got up off the stool and pulled a mug from one of the dark wood cabinets, pouring himself a cup of coffee. He reached over to the counter and snagged his cell phone, sticking it on the charger. He added his wallet to the basket of keys that was next to the charger. Sitting back down on the stool with his coffee, that left him with the things he'd salvaged from Gus.

Taking a sip of coffee he continued to stare at the things on his counter, wondering what to do next. Part of him knew he could simply sweep all of them off into the trashcan and carry it out to the big green receptacle he had in his garage, ignoring the fact that Gus had ever shown up on his doorstep the day before. The odds of law enforcement ever figuring out who he was or his connection to Gus and chasing him to the ranch were minuscule at best. He could go out to the barn, get his chores started and go back to living his life the way he had been just the day before.

But that didn't solve the problem of Elena.

In a single smooth motion, Travis picked up the pile of evidence on his kitchen counter, carrying his coffee in his other hand and heading to the other side of the house.

In the few years that Kira had been gone, he had made some adjustments to the floor plan he thought she would approve of. In addition to sanding down all of the original wood floors in the house and staining them a deep chestnut color, covering them carefully with a luster coat of polyurethane, he'd also redone all of the woodwork in the family room, buying new furniture as he found pieces he liked. There was a large stone hearth at one end of the room, the fireplace not yet used during the season, but ready, a long pile of seasoned hardwood nearby. In front of the fireplace were two long couches and two chairs, a coffee table in the middle sitting on top of the rug in reds and browns and navies. There was plenty of seating, although it had been years since anyone had walked into the ranch house other than him.

Along the wall between the kitchen and the family room there was a set of bookshelves. Travis had spent a month the year after Kira died taking them apart and carefully sanding each plank of wood, rubbing dark stain into each one and putting them back together again.

Walking toward the bookshelves, Travis stopped at the one nearest the kitchen, reaching his left hand toward the wall, fishing his fingers into a small crevice that had been hollowed out. He pushed a button inside, hearing a snap. The bookshelf came loose from the wall and Travis gave it a tug. The shelf rolled away from the space behind it. In front of him was a single door, a matching keypad lock attached to the doorknob. The only difference between this lock and the other ones on the house was that this one featured a fingerprint reader as well. Travis keyed in the code and then rested his right thumb on top of the optic. There was a beep and then a pause and then another beep as the door unlatched. He pushed it open, closing the door behind him. The shelf would close in ten seconds, hiding his entry point.

Inside, the lights flickered on automatically. As his eyes adjusted, he took in his surroundings. Originally, what he now called his war room had been a pantry area for storage behind the kitchen. After Kira had died, Travis decided to use the room for a different reason, closing off the doorway in the kitchen and installing a brand-new door behind the bookshelf in the family room. Every man had their secrets and he needed a place to keep his.

The center of the room featured a large island, not unlike the island he had in his kitchen, except that the top was burled wood supported by a square block of cabinets. At one end of the room, there was a long desk with shelves above littered with books on a variety of topics, most of them having to do with fugitives, surveillance, and cybercrime. On the opposite wall were two computers positioned next to each other, a desktop and a brand new laptop. On the other side of the room, there were three monitors plugged into the surveillance cameras he had around the ranch as well as giving him the ability to watch the news or access the Internet. Cabinets floor-to-ceiling opposite the door stored a wide range of equipment — everything from paper and pencils to locked racks filled with a variety of pistols, rifles, and enough ammunition to either start or stop a small war. His war room had it all.

Travis tossed the items he'd scrounged off of Gus's body and from his hotel room onto the center island, carrying his coffee mug over to his desk. He flipped on a small ceramic pad, the red light glowing near the edge. He set the mug on top so his coffee would stay hot. Travis could tolerate many things, but cold coffee was not one of them. At the center of the worktable, he flipped on one of the gooseneck lamps he'd clamped to the edge. It offered a harsh light but was perfect for reloading ammunition, examining maps, or any other detail work that Travis needed to do as part of his skip tracing business.

Pulling open the edges of the white plastic bag he'd taken from the hotel, he heard the thick plastic crinkle under his fingers. He pulled Gus's toiletry kit out from inside and set it on the table, crumpling the plastic bag and tossing it in the nearest trash can. He knew there was nothing interesting about the plastic bag in itself since he had snagged it, so there was no point in examining it. But the toiletry kit might be something else.

Travis furrowed his eyebrows as he directed the work lamp over top of the kit itself. He turned it over, looking at it from all sides before opening it. On the face of it, it was not that unusual — a brown fake leather case with a single, brass-colored zipper running from one end to the other lengthwise. It was probably something that could be picked up at any large retailer in any city around the world. Travis took a sip of his coffee, staring at it for a second. How common it was seemed interesting in itself,

Travis realized. With how carefully Gus had been dressed in his pressed sport coat, his starched white shirt, and his shiny designer tennis shoes it was surprising that Gus would have settled for a toiletry kit that was clearly not very well made. He pushed the thought aside. There could be a million reasons why Gus didn't choose a designer option, but why wasn't clear at the moment.

Tugging at the zipper, Travis could hear the teeth clicking as he opened it up. He used both hands, his fingers in a claw shape, one on either side of the zipper, to open up the toiletry kit, staring inside. Much like he'd done with the items on the kitchen island, Travis took the contents out one by one, lining them up in front of him. There was a razor with a plastic shield over the blade, not that Gus's beard had shown any evidence of using it, a black plastic soap holder with the rattle of a bar of soap inside, a washcloth, and several bottles and jars littering the bottom.

Travis stepped back from the worktable and crossed his arms in front of his chest then took another sip of his coffee. Part of him had the urge to rip everything apart and examine it all at once, but he knew that moving too quickly might cause him to miss details. Details were what mattered, whether he was trying to figure out what Gus was up to or where Elena was. Moving too fast would blur his ability to see what was right in front of him.

Travis picked up the empty toiletry kit and felt around on the inside, making sure he hadn't missed anything. Wrapping one hand on the inside and one hand on the outside, he pressed on the cheap, fake leather, feeling the rubbery texture between his fingers, making sure that Gus hadn't hidden anything in the lining. CIA agents were trained to put things where people wouldn't necessarily look for them. Travis blinked, thinking back to the hotel room. Whoever had searched his room was looking in all of the typical places — on the back and underside of the drawers, in the safe, and Gus's luggage. Anything Gus wanted to hide wouldn't be there. Travis wondered what that said about the people who had broken into his room. Had they been short on time? Not trained thoroughly in espionage?

If Travis had to guess, it would be the former and not the latter, especially if the people chasing Gus were the same ones chasing Elena. KGB agents were trained nearly as well, if not better, than CIA agents. It was hard for him to admit, even to himself, because he liked to think Americans always had an edge, but he'd been in enough conflicts during his time with Delta Force and the Agency that he knew it was like a neck and neck horse race, often the agency who won the day only edging out the other by a nose. It was a point of pride with the agents on both sides, one part of the job he was glad he didn't have to deal with anymore.

And yet here he was trying to get ahead of whoever had killed Gus and was hunting Elena.

Travis tipped his head to the side, his eyes glued to the items on the table, the same calm feeling he used to have after finishing a mission. He took another sip of coffee and then set his mug back down on the warmer. He examined each one of the items in detail. He held the razor under the work light, flipping it over, looking for any holes that might have been filled by material he didn't recognize and didn't look native to the original design. He didn't find any. He laid the washcloth out flat on the workbench, flipping it over a couple of times, but it didn't look unusual either. The soapbox was next. Opening the black plastic case, Travis's head pulled away instinctively, the strong smell of the scented soap stinging his nostrils, "What is this?" Travis mumbled, turning the bar over in the case and then quickly snapping it shut again.

That only left the bottles and jars. He picked them up in succession, feeling the cool plastic under his fingers. He shook each one of them and heard nothing until he got to the third, a short, squat white bottle with a screw-on cap. It offered a muffled rattle. Travis curled his lip, staring at it. On the outside, it was labeled, "Watson's Organic Men's Shampoo, Lavender Scent."

"What kind of guy uses lavender shampoo?" Travis mumbled, shaking his head and staring at the bottle. Unless the shampoo came in some sort of a solid form, which he wouldn't put past Gus, there was definitely something inside of the bottle that wasn't meant to be there. He started unscrewing the top and looked inside, raising a single eyebrow as he peered in. Definitely not shampoo. He turned over the bottle, finding a wad of something that had been jammed inside. Paper had been wrapped around something hard, probably to ensure that anyone who looked at the bottles wouldn't necessarily think it was empty and that it would keep the contents quiet, but Travis had shaken it just hard enough to hear the contents inside.

Using his forearm to sweep the rest of the items to the other side of the worktable to clear some room, Travis began to unroll the paper that was surrounding whatever had been hidden inside of the bottle. Gus had used a narrow strip of white toilet paper to create a cushion around the item. It was a basic, but effective way to muffle the noise. Travis unrolled it slowly, looking at the surface for any markings. There weren't any. He pushed it off to the side. Underneath the toilet paper cushion, there was a small piece of white paper, ragged at the edges as if it had been torn off a larger sheet. There was a single brass key inside.

Cocking his head to the side and adjusting the lamp over the slip of paper and the key, Travis stared at it, chewing his lip. His thoughts raced ahead of him. Was this what the people were looking for when they trashed his room? Was this why Gus had been killed in the first place? At that moment, Travis had more questions than he had working theories.

Staring at the paper, he saw a set of numbers scrawled on it across the diagonal, as though Gus had jotted it at the bottom of a larger tablet of paper and then had torn it off in a hurry. There were rows of numbers, five of them, each in varying lengths. A few of the lines had three digits, a few of the lines had four digits, and two of the lines, interspersed between the others, had five digits. Travis's mind tried to decipher what the numbers meant. It definitely wasn't a phone number. Beyond that, his initial impression was that it was important to Gus and probably to finding Elena, but no other inspiration came to him by glancing at it.

Pushing the piece of paper off to the side, Travis stared at the brass key. It had a round top and a hole drilled in the center of it as if it was meant to be on a key ring. It was a standard size with no other markings, including no brand name on it. There was no key ring attached that could help him identify what lock it could open. Travis stood back from the worktable and took another sip of his coffee. With no markings, the key could belong to anything from a safety deposit box to a door somewhere, and maybe not even in the US. And why did Gus have it in the first place? He'd said he had something that could help Travis find Elena. Was this it?

Tension filled Travis's chest. Once again, Gus had left him with more questions than answers. He looked over at the wall, a battery-run clock with a second hand ticking in the background. A couple of hours had gone by since he managed to make it home after firebombing Gus's car. No one had shown up on his doorstep yet. That was at least one good sign. Travis took two steps over to the computers, opening the laptop and queuing up the surveillance feeds for the barn. It was all clear. No one was around, not that he was expecting anyone, but given the night he'd had, it seemed wise to check. Checking the time, he realized he needed to get the horses fed. He was already behind schedule for the day. He stared at the items on the worktable again, but no answers were coming to him, at least none that would make putting off his chores worth it.

Travis flipped off the work light and grabbed his mug of coffee, shutting off the heater. He walked out of the room, locking the door behind him. Gus's secrets would have to wait, at least a little while.

22

Patrick Mills, the NTSB investigator assigned to the twin-prop plane crash near the Camp Swift Army base, was exhausted. Beyond tired. Every inch of his body ached. And it wasn't the average level of exhaustion he was feeling. Driving his navy-blue NTSB SUV out a long dirt road in the middle of nowhere in Texas, he felt like he was getting a stomach bug, with waves of nausea and a headache plaguing him. The only thing was, he knew it wasn't. Lack of sleep, lack of food, probably not enough water, and way too many questions were lurking in his mind about the crash site he'd found the night before. He'd been there all night long taking pictures and staring at what was left of the small plane until he'd snagged the SUV from one of his replacements.

Patrick adjusted the radio, tuning in a country station, wondering if that would help soothe his frayed nerves. It didn't. He flipped over to talk radio and turned it way down so that every word that came out of the announcer's mouth sounded like nothing more than an indistinct mumble.

He rubbed his chin. The thing about most plane crashes that people didn't understand was that the wreckage told the story. It wasn't really the black box, though it was nice to have the recordings of the pilot talking, but it was the damaged fuselage itself that gave investigators like him answers. It was usually a story of mechanical failure, a poor in-flight decision, or even a weather event that impacted the plane's ability to stay in the air. In the case of trains, shoddy maintenance on even a sparse, foot-long space of track could easily take a four-hundred-ton diesel train and twist it into nothing more than what looked like scrap metal crushed by the meaty hand of an angry giant. Planes weren't any different. For as many people as got on planes every single day, it was nothing short of a miracle that there weren't more incidents and more lives lost. Even something as small as a bird strike could land an enormous jet in a hurry. Patrick glanced down at his GPS. Based on the coordinates, it looked like he still had about seven or eight miles to go to his destination. He leaned his elbow on the windowsill, resting his head on it as he used his right hand to steer.

One thing he knew for sure – the plane crash from the night before definitely hadn't been a bird strike. The most significant one of those events had been when Captain Sully Sullenberger had landed his Airbus 320 passenger jet in the middle of the Hudson River after hitting a flock of geese on takeoff out of LaGuardia.

Patrick sighed. Bird strikes could break off the propellers from a small prop engine like they were twigs, but that wasn't what they were looking at here. No, the crash from the night before was something completely different.

The lights the fire department had left behind illuminated a strange char pattern on the skin of the plane, one he hadn't seen since he was in training, that of an exterior weapon strike. Probably a missile. The way the edges of the fuselage were blackened told the story of an explosion from the outside of the plane impacting its ability to fly. Buddy was probably right. This was no weather event or mechanical malfunction. Something had blown a hole in the fuselage opening it up like a can of soup, spilling whatever was inside out onto the ground, except for one thing.

The pilot.

Patrick glanced over at the passenger seat. On it was his backpack and a small clear plastic bag with a red strip at the top that he'd sealed at the scene. The silver bracelet with inlaid red and green and blue turquoise glimmered through the sunlight streaming through his windshield. He thought back to the moment Marcos had shown him the bracelet. And although Marcos was a firefighter and not an NTSB investigator, he'd bet his life that the man's instincts were correct — there was no way that bracelet could be left so artfully on a boulder next to the plane crash without there being a point to it.

Which left him with a question – what was the point?

Patrick sighed, glancing at the GPS again. Three miles to go.

By the time he left the scene, Doug Parsons had arrived with two other NTSB agents to relieve Patrick. "Head on home, Patrick," Doug said, resting his hand on Patrick's shoulder. "It's been a long night. We'll get this packed up and back to the hangar for you. Take the day off and we'll regroup on this one tomorrow."

While Patrick appreciated the sentiment and the fact that Doug was willing to come out to the crash site to relieve him, part of Patrick felt the sting of resentment. He'd been assigned the crash. He wanted to finish what he'd started. Before Patrick had left, he'd shown Doug Parsons the bracelet. Doug shook his head, "I don't think this is anything, Patrick. It could've flown out of the cockpit at some point or just happened to land on the rock. Maybe some hiker left it there. You know how these things go. We find the strangest things positioned in the strangest places at these crash scenes."

At the time, Patrick had nodded, pretending to agree, but

the knot in his gut told him that Doug wasn't thinking clearly about it.

As he drove, Patrick thought back to a documentary he'd watched on James Cameron's exploration of the Titanic. A miniature submarine was sent to investigate the wreck site nearly one hundred years after it had sunk in the icy cold Atlantic Ocean on its way from Southampton to New York harbor. Patrick remembered sitting on his couch, a cold beer in his hand, watching the footage as the first remote cameras had been inserted inside of what was left of the deteriorating hull of the ship. He remembered taking a sip of the beer and then setting it down on the coffee table, too engrossed in what he was seeing to drink it. He leaned forward, staring at the screen for what felt like hours.

The most staggering thing about the Titanic wreck was that the loss of all of the lives could've been avoided if humans hadn't gotten in the way. Next to that was what the Titanic wreck revealed. Shoes, hairbrushes, purses — all of the everyday items that had stayed in the rooms where their owners had drowned a horrific death, a section of the shattered steel rising out of the water at nearly forty-five-degree angle before plunging to the bottom, passengers still in their rooms. Patrick couldn't imagine what those last few minutes of life had been like for the people on board. The only evidence left of their horrifying experience was their abandoned personal belongings.

So moved by the documentary, Patrick had found the closest display of Titanic wreckage and went to go see it, driving three hours and paying an exorbitant amount of money to walk around with a muffled recording pumping into his ears listening to a narrator tell him everything he already knew about the disaster, dramatic music playing in the background, displays filled with abandoned shoes, jewelry, and hairbrushes.

Leaving the museum after seeing the Titanic wreckage gave

him the same feeling he had at that moment, a vague sense of unrest he couldn't shake.

Patrick shook his head, maybe he was just overtired and his mind was simply dredging up old memories to try to keep itself occupied as he drove. But as he glanced again at the bracelet on the seat of his SUV, the knot in his gut didn't dissipate. He knew if he didn't get answers soon, he probably never would.

23

B y the time his mind got done cycling through the latest batch of Titanic memories, the GPS in Patrick's assigned NTSB vehicle beeped. He'd been driving for nearly an hour in a direction that was north-northwest of the crash site and the Camp Swift Army base. There wasn't much of anything around, at least that he could see. The last three minutes had been spent navigating a plethora of potholes on an old dirt road that should have been newly graveled, but wasn't. The jarring as the vehicle dodged the holes tossed his body left and right as the suspension tried to absorb the shock. The driveway, if it could be called that, was probably better suited to either an ATV or a horse than a vehicle.

Stopping the SUV, Patrick looked around him, double-checking the coordinates he'd put into the GPS against the numbers that were engraved on the back of the bracelet. They were correct. He waited for the cloud of dust to gather itself and curl away from him to clear his line of sight. Looking out over the hood of his SUV, he saw a faint coating of yellow grit had already covered the shiny navy-blue paint job.

As the cloud of dust blew off in the distance, Patrick

narrowed his eyes. Ahead of him and to the right, there was a farmhouse that looked to be original to the property, made of old hewn logs and a wide front porch on the front of it that spanned the entire width, complete with rocking chairs. Down the driveway and off in the distance to his left, he saw a newer building, a white barn with a sign out front that he could barely make out. Squinting, he realized it said Bishop Ranch. "Bishop Ranch? Where the heck am I?" he mumbled, shifting the SUV into gear.

Avoiding the rest of the potholes the best he could, Patrick stopped at the house first, jogging the sidewalk to the front door and pounding on it with his fist. No one answered. He looked around, listening. There were no dogs barking and no noise from any trucks or tractors, only the faint sound of chirping from a few birds in a stand of trees nearby. Whoever lived there clearly wasn't home. He walked back to the SUV and turned around sticking his hands into his pockets, looking toward the barn. The door was open. Maybe whoever lived on the property was at the outbuilding.

Parking in a spot in front of the white barn, Patrick sat in the SUV for a second assessing what was in front of him. He could feel the tension in his chest. He felt edgy, like every nerve in his body was charged with electricity. There were too many questions about this plane crash, and the fact that they'd found no blood and no evidence of anyone in the plane left him with more questions than he could answer. And the mysterious bracelet at the scene only made it worse, no matter what Doug Parsons said.

Patrick stared at the building, waiting to see if anyone would come out, wiping his sweaty palms on his pant legs. The barn stretched wide in front of him, white aluminum clapboard covering the exterior. There were two sliding doors on the end of the barn facing him. Only one of them was open. Inside, he could see the glint of a concrete floor and dark gray metal bars installed over what looked to be stained wood for a stall. Patrick glanced back at the sign. There was a horseshoe intertwined in the lettering. "Definitely a horse barn," he mumbled, feeling his chest tighten again. Horses weren't his favorite. They were too large, too fast, and too unpredictable. And yet, he worked in Texas where there were only a few things that were assured – that the person next to you in line at the grocery store had a rifle rack in their truck, that they loved their smoked brisket, and that they'd probably ridden a horse at one time or another.

Patrick shook his head. No one was coming out of the barn. He'd have to go in.

Stepping onto the concrete aisle, Patrick could smell the distinct odor of the horse barn, a combination of the sweet-smelling hay and grain along with the sour tinge of stalls that needed to be cleaned. He could hear faint rustling in the background; as if one of the horses near him was nibbling on a flake of hay that had been dropped into their stall. There was an occasional bang coming from somewhere down the aisle; as if a metal shod hoof was kicking angrily at the back wall of the barn. Patrick shook his head. He wouldn't want to be on the wrong end of that horse.

He stood, waiting for a second, his hands shoved in his pockets. At the other end of the aisle, he saw a brown cart with tall wheels pushed off to the side, empty from the morning's feeding. He turned his head as he heard the creak of hinges and a door open. A figure emerged about twenty feet from him, wearing a thick flannel shirt and a baseball cap. The way the man stared at Patrick gave Patrick the sense that the man knew Patrick had been standing there all along and he'd been waiting to make his appearance.

As the man approached, Patrick looked him over. He had broad shoulders and a narrow waist covered by a pair of worn denim jeans, a leather belt with a wide silver belt buckle attached in the front. His dark cowboy boots looked scuffed by years of wear. A baseball cap covered a fringe of dark hair and a square jaw. The man's sleeves were rolled up halfway up his forearms, the veins of hard work sticking out in a spiderweb. He walked toward Patrick and stopped, leaving a gap of about ten feet between them, squaring off, "Can I help you?" the man asked gruffly. The words might have been polite, but the delivery was not.

Patrick reached for his back pocket, flipping his jacket out of the way. He saw the man flinch, the man's right hand reaching back for what Patrick could only assume would be a pistol. Patrick sucked in a breath and returned his hands in front of him, "Easy. I'm just reaching for my identification."

"Get to it. I don't have all day." The man's hand rested on his right hip. If Patrick had to guess, it wasn't actually his hip, but the butt of a gun.

From Patrick's back pocket, he pulled the leather folded wallet with two fingers and held it up in front of him, "Patrick Mills. NTSB. Who are you?"

The man in front of him raised his eyebrows as if he was surprised by the question. He still hadn't moved his hand off of his right hip. "You're standing on my property and you have no idea who I am?" The man narrowed his eyes, "Why are you here Patrick Mills? What business does the NTSB have on my property?"

For some reason, Patrick had the distinct impression that whoever the man was standing in front of him knew more about him than he knew about himself. Whether it was the penetrating glare or the way the man held himself, he wasn't sure. A tingle ran down Patrick's spine. He looked at the floor for a second and then reached into his jacket pocket with his right hand, holding his left one up again. "Maybe this will explain better than I can." From inside his pocket, he pulled the sealed clear plastic bag with the red stripe on it, the bracelet curled in the corner like a snake. He tossed the bag to the man.

Patrick stared, waiting. The man looked at the bag and then glanced up at Patrick and then back down at the bag, turning it over in his hands, pinching the bracelet through the plastic as if it was something that he'd lost many years ago and felt sad at its return. The man lifted his head slowly, his chin jutting forward, "How did you get this?"

Patrick swallowed, considering his options. He could press the man for his identity again, or he could wait it out. He glanced outside. Either the man standing in front of him had the name Bishop or he was someone else. Either way, at least the man was talking. That had to be a start. "Like I said, my name is Mills. I'm an NTSB investigator. There was a twin-prop crash last night not too far from here, near Camp Swift Army base. Do you know it?"

The man gave a single short nod.

"The bracelet you're holding was found at the scene. It was draped on a boulder nearby as if it had been left there intentionally. When I examined it, I found the coordinates engraved on the back. That's how I ended up here."

Patrick stared at the man, feeling like he had just given up state secrets to an enemy. His thoughts crashed about inside of his head, chastising himself or revealing so much information without even knowing who was standing in front of him, but he could tell the man recognized the bracelet. He could also tell the man wasn't the kind to give up information if he didn't have to. Patrick waited for a second and then cocked his head to the side, "By the look on your face, I can tell you recognize the bracelet."

"I do." The words were barely louder than a whisper.

"Would you like to fill me in on how it ended up at my crash site?"

A hint of pain covered the man's face before he answered. "I have no idea."

24

P atrick stood, his eyes wide as the man brushed past
him and walked out into the sunshine, still holding the
bag with a bracelet in it. He'd wrapped his thick
fingers around it, only a hint of the red band on the bag evident
he had anything in his hand at all. Patrick trailed behind him,
"Where are you going?"

"You're driving me up to the house," the man said as Patrick
joined him by the side of the dust-covered SUV.

Patrick nodded, his eyebrows raised, a surge of surprise in
him. "Okay," he said, sliding inside. As he started up the engine,
he looked at the man again, "I didn't catch your name."

"That's because I didn't offer it," the man said, glaring at
him. He turned, staring straight ahead. "Travis Bishop."

"That's your name?"

"Yep." He raised a finger and pointed, "Park over there.
We'll go in the back."

Patrick didn't say anything else to Travis as he parked the
SUV exactly where Travis told him to. Patrick had the distinct
impression that if he didn't do exactly what Travis asked, he

wouldn't get any of his questions answered and would find himself unpleasantly escorted off of Travis's property.

As he got out of the SUV, he watched as Travis walked around the back of the house. Travis only glanced over his shoulder once, as if saying to Patrick, "Aren't you coming?" but the words never came out of his mouth.

Patrick followed Travis, watching as he keyed in a code to get inside. He flipped on the light, illuminating a pristinely kept garage with a Jeep and a pickup truck inside. There wasn't a speck of dust on either vehicle or in the garage. Patrick bit his lip. Whoever Travis was, he had serious control issues, and that was a fact.

Stepping inside the house, Patrick watched as Travis kicked off his boots and looked at Patrick as if he expected him to do the same. Patrick complied. There was no reason to argue. He'd gone from not knowing who the man was a few minutes before to being invited into his house. Travis went into the kitchen, pulling open the refrigerator door and handing Patrick a bottle of water. He set the bag with the bracelet down on the island, using the tips of his fingers to square up the bag on the kitchen counter. Cracking the bottle open, Travis looked at Patrick, "Tell me how you got the bracelet again," Travis narrowed his eyes at Patrick. "While you're at it, hand me your ID again."

Patrick pulled the ID out of his back pocket again and tossed it to Travis, "As I said, my name is Mills. I'm an NTSB investigator."

"I got that." Travis studied the folded ID, pulling the laminated cards with Patrick's picture out of the flimsy leather holder. Patrick frowned. No one had ever bothered to look that closely at his documentation before.

"Something wrong?"

Travis pressed his lips together and shook his head, "Nope. Looks pretty legit."

Patrick felt the heat rise to his cheeks. He gripped the edge of the countertop. "It is. I've been with the NTSB for ten years."

A scowl covered Travis's face. "Good for you. Now tell me about this bracelet again. Start from the beginning."

Patrick licked his lower lip, narrowing his eyes. "There's not a lot to tell. We got a call as I was leaving work last night —"

"What time?"

"I don't know. Maybe around six. It'd just started to get dark out."

"Continue."

Patrick felt like he'd been granted an audience with the emperor of a small country the way that Travis was talking to him. He couldn't help but acquiesce. "My boss called me, asked me if I'd look into it. At that point, all we had were a few 911 calls. Buddy Driscoll, one of our pilots, came to get me in the chopper and we spent a couple of hours looking for it." Patrick took a sip of the water Travis had offered him, "We found one of the rear seats and toolkit about a mile out from the actual crash site."

"And the condition of the plane?"

"Largely intact. Missing the right prop and the majority of the right wing, but the rest of the fuselage was in one piece."

Travis leveled his gaze at Patrick, "Bodies?"

Patrick paused, blinking. The way Travis was asking questions made Patrick think he had some sort of military or law enforcement background. There was no way that a simple guy running a horse barn would talk with this much confidence about a plane crash. And they hadn't even gotten to the bracelet yet. Patrick cleared his throat, which had suddenly gone dry. "None."

Travis didn't say anything. Patrick watched as Travis touched the bag with the bracelet in it again; as if it was an invisible force field keeping him from feeling the metal inside.

In one smooth move, he tugged at the red evidence tab and opened the bag. Patrick held his hand up, "You can't —"

Travis glared at him, "Really? You gonna stop me?"

Patrick didn't respond, his shoulders slumping. He knew he was beaten. He'd lost control of the situation, but he had no idea what he'd actually lost control of. He watched as Travis pulled the bracelet out of the bag and laid it flat in the palm of his hand as if it was a baby bird that had fallen out of a nest that needed some love. Travis ran a single index finger over each of the stones and stared at it before setting it down on the counter in a straight line.

"Where did the bracelet come from, Travis?" Patrick whispered.

When Travis looked up, Patrick could have sworn he saw a tiny glint of sadness in Travis's eyes. It disappeared as fast as it arrived. "I had this made for my fiancée. We bought this ranch together a few years back. That's why the coordinates were engraved on the back. It was so she'd always know how to get home."

Patrick stared at Travis and then glanced around the house. It was compulsively neat and tidy, as though no one ever lived there. Beautiful, yes. Homey? Maybe not. "And where is your fiancée now?"

"She's dead."

25

"Dead?" Patrick's eyes narrowed.

Travis watched Patrick for a moment to see what his reaction would be. Travis knew his demeanor and questions were testing Patrick a little. Travis was only feeding him teaspoonfuls of information at a time, but he needed to be tested. Travis could tell the guy was legit. He definitely was an NTSB investigator, but the fact that he'd shown up uninvited with a bracelet that Travis thought he'd never see again had been unnerving, to say the least. That didn't even begin to take into account the fact that Gus had shown up not even twenty-four hours before and was now dead. Questions thundered inside of Travis's mind. He tried to wrap his brain around how a bracelet he'd had handmade for Kira had been found at a crash site five years after her death. How was that even possible?

"Yes. She passed away a few years ago. I haven't seen the bracelet since."

Travis could tell by the look on Patrick's face that the NTSB investigator felt like he had been dropped squarely in the middle of a minefield and wasn't exactly sure where to turn or step next. Travis was starting to feel the same way. He sucked in a sharp breath, pressing the tips of his fingers into the stones on the bracelet, "The crash site — where is it?"

"About an hour from here."

"Let's go."

Travis left the bracelet on the counter of the kitchen, sweeping the evidence bag into the trash. Patrick paused, looking at him, his mouth slightly open, "I need that for the report."

Travis adjusted the baseball cap on his head, "No, you don't. It doesn't have anything to do with your plane crash. The bracelet didn't make your plane go down. Something else did. Now, let's go."

Travis followed Patrick as they walked to the back door and slid their boots back on. Travis did a mental check of where he was with his chores. The horses had been fed and watered and half of the stalls had been cleaned. An hour's drive to the crash site and an hour back, plus probably not more than a half-hour looking around, would only put him a few hours behind. He could always have Ellie school horses that afternoon if he needed to catch up. The fact that Kira's bracelet had shown up at his ranch was more important than anything else at the moment, even the horses.

Travis didn't say much to Patrick as they got back into Travis's truck and started down the driveway. Tension rode on Travis's shoulders like a heavy pack. Patrick tried the typical conversation starters, asking Travis basic questions and commenting on the weather, but Travis simply stared out of the windshield, watching the fields go by.

Travis checked the time on the console of the truck. Twenty-four hours before, everything in his life was orderly and arranged. He got out of bed at five-thirty each morning, made a cup of coffee, and headed out to the barn, getting his chores started by six a.m. And then Gus arrived throwing a wrench in the works, the likes he hadn't experienced since he was part of the Agency. He swallowed, wishing he'd grabbed another bottle of water before they left. And now, Kira's bracelet had appeared out of nowhere. Had Gus known about the plane crash? Travis remembered Gus mentioning a newsflash about the crash, but Gus had played it off, chuckling that it was probably some kids going on a joy ride with their daddy's crop-dusting plane.

Travis rubbed the back of his neck. Everything circled back to Gus, or did it?

26

E lena woke up with a groan, her eyes bleary, achiness covering her body like a wet blanket. She laid on the church pew for a minute, blinking, a few rays of dust-filled sunlight streaming in through the open windows above her. She heard the flutter of wings above her and then saw a single yellow feather float down near where she was laying, landing on the dirty wood floors of the abandoned church.

Before daring to move, Elena took stock of her body. She started by wiggling her toes in her boots. No pain there. She rolled her ankles, realizing the right one was a little stiff. She'd probably jammed it on the floor during the plane crash. Shaking her legs a little bit, she realized they were in good shape except for the stiffness in her back. Whether that was from sleeping on the hard wooden pew or from landing the plane the night before, she had no idea.

Yawning, Elena used her left hand to push herself upright, lifting herself off the backpack she'd used as a pillow overnight. As she did, a sharp groan came from deep inside of her. Her shoulder ached and pulsed with pain. She looked down, wondering what was wrong with it, but there was no way to tell.

The good news was she was able to wiggle her fingers on her right hand. Much movement beyond that tore into something inside her body that was clearly unhappy.

She sat for a minute, or maybe five. It was hard to tell with the cobwebs littering her mind. She listened, trying to determine if there was anyone moving in or around the building. The only thing she heard was a slight buffeting of a breeze against the wooden clapboard outside. Elena's mind circled back to the day before, trying to get away from the military police at Camp Swift, stealing the plane, and then the deafening boom and the shudder of the plane as the missile hit it. A tingle ran down her spine. It was a miracle she was alive and relatively uninjured.

Staring at her backpack, Elena knew she couldn't stay at the church for long. She felt the need to go to the crash site again. Why, she wasn't sure, but the need was like a rock in her gut. Her escape in the dark had been less than well-planned. But then again, who plans on getting shot down by a missile?

Standing up, Elena wondered exactly who had shot at her. When she'd gone dark, she knew the rest of her colleagues at the Agency would have questions, especially because it wasn't part of the operational plan she'd set out with. How they could question her loyalty to the United States mystified her, but it did happen. It was a normal part of working for the CIA. The decidedly abnormal part was the fact that she was operating on American soil and that she wasn't entirely sure it was only Americans that were chasing her.

Replaying the last few seconds before the missile hit in her mind, a surge of bile rose in the back of her throat. She'd seen the trail as it raced toward her, remembering the feel of the controls in her hand and how she'd banked hard to the left. It'd happened so fast that she didn't even have time to be afraid. Closing her eyes, Elena swallowed and sucked in a sharp breath. She was alive. Injured, but alive. She'd lived to fight another day. How she managed to get the plane on the ground without smashing it into a million little pieces had been nothing short of God's grace. Lots of people didn't believe in guardian angels. Elena couldn't help but believe in them.

Her gut told her it was time to go. Elena reached for her backpack, holding the right shoulder strap out away from the bag and carefully moving her right fingers inside of it using her left hand to pull the padded strap up on top of her shoulder. She gritted her teeth as she did and then swung the bag around her left side catching it with her left hand. Once the backpack was on, her shoulder didn't hurt too bad.

Stepping outside into the morning sunlight, Elena stood for a second and blinked, looking around her. It was her first full view of where she was. In the dark, it'd been almost impossible to see anything. She remembered coming up the hill to the little church, which meant she needed to go down the hill to head back the way she came. Looking in the grass, she picked up her trail relatively easily, checking for the crushed stalks of grass and weeds that were matted to the ground. She started off down the hill, striding at a quick pace, getting to the spot where she'd kicked the post for the barbed wire fence over to get through.

As she walked, she did a few tactical calculations in her head. By now, someone would have found the crash scene, whether that was the local fire department or a federal agency, like the NTSB. With any luck, the fuselage would still be there. There might be people hanging around the site. If they were, there would be no way for her to approach it to search it again. She thought back to the bracelet she'd left on the rock the night before. Had anyone found it? Had they deciphered the coordinates on the back? If they had, Travis might know that she was in the area and was in trouble.

Or maybe not.

Elena shrugged as she walked. Leaving Kira's bracelet on

the rock was certainly enough to get Travis's attention if someone took it to him, but would he ask the right questions? Elena shrugged the backpack up a little higher on her shoulders, watching the ground for the next section of her path, following her footsteps back the way she came. At the bottom of a hill, there was a little stream. Seeing it, she realized how thirsty she was.

Swinging the backpack down off her shoulders, she opened up the front pocket and pulled out a plastic case, popping the top open with her left thumb. She flipped it over and pulled out thick straw that had a filter attached to it. She was so thirsty it didn't really matter what she drank, but if she could avoid getting sick that would be even better. The self-filtering straw would at least give her half a chance to stay healthy while she tried to escape. Getting on her hands and knees, Elena bent over, using only one hand to balance, sticking the straw in the water and drawing on it with her lips. A second later she tasted the first cool mouthful of water. Running it through the filter made the process a little slow, but at least she was able to get some hydration in her. After a few minutes of drinking, she replaced the straw in the case. Elena stood up, brushed a few pieces of dead grass off the front of the green uniform pants she was wearing, and started hiking towards the crash scene. Right before the plane had been hit, she saw a small town nearby. That's where she'd head afterward. But she had to see the scene first and hopefully find a vehicle in the process.

As she got close, she could smell the faint hint of smoke in the air, as if something far off was smoldering. Elena decided to climb up a hill and try to look down on the crash scene instead of walking right up to it. Army uniform or not, she imagined she looked so disheveled that it wouldn't take a Sherlock Holmes level of investigative skill to figure out she was the pilot. Although she'd like to be able to examine the plane again up close and retrieve anything she could from it, it might not happen.

Hiking to the top of the hill, her legs burning, Elena crouched down. There were some scrubby shrubs perched at the top of the rise, and a few twisted trees, their leaves thick and green. She darted for the underbrush and scooted forward on her belly until she could see over the edge to avoid being spotted.

Down below her, it was as if a small city had grown overnight at the site of the plane crash. She could hear the hum of generators in the distance, work lights erected on tall poles pointed at the wreckage. With the sun up, the lights had been turned off, but the generator was still running in the background. There were two police cars parked nearby as well as a blue SUV with yellow letters that said NTSB on the door. An ATV had been abandoned on the side of the wreck closest to her, hidden behind the generator.

Elena scanned the ground, looking for the boulder where she'd left the bracelet. Spotting it from the top of the hill, she noticed it was gone. Although she was quite a distance away, there was no glint of silver in the bright sunlight as there should've been. Her heart skipped a beat. Someone had found it. That was good news.

There were two clusters of mostly men hanging out at the crash site. Three of them were standing in a small group near the tail section of the plane. Elena squinted at it, seeing the charred outline of where the missile strike had hit the top of the fuselage right above the rear seats. Seeing it in the daylight only served to show how serious the incident had been. Only one of the rear seats was still bolted in place. Where the other one was, she had no idea. A shiver ran down her spine. It was a miracle that she'd gotten away, given what the plane looked like. Had she not banked the plane at the last second, it would've been a direct hit, probably shattering the entire thin metal frame into a million pieces. What was left of her shredded body would have landed somewhere in a field. Whoever was coming after her was serious. Thinking about the laptop in her backpack, she knew why. Her need to see the scene again had been satisfied. It was time to go.

The three men talking had become four men plus a single woman. All of them walked together toward the back of the NTSB truck, popping the back open, a few of them sitting on the back gate. Elena narrowed her eyes. What were they waiting for? As she glanced around the area, she saw a service road nearby. They weren't going to abandon the plane out in the middle of the field. No, they'd have to bring in a semi-truck fitted with a flatbed and a crane to retrieve the wreckage.

As Elena glanced below her, she realized the ATV was parked out of the eyeshot of the group clustered behind the NTSB's SUV. She licked her lips. An ATV would get her where she needed to go a lot faster than if she had to walk, that was for sure. She glanced down at her right arm. Whether she could actually drive it with only one hand, she wasn't sure, but she'd have to make do.

Standing up from where she was hiding, Elena jogged down the hill on the opposite side of the crash site, pain from her shoulder pinching at her with every step. Getting to the bottom, she circled to the right, staying close to the line of bushes and short trees. Not that she was expecting anyone would see her, but the element of surprise was always better.

The thrum of the cycling generator got louder as she got closer to the ATV. It was so loud, she was surprised anyone could hear themselves think. It certainly would drown out the noise of the ATV starting. Stopping behind the trunk of a tree, she glanced past the plane to see the NTSB people still behind the truck. They had no line of sight. Running as fast as she could, Elena took off for the ATV, sprinting the fifty yards to where it was parked, feeling her legs pump like she was getting ready for a tumbling run at a gymnastics competition.

It took a millisecond to get on. Straddling it, she reached forward with her right hand, giving a groan as her shoulder protested, pressing the start button and putting it into gear. Twisting the handle, she felt the powerful engine lurch forward. She immediately turned the ATV back the way she came, using the hillside as cover. Her skin tingled. At least she had wheels now. She had a chance to get away.

27

Travis didn't say much on the remainder of the drive out to the crash site. He listened as Patrick gave him mumbling instructions that included, "Turn right there," and "Hang a left over there," only responding with a grunt and even that only happened occasionally.

It took the full hour Patrick predicted before they arrived, spending much of it weaving and winding their way through country roads that Travis was surprised actually showed up on any GPS. It hadn't been too many years that cell phone service was available out where Travis lived. When he and Kira had bought the place, they had to keep a landline to make any calls at all. Tech hadn't arrived fully in central Texas, at least not yet. That, plus the beauty and solitude of the rugged countryside, was what drew Travis to the ranch.

As they pulled up to the site in Travis's pickup truck, he scanned the scene in front of him. There were a couple of local police cruisers and a blue NTSB SUV that matched the one Patrick had left back at his ranch. There was, of course, the plane.

Travis swallowed.

He could only bear to glance at the fuselage at first. He had to keep telling himself that Kira was dead. She hadn't been on the plane trying desperately to get home. She was long gone. She'd been in Ecuador when she died, not in the plains of Texas close to the ranch they wanted to make their home. The breath caught in his throat, thinking about the first time they'd met and the way she'd smiled at him. It was only a week later they were having dinners together, much to the ire of the Agency, but that didn't stop them. The tightness in his chest felt like someone had wrapped a huge grip around his heart and was slowly crushing it.

Travis pulled up the truck near the other vehicles and got out. Patrick slammed the passenger door to the truck at the same time and beelined for the people clustered behind the SUV. They were staring at Travis with a combination of curiosity and anger, as though he had crashed a private party he wasn't meant to know about.

Travis walked straight over to what was left of the plane, pulling the brim of his baseball cap down on his forehead a little lower. He circled it with the wariness of a bullfighter approaching an angry bull, starting at the front. He took a single step at a time, cataloging everything he saw before moving again.

At the pilot's side door, Travis stopped and opened it. After a yank, it came away from the rest of the plane with a loud creak, the door sagging as it separated from the body of the fuselage. Peering inside, he saw exactly what he expected to see. Nothing. There was no blood, no personal items, and no body parts left behind. It was as if someone had dropped the plane magically out of the middle of the sky, transporting the pilot to another location. Giving the door a little push back into place, Travis continued his walk, spending the most time at the spot where the hole in the top had exposed the interior of the aircraft to the elements. He rubbed his finger against the black charred section, lifting it to his nose and sniffing it. It smelled acrid, like a combination of fuel and something burning. He chewed the inside of his lip. There was no doubt in his mind – it was weapons residue.

Continuing his survey, he made his way to the tail section. Using two hands, he manipulated the rudder as well as the elevator. Both were functional, and probably one of the reasons the pilot was able to get the plane on the ground; unless it was just dumb luck. On the other side of the plane, Travis leaned inside scanning the interior. Most small planes included at least one jump pack just in case of emergency. There was no jump pack left in the plane.

"You find anything interesting?" Patrick's voice interrupted Travis's thoughts.

Travis grunted. He'd felt Patrick coming up behind him, but was trying to ignore his presence. He didn't want to be interrupted, not while he was trying to assess the damage. And yet, there Patrick was. Travis turned, his eyebrows knitted together. Worse yet, not only was it Patrick, but there was a short blonde man with floppy hair wearing an oversized NTSB jacket, the sleeves rolled up at the wrists as if he'd borrowed it from someone three sizes bigger than him, following along. Travis briefly lifted the baseball cap off his forehead to wipe some sweat away. "I'm not sure."

Patrick raised his eyebrows, "Okay, well, let me know if you find something. By the way, Travis, this is my boss, Doug Parsons."

Doug leaned forward, extending his hand. Travis didn't take it, not interested in making friends. Doug's voice sounded like one of Travis's foster brothers, the one that always got Travis in trouble, left beaten and bruised. Doug pulled his hand back and wiped it on his pant leg. "Patrick tells me you're the owner of the bracelet."

"You could say that," Travis said, pivoting away from Doug

and continuing his walk around the plane. His mind was racing.

"Any insight you can offer as to how the bracelet got on the plane would be helpful to our investigation," Doug mumbled.

Travis glanced back at him. Whoever Doug Parsons was, he was bordering on delusional if he thought that Travis was there to help their investigation. "Oh, I'm sure you'll figure out things well before I do." He stared at Patrick, "Does this model plane come standard with jump packs?"

Patrick's chin bobbed, as if he was surprised by the question. "I didn't think about that. Let me check." Patrick pulled his phone out of his pocket as Travis kept walking around the plane. "Yeah, it does. The manufacturer specs say that it comes with one jump pack preloaded. It should be strapped to the back of the pilot's seat."

"Is it there?" Travis said, not bothering to look. He was standing near the nose of the plane. Although the landing gear was buried in nearly a foot of soft dirt, probably from the speed and impact of the landing, the front of the plane was largely undamaged, only a few cracks in the windshield likely from the fuselage flexing as it hit the ground. Flexing was far better than breaking apart, Travis reasoned, waiting for Patrick to answer him.

Patrick had his head inside the hole in the back of the plane. "No. There's no jump pack here. Are you thinking the pilot bailed?"

"Do you have a better theory?"

"I don't. Except for the fact that it still doesn't explain the bracelet."

Travis shrugged, "Unless the bracelet is completely unrelated to the crash." As the words came out of Travis's mouth, he knew they weren't true. He didn't believe in coincidences. There was no way that Gus showed up on his doorstep and Kira's bracelet appeared magically out of nowhere in the same twenty-four-hour period without some correlation, but Patrick didn't know about Gus and his connection to Travis — and he didn't need to. Travis cleared his throat. "Maybe whoever had the bracelet left it here a while ago."

Patrick twisted his lips to the side of his face as if he was thinking, "I guess that's a possibility. In that case —"

Travis felt the first bullet whizz by his right ear before he heard it. "Cover! Get cover!" he yelled as he dove for the ground.

The crack of gunfire coming down from above them sounded like they were in a war zone. Travis looked to his left. Patrick and Doug were huddled near the tail section of the plane. The plane would give them some concealment, but the skin was so thin that any type of long-range bullet would likely plow through the paper-thin metal and right into them, tearing them into shreds. Travis shot up into a squatting position and started moving towards Patrick and Doug, eyeing up his truck, which was parked next to the other vehicles. The others had dropped to the ground, kneeling behind their vehicles, the two local police officers drawing their weapons, their mouths up to their radios. He was sure they were calling for backup, but this far out in the middle of the countryside, it could take a while to get any help.

Passing Doug and Patrick in a crouch, Travis barked, "On me," as he stopped just in front of them. He pointed as another round of gunfire came from up above him, ducking as he spoke. "Someone took a position on the top of the hillside. We need to get to my truck."

Doug whined, "How do you know they're up there?"

Travis shot him a look, "Use your ears!"

Not waiting for any more unnecessary comments, Travis bolted, sprinting the gap between the plane and his truck. Patrick was on his heels and Doug was bringing up the rear. Travis glanced toward the back of the SUV, making eye contact with one of the officers. The man, with dark hair and sallow skin, gave him a nod. Travis opened the rear door of his truck, flipping the seat forward in one smooth movement. Pressing his finger on the fingerprint lock, it popped open half a second later, revealing a cache of weapons he always kept with him. He pulled out a shotgun and tossed it to Patrick. "You know how to use this thing?"

"Sure do," Patrick nodded, pumping the stock.

Travis followed up by tossing him a box of ammunition and a pistol preloaded with nine-millimeter rounds. He grabbed another pistol and almost handed it to Doug until Travis glanced at Doug's face. Doug's eyes were wide. "Go over there and crouch behind the officers," Travis shouted, ducking behind the side of his truck, hearing another volley of gunfire, this time from the officers near him returning fire. Travis leaned inside of the truck and pulled out an AR-15 and four, thirty-round magazines, jamming the first one inside and pulling back on the charging handle.

Lining the muzzle up on the back rim of his truck's bed, Travis stayed low, trying to visualize where the shots were coming from. He scanned the hillside. Whoever was up there was well covered. As he studied the area, more shots came from the right side of the hill, closer to where the fuselage had been abandoned. Travis pivoted the muzzle of the AR-15 and looked through the sights. He sent a couple of rounds in the direction of the shots, a warning that their force would be met with his own. Travis narrowed his eyes. Return fire came, but it was well above his head, the rounds zipping by leaving little clouds of dust as they hit the ground. Even using the scope, Travis couldn't see the shooters. Whoever was aiming at them was well camouflaged.

Another round of shots came from his left. It was the police officers firing back at the people on the hillside. Travis knew the bullets from their pistols didn't have enough distance to take out the shooters. They were doing nothing but making a lot of noise. A few more shots zinged past him, this time from the top of the hill. The shots were well-placed, but slightly off. Travis narrowed his eyes. It was almost as if whoever was shooting at them from the hillside just wanted to scare them, not actually kill anyone. Travis pulled the AR-15 down with him as he slid to the ground, wiping sweaty palms on his jeans. On his right, he saw Patrick, who had knelt near the front bumper. He had a shotgun at the ready, but hadn't pulled the trigger yet. Travis glanced at him. Patrick yelled, "They're out of range."

Travis gave a sharp nod. Patrick was correct. Travis glanced at the police officers, who were firing a little more indiscriminately than he would have liked, the action on their pistols flapping back and forth like the wings of a bird. The police officers were clearly not combat trained. Travis didn't move for a second, sitting in the pale beige dirt, listening. All the rounds headed in their direction were slightly above the targets. He'd have to be a foot taller than he was in order to get hit. That couldn't be a mistake. He felt his heart rate slow in his chest as shots rang out on both sides of him. He looked at Patrick, narrowing his eyes. "We gotta get outta here!" he shouted above the din of the police officer's guns firing. Patrick gave a single nod and retreated to the back door of Travis's truck, putting the shotgun on the floor. Travis moved at the same time, opening the driver's side door, staying low. The keys were still in the ignition. As soon as he saw Patrick was laying on the floor of the backseat of the truck, the shotgun still in his hands, Travis crawled into the driver's side, crouching down. He revved the engine and put it into gear, turning the wheel sharply to the left to avoid the police officers who were still shooting at the ghosts on the hillside. Travis tromped on the gas pedal.

The truck took off like it had been blasted out of a cannon, the stiff suspension bouncing over the uneven ground that covered the field where the plane had gone down. Lifting his chin slightly from his crouched position so he could see better, Travis angled the truck for the service road, increasing his speed. The truck took two significant bounces over the ruts in the road causing Patrick to grunt from the back seat, and then managed to get its footing as Travis slid to his full posture in the driver's seat.

Glancing behind him, Travis saw they were out of range of the firefight unless the assailants in the hills were planning on launching an RPG at them. Given the assault they had just experienced, Travis wouldn't put anything past them. The best solution was distance.

Travis veered the truck onto the service road, kicking up a plume of dust behind him, handing the AR-15 back to Patrick who had pushed his way up into a seated position on the backseat. Travis watched in the rearview mirror as Patrick laid the weapons down and shimmied his body through the narrow gap between the two front seats, landing in the passenger seat and clicking on his seatbelt. Travis did the same. "What the hell was that?" Patrick mumbled, his eyes wide. "Can't ever say that's ever happened to me before at a crash scene."

Travis was quiet for a moment, thoughts gathering in his head like oncoming storm clouds. He drummed his fingers on the steering wheel. "You notice anything strange?"

"Other than everything? What do you mean?"

"About the shot pattern." Travis glanced over at Patrick and then back to the road, nearly hitting a boulder. They both leaned to the left as the truck lurched.

"It was cover-fire."

Travis gave a single nod, "Whoever was shooting at us couldn't hit the side of a barn."

Patrick knitted his eyebrows together, "You don't mean that literally, do you?"

"Of course not. Whoever was shooting at us was trying to scare us away. It wasn't like they had revolvers up there on the hillside. They weren't potshots. Whoever that was had high-powered rifles and camo."

Patrick groused, "Yeah, I noticed you didn't take very many shots."

Travis shook his head, "No point in wasting good ammo on a target you can't see." Travis got lost in his thoughts for a minute. He licked his bottom lip, tasting the salt of perspiration that had run down his forehead. He hadn't even noticed he'd been sweating.

Travis glanced over to see Patrick fumbling with his phone. "Any news from your boss?"

"Other than him saying he can't believe I left him there?"

"Yeah."

"Nope. I told him he should relax. He was with the police."

Travis raised his eyebrows. Doug was definitely someone Travis wouldn't want to go to war with.

"Where are we going now?" Patrick said, staring out the windshield.

"Back to the ranch."

28

After a few minutes of silence, the two men veered their way into an easy, if stilted, conversation about football and the weather. Patrick had more words in him than a frustrated novelist, but there was something about it that was comforting. Travis knew it was nothing more than post-incident letdown, as if their bodies and minds needed a break after what happened at the crash site. But despite the banal words coming out of his mouth, Travis could feel his mind working; as if the wheels of his thoughts were clattering somewhere in the background. He was sure that at some point something would start to come together. After the gunfire, the one thing he was sure of was that somehow Gus and Elena were linked to what happened at that crash site. That was no joyride in daddy's crop duster, that was for sure.

Travis expertly avoided the majority of the potholes on the mile-long driveway to his log cabin, the truck coming to a peaceful stop next to Patrick's dust-covered NTSB SUV. "How did you do that?" Patrick said, slipping out of the truck.

"Do what?"

"Managed to get us down that long driveway without snapping our jaws together in those ruts."

Travis smiled, "It's a deterrent, Agent Mills. Haven't you figured that out already? Like a minefield with no mines."

Patrick didn't say anything as Travis walked around the back of the house after pulling the AR-15 and the shotgun from the back seat of the truck. He nodded at Patrick, "You still have that pistol?"

"Yeah."

"Bring it with you."

Hanging the AR-15 on his shoulder and carrying the shotgun, Travis went to the back door of the house, entered the code, and went inside. He could feel Patrick behind him. Going into the kitchen, Travis laid the two weapons down on the kitchen counter and stared at the bracelet he'd left behind. Patrick laid the pistol down on the counter and stood for a second, staring at Travis. "Okay, so what was that about?"

Travis cocked his head to the side, "You think I have all the answers? I'm just a horse trainer."

Patrick's shoulders slumped, his lips parting slightly, "And I just took a walk on the moon. Listen, Travis, I don't know what you've got going here, but something doesn't seem right. I've been an NTSB investigator for ten years and never once have I had anyone start firing at me at a crash site. It doesn't make any sense. That, plus the fact I ended up here a few hours ago after tracking this mysterious bracelet all points back to you. You're the common denominator."

Travis stared at the ground for a second, contemplating a knot in the wood floors near the edge of his sock before answering. "I'm not the common denominator, I'm more of a nexus."

"What does that mean?" Patrick groaned.

"It means that everything you've seen has some sort of a central connection to me."

"Can you tell me what this nexus is? I mean, I can't exactly go back to the crash site and finish my job while getting shot at."

"You did seem pretty comfortable handling that pistol and the shotgun." Travis narrowed his eyes, "You have training?"

"I was in the Marines." Patrick stretched his neck and then cracked his knuckles, "After my four years I went back to college on the G.I. Bill. Got a degree in Avionics, but didn't want to be a pilot. The NTSB came calling and I've been there ever since."

"Makes sense." Travis thought for a second, wrapping his fingers around the edge of the chocolate-colored granite countertop, staring at the guns and Kira's bracelet. He'd gotten in the habit of stopping and thinking before making any moves whether in his personal or professional life. The image of a pocket-sized rectangular brown notebook with the word "think" embossed in black lettering on the front popped into his memory. It was a notebook his grandfather had given him after meeting with some executives from IBM at a conference. The way his grandfather told it at the time, IBM discovered that most of their internal issues could be solved if people would just slow down and stop to think before they did something. Their answer was simple. They printed a couple of thousand small notebooks with the word think on it and started a campaign to get their people to think through the issues in front of them rather than plowing ahead and costing the company thousands upon thousands of dollars because of a rash decision. Travis remembered the feel of the notebook as his grandfather handed it to him, the nubby texture of the cocoa-colored leather and the way the five letters were pressed into the center of the cover. He still had it in a drawer in the war room. Thinking had saved his skin more than once. He wondered if he could think his way through what was going on now, in time to save Elena.

Patrick leaned his hands on the counter, staring at Travis, "Listen, you need to tell me what's going on here. I nearly got shot at the crash site after finding that bracelet. Somehow, I think things are all tied together. Now you're saying you're the nexus. Maybe we should have stayed."

Travis rolled his head to the left, trying to loosen a muscle on the side of his neck, "There wasn't any need to stay. You know as well as I do, they weren't in any danger. Besides the fact, the officers had already called in for backup. If we'd given them another two or three minutes, whoever was shooting at us probably would've skedaddled and hightailed it off of that hillside."

Patrick frowned, checking his phone. "Backup got there a couple of minutes ago. The shooting stopped."

"That's good."

"But that's not good enough. What does being the nexus mean exactly?" Patrick said, starting to pace. "All roads seem to be leading right back to you."

Travis shrugged, "That's the point of being the nexus, Mills."

Patrick shook his head, "Cute. Yeah, I got that. But what is your involvement? And who exactly was this fiancée of yours? And how did that bracelet end up at my crash site?" He held his hands up, "And don't try to tell me she left it there when she was hiking. That's about as plausible as a blizzard in the middle of Houston in July. So, cut the nonsense and tell me what's going on here."

Travis turned around toward the refrigerator, not saying anything. He reached in and pulled out two cold bottles of water. "Aren't you the least bit concerned about Doug?"

Patrick's face got red, "Don't try to change the subject on me, Travis. You know as well as I do that was cover-fire." He stuck his hand out in the middle of the air; as if pointing to a piece of evidence in a courtroom, "You said yourself a second ago that they were in no real danger. I agree. But that doesn't change the fact that some lunatics in camo were hidden up in the hillside trying to scare us away from the fuselage."

"Maybe they were drug runners. Maybe you tripped over their stash, Mills. That might irritate them a little bit. Maybe it was cartel members and they were trying to scare you off so that they could get their pot, hash, coke, smack, molly, or whatever else they were transporting and get it out of the plane."

Patrick's face got even redder. He slammed the palms of his hands down on the granite countertop with a slap, "Don't give me that! If that was the cartels, first of all, they wouldn't have blown the plane out of the sky with a missile and risked losing their load. They're interested in keeping their merchandise, not crashing the plane. And secondly, the cartels are brutal. That wouldn't have been cover-fire if that was them. You know that as well as I do. Tell me what's going on!"

Travis twisted the cap on his bottle of water off and took a long drink, draining half of it and wiping his mouth with his sleeve before answering, "Follow me. Bring the shotgun and the pistol." Travis said, striding away from the counter, catching the strap of the AR-15 as he did and slinging it over his shoulder.

Walking into the family room, Travis headed for the bookshelf. He slid his fingers behind the woodwork and pressed the button. As the door popped open, he heard Patrick suck in a breath, "What the —?"

Travis glanced over his shoulder, his face blank. He looked at the locked door, punched in the code, and set his thumb on the fingerprint reader. The door clicked open.

"Travis, what is this?" Patrick froze in the doorway.

"You're right, I'm more than just a horse trainer."

29

Travis watched Patrick as he took in the war room. "Who are you?"

"I run a little side business as a skip tracer." There was no need to say anything more about his background, at least not at the moment. The war room would speak for itself.

Patrick frowned. "What's that?"

Travis motioned for Patrick to put the guns down on the worktable. Travis unloaded all of them, checking to make sure they were clear before he said anything else. He had a rule about his guns. If they came out of where they were stored, they got cleaned before they were put away. A gun was no good to him if it wouldn't cycle properly and in the Texas dust and grit, things could jam, the combination of gun oil and the sandy dirt turning into a sticky paste.

Opening the cabinet behind the worktable and pulling out a clear plastic container, Travis scooped up the loose ammunition and dropped it inside, the clatter of the metal jackets against the sides of the hard plastic container bouncing off the walls. "A skip tracer is someone who finds things, things that have skipped town."

Patrick shrugged, "Like a bounty hunter?"

Travis turned away from Patrick, keying in the combination for a locked cabinet. He set the rifle, shotgun, and ammo inside and closed it again. "Kind of, but usually with no attachment to the court system. Bounty hunters are looking for people who skipped bail. I can do that, but I prefer not to. I like taking on private cases better."

"Like what?"

Watching Patrick, Travis saw his head was on a swivel. He was cataloging everything in the room. Travis ignored his watchful eye for the moment. "Like things that have been stolen people want to find but they don't want to involve the police." Travis was intentionally vague about his answer. Although he trusted Patrick enough to bring him into the war room, he wasn't ready to reveal everything. He doubted he ever would. Not to anyone. Not after what happened to Kira.

"What? Jewelry? Horses? What are we talking about here?"

Travis cocked his head to the side and scratched his face feeling the rough whiskers on his chin, "Could be anything — all the stuff you mentioned, or people." The way the word hung in the air, Travis knew Patrick would start to quickly put the pieces together.

"So, people are tied into this big old mess. Is that what you're telling me?"

"You could say that." Admitting the fact that he was looking for someone sent a knot down into the pit of Travis's stomach. He slumped down onto one of the stools near the worktable, looking at the bracelet again. He ran his fingers slowly over the stones, touching each one of them in succession – red, blue, green – the same way he had before he gave it to Kira. The memory of the day he'd given it to her flashed in his mind. They'd had a quiet meal just the two of them after a long ride on their horses that afternoon. Kira was leaving for Ecuador the next morning. It was supposed to be her last mission. The two of them sat outside on the front porch of the log cabin, talking about the things they would do when she got back — the renovations they wanted to make to the house, how they wanted to expand the training program, and even the possibility of adding a breeding program. Kira was talking about adding a second barn when Travis got up in the middle of her sentence and walked into the house, retrieving the bracelet. He'd picked it up that morning, planning on giving it to her when she got back from Ecuador as a welcome home present, but he was so excited he couldn't wait any longer.

"Travis Bishop, are you always in the habit of walking away when the love of your life is speaking to you?" she said, her voice dry and gravelly with the slightest hint of a Russian accent.

"Only because I wanted to give you this..."

"TRAVIS?"

Patrick's voice cut through Travis's memories. He lifted his eyes from the silver bracelet. "What? I was thinking."

"Yeah, you were totally ignoring me. Where did you go?"

"Nowhere you want to follow." Travis turned to his desk, opening the drawer where he'd stashed the key and the slip of paper he'd found in Gus's belongings earlier that morning. "This may be part of the puzzle."

"What's this?"

Travis sat back down on the stool next to the worktable and hooked his thumbs in the front pockets of his jeans. "It's a key and a set of numbers. For what, I don't know."

Patrick picked up each of them in succession, staring, turning them over in his hands. "Do you think this is somehow linked to the plane?"

"Maybe. Like you said, I'm the nexus, but that doesn't mean I've got the whole story figured out." Part of Travis wanted to tell Patrick the whole story — about Gus showing up the day before, Gus getting shot in the park in Austin, and about Elena, but Travis had no idea how much of the information he had was still classified. He swallowed. If he had to guess, the answer was all of it, minus the park shooting, which would make the news nationally if it hadn't already. Gus had come to him with the assumption that Travis would keep the information about Elena to himself. But things changed when Patrick showed up on his doorstep with Kira's bracelet.

"What are we supposed to do now?" Patrick said, slumping down on the stool across from Travis at the worktable.

Travis lifted the brim of his baseball cap, scratching his forehead, "I don't know."

30

E lena Lobranova was no fool. She'd worked in the field long enough to know she needed to have more than one place she could hide in case of emergency. The Agency had taught her that. And this was an emergency.

After driving the ATV a painfully bumpy and circuitous route to the nearest town, she'd found a farm on the outskirts and promptly traded the ATV for a gray sedan she hotwired. She thought it was a good trade. Her grandmother, a shop-keeper in a small town in Russia, would have approved. At least she hadn't left the owner of the car she'd stolen without wheels, even if it wasn't exactly what they were looking for.

Pulling away from the farm, she drove into town, heading back toward Austin. The cover of being in a bigger city would give her options she didn't have out in the countryside.

Elena turned the radio on to a local news station as she checked the fuel gauge on her newly acquired vehicle. It was half-full, more than enough to get her back to Austin. That beat the time when she had stolen a motorbike in Chechnya only to discover it had barely enough gas to get her around the corner. She shook her head a little and smiled, remembering the moment of frustration when she'd had to ditch it and grab a different motorbike to get away from the gang members chasing her. No matter how it looked in the movies, agency missions rarely went according to plan. Sometimes the unpredictability was fun, sometimes not.

Heading into the city, Elena weighed her options. The benefit to staying further out in the countryside was the space. She wouldn't be seen by as many people. There simply wasn't the population to support it. On the flip side, everyone seemed to know each other, so she stuck out like a sore thumb, her cropped blonde hair and petite muscular physique nothing like most of the ranch girls she'd seen, with their long legs, big hair, worn denim jeans and matching boots. The best cover for her had been as an Army captain, but looking down at the soiled uniform she was wearing, she knew she would need a change of clothes soon. At least getting into the city gave her more options, although there was typically more surveillance and more law enforcement as well. It was something she'd have to weigh.

No matter where she was, she'd have to deal with the issue of her shoulder. Piloting the ATV into town had done nothing for it. She chewed her lip. She had cash in her backpack. She could stop at a drugstore and at least get a bottle of painkillers that would get her through until she could get some medical attention. She rolled it a little, trying to figure out what she'd done to it. She winced as she felt a shooting pain slightly below where her collarbone intersected with her shoulder joint. It didn't seem like her collarbone was broken. At least that was good news.

At the next red light, Elena twisted in her seat, pulling her backpack toward her, a wave of exhaustion washing over her. From inside, she fished a small black box, powering it on. It was a GPS unit, a standalone model, not the typical piece of equipment that agents carried with them, but she liked it. There were times she didn't want to power up her cell phone. This was one of those times. There was no tracking the GPS equipment, at least none that she knew of. Glancing up at the stoplight, she realized she only had a few seconds so she quickly keyed in the coordinates she'd memorized, feeling in the front pocket of her backpack for the key that she'd been given. It was still there. She let out a sigh of relief.

As the light turned green, Elena heard the GPS chirp. Moving her right hand slowly, she gripped the GPS and dropped it into the cup holder between the seats where she could glance at it to see where to turn next. According to the green lights on the display, she was about eight miles from her destination.

For the next few minutes, Elena alternately checked the GPS and her surroundings. Her training had taught her to look for more details than most people, everything from noticing traffic patterns and what people were wearing, to how they were moving. Circling the outskirts of Austin, Elena didn't see anything that looked suspicious, at least not at the moment. She checked her rearview mirror and looked for tails every sixty to ninety seconds. It seemed the traffic behind her was constantly shifting and changing. No tails. There hadn't been anyone watching the farmhouse when she'd taken the gray sedan either. Even if they had been, they were unlikely to be the people that were hunting her.

When the GPS indicated she was only a mile out from the safe house she'd set up for herself, Elena could feel the tension building in her chest. Circling the block a couple of times, Elena saw the narrow townhouse building the GPS was pointing her to. It was worn red brick and three stories total, with peeling white paint on the windowsills and a few drooping mailboxes out front. The narrow driveway on the side of the building was the only downside. While there was parking in the back, Elena passed it by. There was no way she was going to park there. If she had to get away quickly, it wouldn't take anything at all to block her in between the two buildings.

Rounding the corner she saw a flower shop. The owner had put a line of potted plants by the front door, their wide green leaves lifting gently in the breeze. The dry cleaners next to the florist had propped their glass door open with a bucket, a well-dressed woman in a pantsuit leaving with an armload of shirts wrapped in thin plastic bags. Elena circled behind the townhouse and pulled into an art supply store directly behind it. The store was closed. The large white lettering on the window across the front of the building said it wouldn't open until later on that day. She parked the gray sedan next to a dented green dumpster with a black lid where it was out of the way. Hopefully whoever worked at the art supply store would completely ignore her vehicle. Elena got out, yanking the backpack with her, walking toward the ramshackle chain-link fence that separated the two properties.

The post in the center of the space between the two properties had tipped on its side, the chain-link pulled away from the bottom of the fence, scraggly grass growing up underneath it. Elena dodged through the small space, careful not to catch her shoulder on any of the metal. She stopped for a second, sniffing the air. Car exhaust surrounded her as if a vehicle had just left the parking lot of the townhouse. There were no cars parked in the lot. The thrum of traffic buzzed on the other side of the building, the growl of engines surging and retreating as they passed by.

Elena strode across the parking lot scanning the area ever so slightly, only using the movement of her eyes to check for people who might be watching or tracking her. There was nothing more obvious than someone whose head was swinging back and forth like a wild dog checking for tails. She knew better. It was a sign of nervousness, one she couldn't afford.

Arriving at the back door of the brick complex, Elena opened her hand, the metal from the key warm from her body heat, and shoved the key into the lock, twisting it. The door popped open after the deadbolt loosened from the doorframe with a decisive click. Elena walked inside, pulling the glass door closed behind her, spinning around to peer at the parking lot. She paused for a second, listening. There was nothing to see or hear, aside from the sound of what seemed to be a washer or dryer running somewhere, the smell of fresh soap faint, but still discernible.

Elena turned and walked to the elevator, pressing the button for the third floor. At the top, the door split open revealing tightly woven beige carpet stretching out in front of her down a short hallway. There was only one door on the entire floor. It was hers.

Elena had rented the small townhouse on her own with no Agency intervention or assistance four weeks before, the moment that she got wind of something going on in the office. Her inkling of trouble wasn't much to the outside eye, just a collection of a few strange looks as she passed people, the sense she was being followed, and a single email she received about her asking for verification of her recent travel to Russia. It was a trip she never made, nor had been assigned. In her business, paranoia was something that could either save your life or cause you to lose your mind. At that moment, Elena didn't know which it was.

Walking silently down the hallway, Elena stopped at the door, using the key to get inside. Closing it behind her, she fastened the locks and pulled a strip of L-shaped metal out of her bag that she jammed under the door. It was designed to prevent anyone from being able to jimmy the door open. Knowing the door was secure, she turned and stood for a second, staring at the loft space in front of her. Her shoulders slumped and she sighed. She was safe, at least for the moment.

After the suspicious email she received at work, Elena went home that night and plotted the next steps of her mission. It was one she's chosen for herself, not entirely unknown to the Agency, but one she had been keeping close to the vest. Based on her early research, she knew there was something going on that had to do with people in her division and their intentions. Some of them didn't appear to be good. Locating the final documentation to prove her theory there was at best a mole in her division, and at worst, a double agent had been the most challenging part of the operation. She knew the files would be in Texas at Camp Swift, and she also knew she'd have to get them in person. These weren't the kind of intelligence files that could be emailed or requisitioned. The thought had crossed her mind to go to her division chief and explain to him what was going on, but the more she dug, the more she realized someone was countering every single one of her moves and pointing the evidence back at her, painting her as a traitor. That was when she rented the loft.

Simple at its core, the loft had the same neutral beige looped carpeting in it that ran down the hallway. The walls were a matching shade of beige, giving the entire place the sense of living in an empty cardboard box. All in all, it wasn't more than about eight hundred square feet, with a single bedroom, a small kitchen, and one full bathroom, fully furnished. The living space included a sitting area that led out onto a balcony that faced the street above the hum of the florist shop and the dry cleaners.

Elena walked to the couch and dropped her backpack. Going into the bathroom, Elena started the shower, stripped off the soiled Army Captain's uniform, and stepped under the hot water, the smell of sweat, dirt, and aviation exhaust fumes stuck to her skin hanging in the air for a second until it was masked by soap. She rinsed off, letting the hot water run over her shoulder, hoping the heat would help loosen it up. Rolling it a little, she winced, the pinch of pain reminding her that all was not well in the joint.

Stepping out of the shower, she wrapped herself up in a towel. When she'd rented the unit, the agent she'd emailed told her it was furnished and sent her a list of what was included. Elena, using the alias Julie Green, emailed back and asked if it would be all right to purchase some things and have them shipped directly to the unit. The agent had quickly agreed, especially after Julie Green had wired the rent money for an entire year to her. The keys had arrived at an anonymous post office box Elena kept in Washington DC the next day.

The rental agent had been so kind as to have the building manager deliver all of the boxes inside the door of the loft prior to Elena's arrival. She'd spent two days driving to Austin from DC, spending the night in Nashville on her way, not wanting to risk anyone in the office tracking her plane flight. She'd made the excuse of a friend breaking up with her boyfriend and needing solace as the reason to take a few days off. As soon as Elena got to the loft, she unpacked the boxes and set up the things she'd purchased – sheets, blankets, towels, a few kitchen supplies, and toiletries – in case she needed them. Normally, there were services within the Agency that managed and stocked all of the safehouses. And normally, Elena would have been more than happy to take advantage of one of them. All she'd have to do was make a call.

But given the fact she was almost sure she was being watched, that was a call she wasn't willing to make.

Pulling on a fresh set of clothes and going into the bathroom and combing her cropped blonde hair away from her face, Elena sighed, looking in the mirror. Tugging her T-shirt away from her shoulder, she could see a dark black bruise that stretched across the right side of her chest. She touched it gently with two fingers pressing on the spot where it hurt the worst, her nose wrinkling as the nerves objected. "Looks like it's from the seatbelt," she mumbled, frowning in the mirror and letting the fabric of her T-shirt go back where it was supposed to be, covering the bruise.

Feeling slightly more human after a shower, Elena walked back into the sitting room area in her bare feet. Her clothes felt stiff, the T-shirt and zip-up jacket smelling like the starch of new clothing, the jeans rigid from lack of wear. But anything was better than the dirty Army Captain's uniform. She'd left it on the floor of the bathroom, crumpled and grimy in the corner.

Unzipping her backpack, Elena pulled out the laptop she'd been carrying everywhere and a pen from a local restaurant. Unfurling the charging cable, she found a plug nearby and attached it to the machine, opening up the lid, hearing its whirr.

While she waited for the machine to load, she walked into the kitchen. Not knowing if she'd ever need to use the safe flat or not, the only food she'd ordered were things that were shelf-stable. From out of the refrigerator, she pulled a bottle of water and found a package of microwavable noodles in the cabinet. She peeled back the corner of the clear covering, squinting at the instructions and then setting them inside the microwave as she cracked a bottle of water open and took a long swig. By the time a minute had passed on the microwave, Elena had consumed the entire first bottle of water. She glanced at the microwave, humming a happy Russian song her mother had taught her as a child under her breath, the light on inside of the compartment, the black tray of processed noodles turning slowly as if it was on display. With still a few minutes to go before her makeshift meal would be ready, Elena walked back into the sitting room and checked the computer. She sat down next to it, barely breathing. The machine and its files were her lifeline. If they had gotten damaged or corrupted during the plane crash or her escape, she might be out of options.

Hearing the microwave beep in the background and smelling the noodles as they finished cooking, Elena's stomach rumbled, but she ignored it. She had to know if the files had survived the crash.

Staring at the home screen, she entered her password and then scanned her thumbprint on the reader in the corner of the keyboard. The computer unlocked and moved to the next screen. Icons for about one hundred different files filled the page.

Frowning, Elena balanced the laptop on her knees. Before leaving DC for Texas, she'd installed specialized encrypted connection software on it, one that would give her Internet access, but in a way that she'd appear to be nothing more than the vapor of a ghost to anyone who was looking. She'd done the research herself, quietly asking questions of a friend she made in the CIA's tech department over coffee the month before, telling her she was doing research on options her division could use when agents were out in the field and feeling exposed. The computer specialist had been more than happy to oblige, launching into a forty-five-minute-long discussion of the limits of air-gapped computers and how some of the newest technology made it much easier for people who didn't want to be found to work on the Internet in stealth mode.

Elena had quickly purchased the software her friend had recommended, buying it under yet another one of her aliases. Before her decade-long career with the Agency, Elena had no idea how easy it was to create a fake identity. People made such a big deal about it, as though they had to rip off someone's purse and get access to their Social Security number or their passport. It was far easier than that, Elena had discovered. She'd simply come up with a name and used her post office box as the address. Using the Internet, she was able to apply for a bunch of different credit cards, putting them under different names within the same account. It wasn't a perfect solution, and definitely not as cleverly hidden as one that was created by the Agency, but it worked, nonetheless. Most people she bumped into weren't that interested in her back story. They were only concerned they could get what they needed out of her, whether that was payment for supplies, rent, or travel expenses.

Turning to the computer again, Elena moved the cursor over the icons one by one, reading them to herself, her lips moving silently. About halfway through, she glanced up, looking toward the kitchen. She stopped what she was doing, set the computer off to the side, and went into the kitchen, pulling the black plastic tray with the microwavable noodles out. The few minutes it sat cooling caused the clear plastic to suck itself down onto the surface of the food, making it look like the noodles were worms swimming in a pond. Elena wrinkled her nose as she pulled the acetate off and tossed it in the trash, finding a fork in the drawer. She wandered back into the sitting room, holding the hot tray gingerly with her fingers, and set it on the cheap wooden coffee table in front of the couch. She took a couple of bites of the noodles and then set the fork down, picking up the laptop again

After scanning the rest of the icons, she realized everything was in place. All of the files she'd loaded onto her computer were still there. But there was one, in particular, she needed to track.

At the bottom of the page, the last file was labeled "TMB" — The Moscow Brief. It was part of the final set of files she'd acquired a day and a half before as she made her escape from Camp Swift.

Double-clicking on the file, she opened it up and scanned the information, setting the black tray of noodles next to her on the couch and picking at it. She was hungry, but what she was looking at was far more important than eating. Elena's eyes moved slowly across the screen, absorbing the information in front of her. Her heart started to beat a little faster as she read the information.

The file itself had been compiled by the DCA, the Defense Clandestine Agency, an arm of the Defense Intelligence Agency. Simply put, the DCA was a bunch of military-grade CIA operatives. They'd put together the Moscow Brief as part of an ongoing threat assessment as Russia made more and more noise from its position on the other side of the globe, seeking to change its position as at least third in line behind the United States and China as a world power. Third in line wouldn't do, at least not where the level of Russian national pride and moxie was concerned.

Once Elena got to the third page, a red light at the top of the computer screen started to blink, drawing her attention. Her computer was programmed to go out every four hours and look for new messages, loading her email within a fraction of a second and then immediately disconnecting itself from the Internet. It was part of the package her friend at Langley had recommended. She was online for such a short time that it was almost impossible for anyone to pick up her presence there. That was part of the simple beauty of it.

Leaning toward the screen, Elena double-clicked on the mail icon and waited for it to load. There was only one message.

"Attack is a go. Twenty-four hours."

Elena sat up, her eyes unfocused on anything other than the words on the screen. The words landed heavy. The email was unsigned, coming from an email address that had no name, only a set of random letters and numbers. But she knew who it was from. Despite the fact that she'd been in the United States since she was a teenager, Elena had managed to keep track of a few of her cousins. One of them, Grigori Stefankovich, had managed to land himself a high position with a matching high salary by Russian standards, with the

FSB, formerly the KGB. Grigori played the part of being sympathetic to the Russian rule and their desire to reclaim the former glory of the Soviet Union, but not everyone in his country, more specifically within his government, agreed. Many of them could see the benefits of capitalism and collaboration that the West enjoyed with other countries and wanted to bring that into Russia, even more so than it had after the original collapse of the Soviet Union.

But Grigori, like the other sympathizers, had to be careful, so careful that Elena only received an email from him on a very highly irregular basis. She stared at the message again, chewing her fingernail. She looked at the time it had been sent. Only a few minutes had passed, so she still had the full twenty-four hours. Glancing at the time on her watch, she started a countdown timer. She still hadn't wrapped her brain around the essence of the assault, only that it was meant to disrupt the American government in a way it hadn't been since the attacks in New York City on September 11, 2001, when Al-Qaeda terrorists slammed two enormous jetliners into the twin towers, crumbling the buildings after internal fireballs melted the supporting ironwork, taking nearly three thousand lives with them.

Elena closed the lid to the laptop, resting her hands on top of it, her fingers gripping the back of it tightly. If the attack was greenlighted by the Kremlin, then the information laid out in the Moscow Brief she'd acquired from the DCS unit at Camp Swift was in play. Elena got up and walked to the balcony, staring out of the windows at the traffic below. The people on their way to home, work, or school had no idea what could happen over the next twenty-four hours. What the Russians were planning could change the very fabric of their lives and the history of their country. The question was, could Elena get in position to stop it, and prove she wasn't a traitor in time?

31

Travis and Patrick hung out in the war room for another hour, going over the information they had between the plane crash, the bracelet, and the shooting they'd experienced at the wreck site. In the middle of their discussion, Travis took a brief pause, calling Ellie and letting her know he needed her to step in and take care of the horses for the next day or two, "That'll work. I'll be out there in the next couple of hours."

"Good. There are notes on the whiteboard about what needs to be done with each of the horses. I got through the morning feedings and then got distracted."

"So you left the stall cleaning for me?"

"That's correct."

"Thanks a lot."

Travis harrumphed as he hung up the phone. Ellie was a good employee and an even better horsewoman. She might have pretended to be grumpy about cleaning the stalls, but on more than one occasion, Travis had caught her in with one of the horses, her picking rake leaning against the wall of the stall, humming quietly and gently stroking one of the horse's necks as if they were having a private conversation. She had a calming presence around the horses, one they seemed to appreciate. Travis appreciated it too. He needed people he could count on in his life, especially after Kira died. Ellie was one of them.

As soon as he got off the phone, he noticed Patrick was staring at him. "Can I use your computer? I want to run these numbers through a program that I have access to through the NTSB." Patrick pointed to the slip of paper Travis had found with the key.

Travis answered with a curt nod but no words. He took three steps over to the desktop and jiggled the mouse as he sat down on the desk chair. He opened up an Internet browser and stood up, making room for Patrick.

As soon as Patrick sat down, Travis could hear the keys on the keyboard tapping in the background. He stood behind Patrick, his arms crossed across his chest, staring at the screen. Patrick was a guest in his war room. Travis felt like he had a right to see exactly what he was doing. He didn't much care if Patrick had a problem with it or not.

Travis watched as Patrick went to the NTSB main site, scrolled to the bottom, and clicked on the login, entering his email and password. A new screen popped up as Patrick waited. He looked over his shoulder, "Can you grab that slip of paper for me? The one that came with the key?"

"Sure."

"By the way, you didn't tell me how you found the key and the slip of paper or why you think they are connected. Where did you get these?"

A frown tugged at the corners of Travis's mouth. It was inevitable questions about the key and paper would be coming, but he had avoided them. He paused for a second, not answering immediately, weighing his words.

"It's a long story," he grumbled. "Suffice it to say, this might have something to do with the plane crash."

Patrick spun in the chair, "Might? Give me something better than that, man. It's my case."

Travis pulled out the stool from the worktable and sat down, staring off into space for a second. He'd only met Patrick a few hours before, but Patrick's presence had definitely shaken up things at the ranch, that was for sure. Or at least, his possession of Kira's bracelet had. Patrick was stepping into the edge of a world he knew nothing about. Travis wondered for a moment if it was fair to let him walk onto a minefield without understanding exactly what type of explosives were laying at his feet.

"You hungry?" Travis said, buying himself a little time.

"Yeah. I'm starved. Didn't manage to get dinner last night with the plane crash."

"Okay." Travis pulled his phone out of his back pocket and thumbed through his contacts, making a quick call to a local restaurant. "Hey, Sarah, this is Travis over at Bishop Ranch." He paused for a second, "Yeah. Things are busy over here. Wondering if you could have Archie run a couple of sandwiches in this direction when you get a moment? Yeah, the regular's fine. Make it full-sized, with the sides." He nodded, listening. "Put it on my tab. Just have Archie leave it by the front door. I'll get them from there."

Ending the call, Travis commented, "Lunch will be here in a little bit."

"You still didn't tell me how you got this key." Patrick had a sour look on his face; like he was suspended on a tight wire between the information on his computer and what Travis knew but wasn't saying. He knew Travis was holding out on him.

Travis stood up, shrugging his shoulders. He started to pace. "You have a clearance through the NTSB?"

"Yeah, they carried my top-secret clearance through from the Marines. Just got it updated."

Travis grimaced, "What did you do in the Marines?"

"STO – Special Technical Operations. I helped plan operations and exercises with our aircraft."

At least Travis could tell himself Patrick had a clearance. That was something. "Like you had your job with the Marines before you went to the NTSB, I had a job too. I was with the Army for a while, was deployed, and managed to pick up a bunch of languages. As my time in the military was coming to the end, I was approached by the CIA."

Patrick's eyes went wide, "Like Langley? Like the CIA, CIA?"

Travis nodded, realizing at that moment he didn't care anymore about Langley's rules about what he could or couldn't say. They didn't control his life anymore. He did. "They were looking for people who could speak Russian and some of the other derivatives — things like Croatian, Hungarian, and a few of the other Russian dialects. I picked all those up in my spare time when I was deployed."

"Did you have a desk job?"

"No, not exactly. I was deployed to the Middle East as a Delta Force operator. When I wasn't out on combat patrol or on a mission, I had trouble sleeping, so I would sit in the comm's office. We had a couple of different people there who were collecting information from informants. The Russians had inserted a bunch of their military people undercover, plus some people from the KGB."

"I thought there wasn't any KGB anymore? Isn't it called the FSB or the SVR or something like that?"

Travis scowled at Patrick, "Supposedly that happened in 1991, but you can change the letters all you want. The KGB is still the KGB, make no mistake about that." Travis stood up, shoving his hands in his pockets. "Anyway, that's how I met

Kira. She was recruited by the CIA too, and I ended up working with her after my time in the military."

Patrick glanced at the bracelet on the worktable, "That's the same Kira that was your fiancée? The one that was killed in Ecuador?"

"Yep. The same one." Travis looked away.

"So you're telling me you were a spy?"

Travis nodded, "Yeah. It's not something I talk about. Honestly, I'm not supposed to now that I'm no longer with the Agency. But given what we're up against, I feel like it's only fair. You need to know who you're dealing with and what could possibly be coming your way – for you or your family." Travis knew the words coming out of his mouth sounded ominous. He meant them to be. Whether Patrick could see the storm clouds collecting on the horizon or not, Travis could. Better to be prepared for bad weather than to be surprised by it, Travis reasoned.

Patrick shook his head. "No family to worry about. I'm a confirmed bachelor." Patrick grabbed the slip of paper in his hand and studied it. "How does all of this tie together?"

"Yesterday, one of the guys I used to work with showed up here at the ranch. His name was Gus. He asked me to track down one of the women that was on our team — Elena Lobranova."

"Sounds Russian."

Travis shook his head, "You must be a genius. Elena grew up in Russia. Moved here when she was a teenager. Really good agent. Saved my bacon a bunch of times. Anyway, they've lost track of her. He said he wanted me to look for her since I'm one of the people that knows her the best and I'm a skip tracer. We ended up driving to Austin to have dinner, but he got shot."

"Wait," Patrick said, holding his hands up. "I heard something about that this morning. There was a shooting in a park in Austin?"

Travis nodded. "Yep. Got him center mass from long range. I booked out of there and ran up to Gus's hotel room and searched it. That's how I found the key and the slip of paper. I have no idea what it is or why Gus had it."

"And you think somehow all of this is tied together?"

"Like I said, I'm the nexus."

32

J ust as Travis finished recounting the story of how Gus had shown up at the ranch the day before to Patrick, there was a beep from the security system in the war room. A small red pickup truck was careening down the mile-long driveway, going far faster than it should have been on the ruts and bumps. Travis stared at the vehicle and stayed on his perch at the stool.

"You know who that is?" Patrick's head spun on his shoulders, his eyes wide, looking at Travis.

"Yeah. It's lunch."

Travis didn't move off the stool until he saw Archie set the bag of food right by the front door, get in his truck, and drive half a mile away from the cabin. "Stay here for a minute," he said to Patrick.

Opening the front door, Travis picked up the bag and stepped back inside. The tangy smell of beef brisket and barbecue sauce floated to his nose. His stomach rumbled. After being up all night long, he needed food.

Yelling over his shoulder, he called for Patrick, "Lunch is served. Come on out to the kitchen."

Patrick wandered out from inside the war room, "Now that I know your background, all your toys make more sense. Want me to lock this up?"

Travis shook his head, "Nope. We can go right back in there after we're done eating."

Travis took two white Styrofoam boxes out of the brown paper bag and set them on the granite. He pulled two more bottles of water out of the refrigerator and set them in the center of the counter. Turning toward the stove, he slid open a drawer and grabbed forks and knives plus a stack of white paper napkins. As Patrick wandered over, Travis lifted his chin, nodding at one of the stools. "Have a seat."

Travis lowered himself down onto the seat opposite Patrick and popped open the white container. The bottom was layered with red and white checked decorative wax paper. On top of it was a sandwich made of tender smoked brisket soaked in homemade barbecue sauce with grilled onions on toasted bread.

"Thanks for this, Travis," Patrick said, lifting half of the enormous sandwich and taking a bite. Travis watched for his reaction. Sarah's barbecue restaurant was nothing to look at, basically a shack on the outskirts of Burton, about fifteen minutes from the ranch. Travis had found it accidentally one day when he was coming back from buying worming supplies for the horses up in Austin. He'd eaten one of her brisket sandwiches standing outside at her counter and immediately bought five more pounds to bring home and stick in the freezer. It made a great meal with a cold beer after a long day.

Patrick grunted, "This has to be some of the best brisket I've ever had."

Travis used the napkins to wipe barbecue sauce off his face. "Yeah, Sarah has it figured out. Best brisket nobody ever knew about."

"Maybe she should advertise," Patrick mumbled, chewing a mouthful of his sandwich. "She could franchise this."

Travis shook his head, "She's not like that. She's a real, old-fashioned pitmaster. Wants to make sure that every piece of meat that comes out of her pit is the best it can be. And no, she doesn't need to advertise. She sells out pretty much every single day. We're lucky we got these."

Patrick's eyes went wide, barbecue sauce on his lips, "We almost missed out on the sandwiches?"

"It was a distinct possibility."

"I'm glad we didn't. This was worth getting shot at."

Travis chuckled, "I'm glad you think so."

The two men sat in relative silence for the next few minutes as they finished their lunches, heaping bites of coleslaw and tangy potato salad into their mouths, punctuated by bites of the smoky brisket sandwiches. At one point, Travis got up and retrieved more water and another stack of napkins. Eating Sarah's sandwiches was a messy affair at best, although a delicious one.

Their bellies full, Travis pulled a trash can out from underneath one of the dark wood cabinets and used his forearm to sweep the containers and stained napkins off the counter, pulling a soft towel and a spray bottle from another cabinet and returning the pristine granite to the way it looked before they ate.

Travis walked back to the war room, Patrick on his heels. Travis sat on the stool, his arms folded across his chest as Patrick repositioned himself in front of the computer. Patrick tapped his fingernail on the paper on the table next to the monitor. "I know this isn't a phone number. Too many digits. And it's almost too many numbers for coordinates, but let me see if I can make this work." Patrick stared at the computer as he keyed in the numbers onto the NTSB website. Travis glanced at the paper again. It was good Patrick thought he had a bead on the numbers. They didn't make any sense to Travis at all. No coordinates he'd ever seen were broken up on several different lines like they were on the slip of torn off paper Travis had found jammed into the soap bottle with the key stashed in Gus's toiletry kit. After a couple of tries, Patrick looked over his shoulder at Travis. "What do you think of this? Looks like coordinates plus the street number mashed into one."

Travis got up, unfolding his arms from across his chest, taking two steps toward Patrick who was still perched in front of the computer. Travis half bent over, leaning his palms on the desk, staring over Patrick's shoulder at the monitor. In front of him was a map with a single red pin. "Can you zoom in on that?"

With a couple of clicks of the mouse, the map pulled in tighter. "Where is this?" Travis asked, cocking his head to the side.

"Best I can tell it's on the outskirts of Austin. Looks to be west-northwest of our current location by about twenty miles."

Travis stared at the screen for another minute without saying anything. The pin had dropped in a suburb he'd never traveled into. Austin was a big and sprawling space, currently the fourth fastest growing city in the United States, with its favorable tax policy, casual western vibe, excellent job market, good schools, and reasonable weather, if you didn't count the occasional hurricane or tornado that blew up through the Texas countryside. In general, the people were friendly, that was if it was possible to find a native-born Texan in the slew of new people that were flooding into the state. With Texas growing so fast, it was starting to look a little more like Florida, where it seemed that at least half, if not more of the people, were natives of other states. And that didn't even begin to touch the issues at the southern border with migrants making their way into the United States in record numbers.

"What kind of building is that?" Travis frowned, staring at the screen.

"Not sure. Gimme a sec," Patrick clicked on the pin again and enlarged it even further. As he did, the street names became visible and a small image of the building in question popped up, courtesy of the browser and some random satellite that had been cruising overhead taking surveillance pictures of every building in the United States for the last decade. Travis pressed his lips together. That same satellite could be sitting over his ranch at that exact moment, taking pictures of his every movement. His shoulders tightened. People didn't realize it, but there wasn't much left of actual privacy anymore.

"That looks like some sort of a building to me," Patrick said, pointing his finger at the screen.

"Get the street name. Let's go make a visit."

33

Instead of taking Travis's truck, this time the two men slipped inside of Patrick's blue NTSB issued SUV, still covered with the pale yellow dust from the dirt on Travis's driveway. Pulling on his seatbelt, Patrick looked at Travis, "Would you mind programming the address in the GPS while I try to navigate this bumpy driveway of yours?"

Travis cracked a half-smile. "Yeah, I'll program it. Good luck with the potholes," he grunted.

After nearly cracking his head on the side window when Patrick took one of the potholes too fast, Travis took up directing him. It was better than getting a concussion. "Veer right here and then left. Then you can go straight for a little bit before you veer left again."

"How do you know where to turn?"

"Practice. Lots of practice."

On the drive into Austin, the two men chatted much like they had over lunch, continuing their argument about sports and talking about not much other than that. Travis checked his cell phone. He only had one message. Ellie had just arrived at the ranch and was beginning to work. "Everything's fine here.

I'll take care of the horses. Go do what you need to do," she wrote. Travis didn't bother replying. They'd already had a conversation. That was enough.

By the time Patrick's SUV rolled into the outskirts of Austin near the address on the slip of paper, Travis was starting to feel edgy, as though prickles from electricity were crawling up the back of his neck. Since Gus had come to visit him, another full twenty-four-hour cycle had passed since Elena had disappeared. Travis still had no idea whether she was somewhere local or halfway around the world. If his life depended on it, Travis would imagine that Gus had come to Texas because that's where he suspected Elena was hiding. Having Travis nearby was simply a side benefit, sort of like a big piece of strawberry shortcake with whipped cream after one of Sarah's delicious smoked brisket sandwiches.

Except that Travis wasn't feeling like there was anything sweet about the situation he was in at all.

As the GPS beeped that they'd arrived at the address from the slip of paper, Travis could tell Patrick was ready to swing the SUV into the parking lot. Travis reached out and caught the steering wheel as it started to turn, the vehicle giving a lurch, Patrick's eyes wide, "What the —?"

Travis growled, "Circle the block."

Patrick kept driving, but managed to shoot a glare at Travis, "What the heck was that about?"

"We're not going to roll up to the front of this building without getting the lay of the land. And I want to check and make sure we weren't tailed."

"What? You haven't been checking? Been slacking off at your job there, Agent Bishop?"

Travis shook his head, trying to ignore Patrick's sarcasm. "Yes, I've been checking. I've been checking the entire time you've been droning on about the Houston Texans versus the Dallas Cowboys. But that doesn't mean we haven't picked up a tail in the last few minutes or that someone isn't watching us. We have to try to figure that out before we go marching up to the door of that building and leave ourselves exposed. We don't know what we're going to find."

Sufficiently chastened, Patrick didn't say anything. He just kept driving.

"Turn right here," Travis said when they had gone down three blocks. As the SUV made the turn, Travis watched behind him to see if there was a pattern to the swirl of vehicles, any particular make, model, or color that seemed to be following too closely, or even worse, just far enough away to indicate they were professionals. After three more turns and another fifteen minutes of circling the block, Travis was satisfied. He spotted a café about a half a block from the building past the florist and the dry cleaner that were next to the address. "Pull in here."

"What are we doing?"

"Buying coffee."

Getting out of the SUV, the two of them went inside the café, Patrick darting off to use the restroom. By the time he was back, Travis had bought two large coffees, lids tightly snapped on and paper cuffs around each one of the cups to prevent the scalding hot liquid from burning their fingers through the thin paper cups.

"Thanks."

"Sure enough."

"What are we doing now?" Patrick adjusted his fingers on the cup and took a sip.

"Follow me."

As the two men walked outside, Travis led them on a slow but methodical path toward the address they'd found. They stopped for a moment to look in the front window of the dry cleaner, engaging in a few sentences of conversation while they stood and then moving on to the florist, Travis watching the building next door as they stepped inside. Travis made a show of walking around and looking at all the different flowers the florist had in the case and the drooping, multicolored bouquets that were ready for purchase. Pulling some cash out of his pocket, he bought a bunch of yellow daisies, keeping his eye on the road and the cars passing by the entire time.

"What are you doing?" Patrick whispered as the girl behind the counter walked away to wrap up his purchase.

"Buying some flowers," he frowned, staring at Patrick, his voice suddenly loud. "I told you that if we were going to go visit Aunt Pauline, we needed to bring her some flowers. Yellow daisies are her favorite."

"Aunt Pauline?" Patrick whispered. "What are you talking about?"

"Play along, Agent Mills," Travis hissed. He shot Patrick a look, "You would've made a terrible CIA agent."

"Thanks," Patrick mumbled, turning away and almost knocking over a potted fern, its long leaves nearly touching the ground from the metal stand it was perched on. "I think I'll stick to plane crashes."

Eight minutes later, after having a lovely conversation with the girl behind the counter about the increase in flower prices at the wholesale level, Travis and Patrick walked out of the shop, carrying their coffees and a bunch of yellow daisies wrapped in a layer of green waxed tissue covered by cellophane, a large yellow bow tying the bunch together. They wandered down the sidewalk, not in any hurry, and approached the building. Travis pointed at something above him and then glanced back at the building. Pointing as though he'd seen a rare bird he wanted to show Patrick gave him the opportunity to scan all three levels of the structure. There was no movement. No one was out on any of the balconies. All of the doors were closed. Given the fact it was the middle of the afternoon, it was likely that most people were at work, that was, if the units were even occupied.

Wandering slowly to the front door, Travis pulled the key out of his pocket. The moment of truth had arrived. Would it fit in the lock? He handed the bundle of flowers to Patrick and inserted the key, giving it a turn. He felt a little bit of tension and then the tumblers moved, popping the door open. "Bingo," he whispered.

Leaving Patrick to carry the flowers, the two of them walked inside. Travis glanced around the small lobby. It looked like there were two entrances to the building, one in the front and one in the back. That confirmed what he'd seen when they were driving around the block. There were no cars parked in the rear parking lot, which was another good sign that no one was home. Or if they were, they had concealed their vehicles elsewhere. The narrow hallway ran through the length of the building, the space of the building as a whole probably three or four times as long as it was wide. The shape resembled something more like a bowling alley than a box. The thought flitted through Travis's mind that the narrowness must have been a nightmare for the architect who designed the space. In older areas, the buildings were jammed together, making the best use of the space they did have.

"Where do we go now?" Patrick said, juggling the bouquet of flowers and almost dropping it. He glanced at Travis, "Can I set these down somewhere?"

"Not yet. Stop fidgeting."

Travis glanced at the bank of mailboxes installed against the wall. There were no names attached, just numbers. It was likely the units were residential, not office space. There were only three of them. "Let's start at the top of the building and work our way down."

Patrick shook his head, "We don't have another key. How are we going to get in?"

"I'm not sure we need one. Let's go see."

Getting in the elevator, the doors slid closed with a shudder. Any other time, Travis would probably have taken the steps. He hated elevators and everything about them, from the dank smell to the incessant beeping as they passed each floor to the tiny, cramped space where everyone trapped inside was subjected to conversation and body odors no one should have to endure without a choice. But taking the steps would arouse suspicion in this small of a building. Since they were going to see Aunt Pauline, Travis knew her two nephews wouldn't take the steps. They'd take the elevator to find their aunt's new apartment.

As the doors on the elevator opened, Travis glanced down the hallway before stepping onto the beige carpeting. There was a single light fixture glowing next to a single door at the end of a short hallway. It looked like the architect had done whatever they could do to maximize the space. No space was wasted on a long hallway, that was for sure.

Still holding the key in his hand, Travis walked to the door and put his ear up to it, listening. There was no noise inside. That didn't mean there was no one there. Someone could have been watching from inside the building as they approached, or they certainly could have heard the chirp of the elevator as it made its way up to the third floor. A tingle ran down Travis's spine. He needed to be careful. Very careful.

Travis handed his coffee to Patrick, who balanced it in the crook of his elbow, still holding his own drink and the bouquet of yellow daisies. Travis took one look at him and shook his head. Patrick blinked, the flash of embarrassment flushing his cheeks as he juggled all of the items, but he didn't say anything. Travis put the key in the lock and twisted it slowly, trying to make as little noise as possible. The lock was stiff, but like the one on the lobby door, it gave way after a moment of pressure, as though it had been newly installed. Travis lifted his chin and nodded at Patrick as he put his hand on the doorknob, giving it a twist, pocketing the key again. He set his jaw. It was time to go in.

Travis didn't say anything as he entered the loft, simply drawing his gun from the holster. Patrick trailed behind him. Travis motioned for Patrick to set the coffees and the flowers down on the floor near the door. If there was someone in the apartment, they'd need their hands free. Taking a few steps forward, Travis cocked his head to the side, glancing around the corners. There was a faint smell of food in the air, as if someone had been in the apartment recently. A single black microwavable tray was on the coffee table, the handle of a fork hanging over the side, along with two empty bottles of water. Travis glanced at the items and left Patrick in the sitting room and went into the bedroom. There wasn't much to see there, just a blanket and a pillow folded up on the mattress. It didn't look like it had been used, at least not recently. Sticking his head in the bathroom told a different story though.

On the floor was a pile of dirty clothes. He recognized it instantly. It was an Army uniform. Hung over the glass of the shower door was a towel. Travis wrapped his fingers around it. It was still damp. Someone had been here, and recently.

Walking back out into the sitting room, Travis motioned to Patrick as he holstered his gun. "We just missed them."

Patrick frowned, "The story I got from the phone call I had with the MPs at Camp Swift said they were chasing somebody from the base who went over to the private airstrip just north of it. That's where they think the plane came from that crashed."

Travis narrowed his eyes. "You didn't tell me that before."

Patrick shrugged, "I didn't really have the opportunity to give you the grand tour of the wreckage while we were getting shot at. After that, it kinda slipped my mind, to be honest."

Travis frowned, "Don't do that. Don't forget details like that. Now tell me all of it one more time."

Patrick blinked, "It's like I said. I got a call a couple of hours after I got to the crash right after the fire department arrived. It was from some guy at Camp Swift. Don't remember his name. One of the MPs. He heard about the crash and wanted to let me know they'd been in pursuit of someone who'd gotten into their tech facility, I think he said."

"Like an intelligence hub?"

"Yeah, maybe something like that," Patrick shrugged. "I can't remember the exact phrase he used. Anyway, he said the person stole a van and drove like a madman over to the airstrip. They ditched the van inside the fence and then ran across the tarmac. That's when they grabbed the plane and took off. The guy that called me was concerned the person that crashed was the same person they were chasing. Wanted to know if they could question them." Patrick looked down at the ground for a second then back up at Travis, "And the other thing he said is that whoever took off was small and fast. Almost like it was a woman."

Travis's mouth went dry. Elena was small and she could move fast if she wanted to. He imagined the scene in his mind, Elena's small frame charging across the tarmac, throwing her body into the first plane she'd found. That sounded exactly like something Elena would do. And to add to that, Travis knew she could fly. Travis's mind flashed to the conversation he'd had with Gus about Elena's disappearance. More and more, it wasn't looking like Gus being in Texas was any coincidence at all.

34

————

"Wnext" — **W**hat do we do now?" Patrick said, taking a sip of his coffee and leaning against the wall watching Travis.

Travis needed to finish his search of the apartment. He strode into the kitchen, looking inside nearly every drawer and cabinet. After a minute of opening and closing doors and drawers, he realized it was mostly empty, a prepacked drawer organizer with knives and forks and spoons slid inside one of the drawers, the plastic pulled off only enough so that someone could reach in to get one of the utensils. That would explain the fork left in the tv room. Inside the refrigerator, the only thing was water. There weren't any condiments, no ketchup, mustard, or hot sauce. The only food in the apartment was a stack of shelf-stable microwave dinners with black plastic trays that matched the one that had been abandoned on the cheap veneer of the coffee table. Two boxes of protein bars and a bag of chocolate were in the same cabinet. Whoever was staying here didn't have a lot of supplies.

Checking the bathroom again, Travis found the same setup — a single toothbrush and toothpaste, a bottle of shampoo, and a bar of soap. A stick of deodorant and a comb were left in the bathroom – ladies' deodorant. Travis swallowed, looking at it and then closing the drawer. Going to the closet, he opened it up to find nothing inside. He frowned as he opened a drawer to the dresser, seeing a package of panties in pastel colors that had been torn open, a stack of T-shirts, jeans, and socks with labels from a big box discount store in the drawer underneath.

Back in the tv room, Travis found Patrick staring out the balcony window. "See anything out there?"

Patrick turned back toward him, taking another sip of his coffee, "No. Looks like regular traffic going by. No one is parked along the street. You find anything?"

"Whoever is staying here is female."

"Think it could be the woman you're looking for?"

"Maybe..."

The tv room was the last place Travis hadn't scoured. Mentally, he felt like a timer was running in his head. He and Patrick had spent enough time in the loft apartment already. Someone could open the door at any moment. But at least he knew if someone was coming back, it was likely a woman. Now whether she'd have backup with her or not, Travis had no idea. He sat down on the olive-green couch that was placed haphazardly against the wall in the tv room, feeling the cheap springs sag under his weight. A large flatscreen monitor had been placed against the wall on the opposite side of the room, on top of a stand that looked like it was supposed to match the coffee table. Above him on the wall was a print of the Austin skyline, hastily hung in a cheap metal frame, slightly off-kilter. Everything about the loft looked like corporate housing to Travis — the kind of place where executives were left to fend for themselves when they were on assignment — except for the fact that he knew it wasn't corporate housing. It was a safe house.

Other than the abandoned empty tray of food on the table, there wasn't any other sign of life. Travis stood up from the couch, feeling between the cushions. He picked them up off the frame, feeling the cheap fabric rough in his hands. As he lifted the cushion underneath where he was sitting, he saw something. A pen.

Patrick walked toward him as Travis picked it up, "What's that? A pen? That could have been left there by anybody."

"No, it couldn't."

35

"It's just a pen, Travis," Patrick said, pressing his lips together.

"Maybe to you, but not to me." Travis stared at the black plastic ballpoint pen he'd found between the cushions on the couch. He was sure it was an accident that it was left behind. The matte black surface of the pen had been stamped with yellow lettering that read, "The Sour Lemon," with an address and a website.

In every city around the globe, it seemed there was at least one hangout that Agency types could rely on as a place to meet others in their industry. For how many intelligence agencies that operated around the globe — whether it was the MI6, the CIA, KGB, Mossad, the R&AW out of India, the ISI from Pakistan, or the MSS from China — all the people that worked for those agencies had one thing in common. Secrets. And because they had so many secrets, they needed safe places to meet others that understood their business. It was a strange thing, these hangouts. In Washington DC, the place to be was The Continental Hotel, an imposing brick structure built in the late 1800s in the Federal style, long narrow windows gracing each one of the hotel rooms above the white linen-draped tables of the restaurant and the brass rails of the bar. At any time of day or night, people could be found in the Continental who represented intelligence interests from around the world. Many a deal had been brokered in hotels and restaurants like the Continental, whether it was for information, the trade of a prisoner, or the assassination of a world leader.

The Sour Lemon was no different. It was just a more modern, Texas version of the Continental Hotel.

TRAVIS REMEMBERED HEARING about The Sour Lemon when he visited Texas on his first vacation from the CIA. On his way out of Langley, someone from another division had stopped him in the lobby, a guy named George he'd gone to training with. He asked where Travis was headed. "Home for a week."

"Where's that?"

"Texas."

"If you're anywhere near Austin, try The Sour Lemon. You might come back with something valuable. You never know..." The comment almost came with a wink and a nudge, but not quite.

On that trip home, curious about George's comment and tired of the parade of family members he'd lied to about his work, Travis had taken an evening and hung out at the bar at The Sour Lemon, drinking whiskey on the rocks, nursing only one for several hours. He watched people come and go and caught them watching him. As he was paying his tab, an older woman sat down on the barstool next to him, her thick gray hair braided just past the back of her collar, caught in a clip, a smear of bright red lipstick on her lips. "Sit down and have a drink with me."

Travis frowned. He was dating Kira by then and definitely wasn't interested in an older woman, especially not one with a mop of gray hair.

"I'm sorry, ma'am. I paid my bill. I'm headed out."

The woman sighed, "Sit down, Agent Bishop. Let's have a drink."

The fact the woman knew his name was enough to get Travis's attention. He sat down, giving the bartender a nod who quickly replaced his whiskey with another. Travis wrapped his fingers around it but didn't take a sip. He stared at the bar, frozen in place, the blood rushing in his ears. Questions were surging through his thoughts, but he held his body perfectly still. It was part of the training he'd gotten at Langley. Don't make any fast moves. Don't make any unnecessary eye contact. Those were all habits of being a good spy. What he hadn't counted on was the fact that someone knew who he was.

After a silence that seemed to stretch for eons, the woman took a sip of her wine and looked at him. "I've been watching you for the last couple of hours. Did you notice?"

"Nope. Can't say I did." He glanced at her. She had clear blue eyes and smooth skin. For all he knew, she could be forty or she could be seventy. She appeared to be ageless. "How do you know my name?"

"That's my job." Her Texas accent had evaporated. The words coming out of her mouth sounded distinctly British.

Travis narrowed his eyes. "All right, I'll play along. You seem to know who I am. Who are you?"

"You can call me Catherine."

"And you're clearly not a Texas native like I am," Travis observed.

"You are a sharp one, Agent Bishop." Catherine cracked a smile, "I keep tabs on who's in the bar. And since you are one of us, I thought I would introduce myself."

Travis didn't say anything, his mind racing. His hand shook a little as he took a sip of the whiskey. Glancing out of the corner of his eye, he was sure Catherine noticed. There was something about her that was intimidating, imposing, even though she had perched herself on the barstool next to him with a great amount of ease.

"Would you like to know why I approached you, Agent Bishop?"

Travis winced. Every time she used his name, she was pointing out the fact that she knew who he was, and probably everything from his file. Confusion swept over him. He knew nothing about her except for the name she'd given him, which he was relatively sure was an alias.

"I'm not sure I do."

A deep, hoarse laugh came out of Catherine's throat. She threw her head back, a broad smile across her face. "Well, at least that's an honest answer." After taking another sip of wine, she glanced over her shoulder. "Your bosses have a project for you while you are on vacation."

Travis raised his eyebrows. The fact that a foreign intelligence operative had exposed herself and was now telling him that his own people at the CIA had a job for him while he was on vacation seemed suspect, highly so, especially since he hadn't been briefed before he left. "They do? How would you know about that?"

"Because they sent me here to talk with you about it. They told me to use the word 'catastrophe" to get your attention."

He snapped his head toward her, then away, catching himself. "Catastrophe" was the code word Travis had been assigned. For all the tech the CIA had, sometimes the simplest processes were the best. Code words were one of them. Travis looked away from Catherine for a moment, peering into the bottom of the glass of amber-colored whiskey he had in front of him. He picked it up and took a sip, barely dampening his lips with it. He needed something to do with his hands while the thoughts raced in his head, not necessarily drink.

"That rings a bell."

"I hoped it would," Catherine said. She stared at the bar, lowering her voice to something barely above a whisper, "There is a file your bosses need you to collect from an army base not far from here."

Travis narrowed his eyes, "Camp Swift?"

Catherine shot him a piercing look as if he shouldn't have said anything that specific out loud. "That's not exactly for me to say. If you feel around underneath the lip of the counter where you are sitting before you leave, you'll feel a flash drive attached underneath. Pocket it carefully and when you get back to wherever it is you're staying, run it on your agency laptop. It will provide you with additional instructions." She glanced at him, "You have your laptop with you, don't you?"

Travis had almost left his laptop behind in DC, not wanting to load himself down with equipment when he'd left to go on vacation, but at the last second, he'd been reminded of the policy to take it with him. "You might be on vacation, but you're never truly off-duty," the assistant to the director of his division said, a woman named Ramona with curly brown hair that stuck out from every direction and a pair of glasses that Travis was relatively sure were only on her face for effect, not for correction.

"I do."

"Good man." Catherine took a long swig of her wine, draining the glass and setting it down in front of her. "Now, give me a kiss on the cheek like we've known each other for a lifetime. Then sit here, finish your drink and go about your business, Agent Bishop."

Travis did as commanded by Queen Catherine, or at least

she seemed like a queen to him. As he leaned in to plant the perfunctory kiss on Catherine's cheek, he could smell lilacs. By the time he sat back on his stool and picked up his drink, Catherine had somehow disappeared in the crowd at The Sour Lemon. He never saw her again.

36

The memory of Catherine was so strong Travis thought he could smell lilacs hanging in the air in the loft where he and Patrick had found the pen from The Sour Lemon. Travis was staring at it, rolling it over in his fingers, thinking, when Patrick pulled his phone out of his back pocket. "I'm sorry, man, duty calls. I just got a text from Doug. They called in the Texas Rangers and got that hillside cleared. I gotta get back."

Travis pressed his lips together, "Did they find anything?"

Patrick shook his head, "According to the text, all they found was a bunch of spent brass. Whoever was up there high-tailed it away, probably right after we left. I guess Doug is mad as a hornet and wants that plane wreckage out of there ASAP before something else happens. I gotta go help with that."

Travis nodded. It was time to leave the loft anyway. Staying much longer presented a risk they would be discovered. Then there would be explaining to do, explaining that Travis wasn't ready for.

Locking the door behind them, Travis padded down the hallway and back to the elevator. He pocketed the pen from

The Sour Lemon. Travis grabbed the bouquet of daisies on his way out of the building, dropping them in a trash can in the lobby. He couldn't very well leave them in the apartment and had no need for them at the ranch.

By the time they got to the ranch, the late afternoon sun had already crested, only a few wisps of gauzy clouds cruising across the blue sky. The wind had picked up. As Patrick's NTSB SUV drove down the mile-long driveway back to the ranch house, the normal plume of dust and grit had whipped itself into something that looked more like a whirlwind, small dust devils like miniature tornadoes cruising behind them as if teasing of a bigger event to come.

Travis got out of the SUV and gave Patrick a brief nod. "I'll be in touch if I find anything. Good luck at the crash site."

"I'll do the same. By the way, thanks for lunch."

"You bet." Travis watched as Patrick pulled out of the driveway. The only thing interrupting the rush of thoughts in his head was the noise of the grinding of the gravel underneath Patrick's tires. Travis stood there for several minutes until the plume of dust following Patrick's SUV had dissipated, blowing off onto the acreage of the ranch next door.

With the driveway empty, Travis stood and stared wondering what might travel his way next.

37

U ri's mood resembled the depth of a blustery Russian winter — cold, grim, and frosty, maybe even threatening. By the time he, Sergey and Alexander made it back to the house they had rented, Uri wasn't sure that his face would ever be capable of smiling again. It seemed like everything on this mission was going sideways, and in ways he could not expect, anticipate, or plan for.

They had dropped Tereza off at the airport. She was on her way to join the second phase of the operation, while Uri finished the first half before traveling to meet her. Uri stood outside of the small white farmhouse they'd rented for a month on the outskirts of Austin at the intersection where the suburbs became the country. When they'd arrived, Uri realized the property reminded him of his grandfather's dacha, something about the flat topography of the land and the sprawling, weed-infested vegetable garden behind the house bringing up memories of summers at the farm during his childhood. That was the last pleasant thought Uri had had since he'd arrived in Texas.

When he was in Russia, he'd heard a lot about Texas. Most

Russians had. It was as if Texas represented the whole of the United States, much the same way as Americans made assumptions about vodka, brutal winters, and being sent to a gulag. The image Russians had of Texas was far kinder, believing that cowboys, guns, and the idea that Texas was the wild, wild West of the real America. But Uri hadn't seen any evidence of that, not in the sprawling shopping centers and clogged traffic, aside from tons of pickup trucks with rifle racks in their back windows. No, America wasn't what it was cracked up to be.

To add to the injury of having to suffer through suburban American life, the team's success had been minimal in this first section of the mission. Yes, they had been able to force Elena Lobranova's plane onto the ground, but they still had no idea where she was, if she was alive, or where her laptop was. And time was ticking. Moscow wouldn't be patient for much longer.

After striding into the bathroom and taking a shower, Uri came out, hoping his mood would improve. It hadn't. Sergey and Alexander were plopped on a blue fabric-covered sectional, the two of them slumped down, watching American TV, a bag of potato chips and a line of empty soda cans in front of them. "Is this how you're going to spend your time?" Uri bellowed. "We only have twenty-four hours left until the second part of this operation and the two of you are going to sit here and eat chips? What is this American junk you are consuming? And where are Elena Lobranova and her blasted laptop?"

Alexander struggled to sit his lanky frame up straighter on the couch. His blond hair was clipped tight to the side of his head, the longer strands sticking out in a jungle-like tangle above his square jaw. "I'm sorry, Uri. Is there something you need us to do right now?" He sounded like a little boy apologizing for spilling his milk.

"No!" Uri yelled, his hands balled into fists. "And even if I did, you two are the last ones I would ask to help!"

Stomping into the kitchen, Uri opened the refrigerator door and then slammed it, a mishmash of jars and bottles rattling as he did. Charging out the back door to the porch, he yanked it closed behind him, hearing the glass clatter in its frame. He stood outside for a minute, taking a deep breath, waiting for his heart rate to come down and the blood in his cheeks to retreat into his chest. His heart was pounding. Alexander and Sergey simply didn't understand. It wasn't entirely their fault, Uri thought, moving to the edge of the porch and crossing his arms in front of his chest. According to the operational procedures his directorate was using, he couldn't read them in on everything that was going on, especially not what they had planned for Washington, a portion of the mission that could change history and push Russia to its rightful place as the global leader. That had been strictly forbidden by General Antonovich before he left.

Uri stared ahead of him, his eyes unfocused on anything other than the spots in front of his eyes as his rage dissipated. Beyond the abandoned vegetable garden, the back of the property where they were staying was nothing but an empty field. It looked like it had been farmed at one time, but there didn't seem to be anything growing at that moment. It was fallow, a tangle of short, broken stalks littering the field. It wasn't unlike the spot they were in with the mission. Would something good grow out of their efforts? Uri didn't know. At that moment, as doubt crept up his back, he wasn't sure it could. He felt acid churn in his belly, the rush of bile at the back of his throat. He swallowed, forcing the burning back down, leaving a sour taste in his mouth.

A moment later, Sergey joined him on the porch, moving slowly as though Uri was a wild animal Sergey didn't want to startle. "Uri Bazarov, what needs to be done?" It wasn't exactly an apology, but Uri didn't expect one. He was known for his foul moods and fiery temper. Most of the people who worked for him for longer than five minutes realized it was going to be part of the process and not to take it personally. He was a lot like the missile he'd launched at the plane, a loud bang, a fiery explosion, and then nothing.

Uri stared out at the empty field for another moment before answering Sergey. Sergey had become one of his most trusted confidants, someone that Uri could rely upon. Sergey had a distinct way of knowing when Uri needed to talk constructively about a mission and when Uri just needed to fume and vent.

Since they'd arrived at the rental house, posing as Russian business people selling replacement parts for grain combines, Sergey had asked very few questions. He'd simply listened to Uri and completed his assignments silently.

But now he was asking.

"This mission is giving me heartburn, literally," Uri said without looking at Sergey. "And I don't think it's only the horrible American food." He glanced at Sergey, "What is wrong with these people? Like every good Russian, I enjoy smoked fish, but these people smoke everything. I even saw a television commercial for someone who was smoking some sort of macaroni."

"Macaroni and cheese," Sergey said, sounding slightly apologetic that he knew what Uri was talking about.

The tangent on American food served a purpose. Uri was letting his mind run in the background, pondering the details of the operation to come into his unconscious. He turned to face Sergey, "Tereza is already on her way. That means the clock is ticking. If we don't find Elena and that laptop, the entire rest of the mission could be exposed, or worse, the Moscow brief could be compromised. And I think you know what that means when we get back to Russia."

Sergey's skin took on a gray pallor; as if death was already hunting him, "Yes. I understand that."

"The thing you may not understand," Uri said, staring at Sergey, "is how much is at stake."

Uri searched Sergey's face for a glimmer of recognition. Staring at him wasn't unlike looking at himself in the mirror. The two of them were similar in features — thick dark hair, square jaws, almond-shaped eyes. In fact, there had been times that they had been mistaken for brothers. But they were far from it. Uri had been raised in a KGB family, born and bred to take up his mantle as part of the long line of agents that were now controlled by the FSB and the SVR. But every Russian and every government agency around the globe knew that the KGB could change its name, but that didn't mean that the KGB didn't still exist. And, in Uri's mind – whether it was the SVR, FSB, or the KGB – it was stronger than ever.

Sergey didn't say anything as Uri stared at him. Sergey had a good military career before joining Uri's team. He was the strongest of the group, physically, thick in his body, revealing Cossack roots, and excellent with weapons. Alexander, with his long limbs and blond hair, wasn't suited for exactly the same kind of jobs as Sergey could do, but that's why they were on the team. Alexander had been assigned to Uri's team to handle the operational side, driving, navigating, and adjusting plans on the fly.

And then there was Tereza. Tereza had been a new addition to their team, calm and strong in her own way, also an expert with weapons and fluent in ten different languages. She had the carriage and the look of an American as soon as they landed. That wasn't what was unique about her, though. Tereza actually could blend in with anyone in any country she was visiting. Therese was what the KGB called a chameleon, someone who could blend into any circumstance. The directorate had recruited dozens of chameleons, using them as sleeper agents or as props to infiltrate governments, whether friendly or enemy.

Uri cocked his head to the side as he thought about his team and their upcoming assignment. Russia didn't really have any allies. There was no such thing as a friendly government where the Motherland was concerned. If a country or an individual wasn't part of Russia, or part of trying to re-establish the Soviet Union, they were an enemy. Plain and simple.

Sergey stood patiently while Uri thought. "We need to find Elena, that blasted laptop, and then get on the road. Time is running out." As the words came out of his mouth, Uri realized he sounded a lot more like an American than a Russian. He frowned.

"I'll get to work on that right away, sir. I'll call some of the local hospitals to see if she's there. I'm sure it won't be long before we have a breakthrough," Sergey said, turning on his heel.

At least Sergey had an idea of how to help. That was, at least, something. Uri turned, staring back at the fallow field. He hoped Sergey was right and that a breakthrough was around the corner.

38

Travis wasn't the kind to go out. He wasn't much for nightlife, much preferring to listen to the mockingbirds' call from the trees nearby from the comfort of his front porch than a band covering the latest hits. After Kira died, Travis pretty much stuck to the ranch, unless he had to trailer the horses to a show somewhere. And although he loved watching the equine athletes perform their spins, slide stops, circles, and rollbacks at reining competitions, there were times he felt the whole show situation was overwhelming. Too many people wanted his attention. Too many distractions. Too many threats. Most of them were women.

After Patrick dropped Travis off at the ranch, Travis walked down to the barn, checking on Ellie. She had the operation entirely under control. By the time he'd gotten back from breaking into the loft, she'd cleaned all of the stalls, replaced the bedding with fresh pine shavings, groomed four of the horses, exercised two of them, and took three more out to the pasture to run on their own while she rode in the arena. "Guess I don't have anything to worry about here, do I?" Travis said, standing inside the edge of the arena, a half-smile pulling at his cheek.

Ellie scratched the neck of the horse she was riding, a black gelding named Gambler, at the opening where the indoor arena and the aisle to the stalls connected to each other. She was as relaxed as Gambler was, her shoulders slumped, the reins long, laying on his muscular neck. Gambler hung his head low, calm after getting his exercise. Travis had shown up in time to see her work through a few of his flying lead changes, Ellie carefully shifting her weight in the saddle and bumping him with her legs, giving Gambler the cue to change his stride. "Those were some clean lead changes."

Ellie reached down and flipped his mane to one side. "Yeah, he's really coming along. You staying here? Want me to tack up one of the other horses?"

Travis licked his bottom lip, "No. I've got some stuff to do. Handle things for me for the next couple of days, okay? I should be around. If not, shoot me a text and I'll figure out what I can do to help."

Ellie frowned, tugging at the tail of her blonde braid. "Something interesting going on?"

Travis glanced at her. It wasn't like Ellie to pry, but she had probably seen the SUV with the yellow letters that screamed NTSB earlier parked in front of the house. He'd have to give her at least a half-truth to chew on in order to get her off his back. "Yeah. A buddy of mine from the Army's having a little problem with a plane crash. Asked me to help them look into it."

Ellie scowled, "You mean the plane I heard about last night?"

Travis blinked. It was hard to believe that it hadn't even been twenty-four hours since the plane crash. It seemed a lot longer. "Yeah. That's the one. I'll be out of pocket here for a bit while I help him. Like I said, though, reach out if you need anything." Travis turned on his heel and walked out of the arena before Ellie asked him any more questions. He didn't mind feeding her a partial truth, enough to keep her satisfied, but the last thing he wanted to do was go into any great detail about what was going on. Not that he had a good grasp on what the truth was in the first place.

Hiking back to the house, a scowl formed on Travis's face. He kicked at a chunk of gravel with the toe of his boot, sending it careening off the side of the driveway, landing under one of the fence posts. Normally, on a day like today, he enjoyed spending hours in the stable, working with the horses, making sure the tack was clean, rubbing leather cleaner on the bridles and saddles, checking to make sure the saddle pads were free of burrs and sweat, even scheduling the vet and the blacksmith for visits to the ranch. He grimaced. As much as he wanted to spend time at the barn, he couldn't. He needed answers first.

39

After a hot shower, Travis shaved, a towel wrapped around his waist. He glanced at his face in the mirror for any spots he might have missed. Although Gus had been shot right in front of him the night before and he'd been under fire only a few hours before, Travis realized he didn't look that much worse for wear. Perhaps he looked a little more tired than usual, a few lines from the corners of his eyes he hadn't noticed before making their appearance. Part of him wondered what that said about him. Had he become callous from the years of trauma to the point where things like watching Gus dying in front of him simply didn't bother him anymore? If that was what was going on, it was a hard truth to absorb. Travis knew underneath it all he was someone that cared deeply about others, but the circumstances in his life had prevented him from getting too involved since Kira.

And while he couldn't do anything about Kira, maybe he could do something about Elena.

Pulling on the single pair of dark wash jeans he saved for special occasions and a plaid shirt, he fished a tooled leather belt through the loops in his jeans, fixing a wide silver belt buckle in the front. In other parts of the country, walking out the door like that would have drawn him a lot of attention, and not in a good way. But that wasn't the case in Texas. Although he didn't generally wear a cowboy hat, finding the brims were awkward, always bumping into things, Travis knew one of the best ways to go undercover was to look like everyone else. And where he was going, wearing jeans, a plaid shirt and cowboy boots would make him look just like everyone else. It was something he'd been good at since he'd left foster care, blending in on the streets, hiding in plain sight.

At seven o'clock that night, after dozing off on the couch for an hour, Kira's bracelet wrapped in a stranglehold through his fingers, Travis awoke with a start. He didn't need to check the time. He knew it was time to go. Travis had an uncanny way of waking up without needing to set an alarm. It was something he'd learned in the military. Operations, while he was in Delta Force, started at odd hours of the day and night, with no real discernible pattern. His team might be required to be at training at seven one morning and then have to be standing on the tarmac ready to be deployed at midnight. There was no rhyme or reason, which made getting sleep a "grab as you go" practice. Travis had found it annoying to have to continually set an alarm. So he trained his body to wake up when it was time to move.

And it was time.

Walking into the garage, Travis got into the pickup truck, using a key fob to secure the house's alarm system, fighting a wave of exhaustion. Pulling out of the garage, he glanced toward the stable. The headlights on Ellie's car were cutting through the darkness into one of the pastures. She'd likely be leaving soon. He didn't wait for her to go ahead of him.

Turning down the driveway, Travis deftly avoided all of the potholes Patrick had so quickly fallen into, finding a smooth path even in the darkness. His headlights cut through the gravel in front of him until he got out on the main road. Turning toward Austin, Travis gripped the steering wheel. With any luck, in an hour he would find what he was looking for.

THE PARKING LOT at The Sour Lemon was completely full. There wasn't an open spot anywhere near the restaurant. As a precaution, Travis circled the block twice and then parked on the opposite side of the street, leaving the truck on the side of the road where he could get to it easily. He'd also have a line of sight from the restaurant if anyone decided to mess with it.

Getting out, he slammed the door, locking it and looking both ways before he stepped into the street. The Sour Lemon grew larger in his eyes with every step he took, light spilling out from the wide front glass windows, a neon sign with a bright yellow lemon outlined in the middle of it flashing on and off with a slight buzz he could hear from the other side of the road, the thump of music from inside reverberating off the glass windows.

Approaching the door, Travis walked slowly. There wasn't anyone else on the sidewalk. Most of the other stores in the area were already closed, save for a fast-food burger joint on the opposite corner. There seemed to be a steady stream of people still cruising the drive-through.

At the door of The Sour Lemon, Travis wrapped his thick fingers on the metal door pull. Stepping inside, he realized it was exactly as he had remembered it except that the restaurant and bar area were completely filled. Travis narrowed his eyes. There was no way that every person that was in the bar had some sort of an intelligence connection. It simply wasn't possible, not with the amount of people in the restaurant. The smell of frying burgers hung in the air. Travis spotted sandwiches laced with piles of french fries going by him as a petite waitress pushed past. "I'll be with you in a second, honey," she said, juggling a tray, a steak knife stabbed in the top of a burger like it was ready to be conquered. Travis didn't wait for the woman to come back. He walked to the bar and edged his way between two guys that were sitting next to each other having a beer and a group of four women who were chatting loudly, flipping their hair in the direction of the two men, who hadn't even bothered to notice. Travis narrowed his eyes. Had The Sour Lemon become a hookup bar in the years since he'd been there? He lifted his attention toward the bartender, "Whiskey on the rocks."

The man, shaved bald and wearing a black T-shirt that looked like it was two sizes too small for him and the shape of his arms suggesting that when he wasn't busy serving drinks, he was likely pumping iron, gave Travis a nod. The drink appeared a second later in a square glass, a matching single cube of ice plopped in the center of the dark amber liquid. It was certainly an upscale version of the drinks he used to get. Travis picked it up and glanced down the bar. He half expected Catherine to show up and give him another assignment, but after scanning the crowd, unless she had completely changed her look, she was nowhere to be seen. The corner of his lips pulled to the side. After what he'd seen in the last day, anything was possible.

Travis wandered down to the end of the bar near the gap where the bartender in the black t-shirt exited into the kitchen. Glancing through the square window that led into the back area, Travis could see bodies moving around. He turned away, not wanting anyone to realize he was carefully mapping the space. He took a sip of his drink and sat down at the edge of the bar. Two of the women from the original group of four walked by him, their hips swaying, presumably on the way to the bathroom. One of them looked over her shoulder at him as she passed, her lips parted as if inviting him to dare to speak to her. Travis pressed his lips together and stared at the top of the bar, running his fingernail over a scratch in the lacquer. He felt a gnawing in his gut and began to wonder if going to The Sour Lemon was a smart move.

Travis nursed his drink for another twenty minutes, waiting. For what, he wasn't sure. He was about to stand up and pay when the bald bartender came up behind him, juggling a tray of sandwiches and drinks, "There's a woman in the back booth that wants to say hi."

Travis tried not to roll his eyes. He mumbled a thanks under his breath. It was probably the same woman who had walked by him earlier on their way to the bathroom. He hadn't seen them come back yet. Maybe it was worth a look. Travis stood up, scanning the crowd. It hadn't thinned at all. If anything, there were more people in the bar than there had been when he'd arrived a half-hour before. Travis decided to take a walk, to see who had requested his presence.

The overall shape of the restaurant wasn't all that different from the loft that he and Patrick had broken into earlier that day. It was long and narrow, probably at least four times longer than it was wide. The bar was smashed up against the wall on the left side of the entrance, booths and tables scattered about. But the bartender had said the person that wanted to see him was at the back booth. Travis walked gingerly toward the back of the restaurant, carrying his glass, twisting and weaving his way through throngs of people who were standing near the bar and those who were seated.

As best he could tell, there were four booths behind the back edge of the bar. The first one was occupied by a man and a woman, holding hands over the table, discarded glasses and plates pushed off to the side. The next table held three women, purses and blazers piled up on the red leather vinyl seats as if they had left work and had decided to stop for a girl's dinner of giggles and gossip. In the third booth were a couple of guys who were toasting with their beer bottles, wearing basically the same outfit Travis had on. What they were toasting to, Travis had no idea and he couldn't care less.

Travis was about to turn around and head back toward the bar after seeing that it looked like the last booth was empty when he heard someone call to him, "Hey." The voice wasn't much louder than a whisper, even in the cacophony of voices echoing off the walls. He took a couple of steps forward, not able to see who was talking to him. Plastered in the corner of the booth on the side away from his vantage point was a small blonde woman with porcelain skin, her hair cropped close to her face. "You looking for me?" A smile stretched across her face.

"You could say that."

40

"How did you know I would be here?" Elena said, pointing for Travis to sit down.

"I found your safe house this afternoon."

A shadow passed over her face, "The loft? How?"

"Gus." Travis stared at Elena as he wrapped his fingers around his drink. She looked smaller and somehow paler than the last time he'd seen her. It wasn't a surprise, though. If half of what Gus said was true, she'd been on the run. That could take the life out of anyone. He spent the next couple of minutes giving Elena a brief overview of what Gus had said about how she'd gone dark and he needed to find her. Travis intentionally skipped the part of the story where Gus had accused Elena of being a traitor. He couldn't imagine she'd take kindly to that accusation. And if it was true, it wouldn't be wise for him to show his hand that quickly.

"I found the key first and then the pen. It was stuck in your couch."

Elena shook her head, blinking her clear blue eyes, "The key? There was only supposed to be one. I have it." Her eyes were unfocused; as if she was staring at something far away.

"And the pen... I wondered what happened to it." She stared at Travis, a smile puffing her cheeks. "No matter how you found me, it's good to see a friendly face." She cocked her head to the side, "At least, I hope it's friendly?"

Travis nodded slowly, rationing his words. "It is, but I think you have some explaining to do."

He saw her stiffen as if his words hit a sore spot. By the look on her face, it was clear Elena was aware of the accusations Gus had made against her. The question was, was she a traitor or was she being framed?

"Tell me what's going on. Why are you in Texas? Why is Gus looking for you?"

"You mean, Gus was..."

Travis swallowed. "You know about what happened last night?"

"Uh-huh. What I don't know is how you got roped into this mess."

41

"Let's get out of here and go where we can talk better," Elena said, reaching for her backpack, almost shouting over the deafening din of conversation and music at The Sour Lemon.

Travis shrugged, pushing away the drink he'd carried with him from the bar. While the constant noise from drunk patrons flirting with each other was probably good cover for their conversation, the questions he had for Elena would be better asked in private. He didn't say anything, only nodding at her suggestion, sliding out of the booth, waiting for Elena to exit in front of him. As she walked towards the front exit, he stopped and put a hand on her shoulder, cocking his head to the side, his face hardening. "Let's use the back entrance." He didn't explain why. He didn't need to.

Elena turned on her heel and walked toward the back of the building. Travis followed, looking at her as she walked ahead of him. She was as petite as he remembered, the black backpack swamping her shoulders, the length of it extending down to her thighs, her almost white blonde cropped hair almost making her look like a middle schooler headed to class. There was dust all over the canvas of the backpack, turning the color from black to charcoal. Following her, Travis raised his eyebrows. If that backpack held the laptop Gus had been talking about, then it probably had been to hell and back with her already.

Stepping outside in the cool night air, Elena turned back to look at Travis. He smiled, "You don't look like you've grown at all since the last time I saw you."

It was an old joke between the two of them. She wrinkled her nose and shook her head, "Very funny." She sized him up, not being shy about staring at him, "Looks like ranch life has been good to you for the last five years. You look great, Travis." She glanced around the parking lot and then back at him, "Where do we go now?"

Travis sucked in a breath and thought for a second. It would be easy to go back to her safe house loft. It wasn't far from there, but if he and Patrick had found it, then certainly someone else could as well. "I think we'd better go back to the ranch."

"Geez, isn't that kind of forward for a first date?" Elena chuckled, "Where did you park?"

"Across the street. Follow me."

Travis started off in the murky darkness towards his truck, hearing the back door to The Sour Lemon open again. The two guys that had been clinking the necks of their beer bottles together just before he sat down with Elena were staggering out of the bar behind them. Travis heard over his shoulder, "Hey! How about some help over here? I'm not sure we'll be able to find our cars." Travis didn't bother to look back.

"The Sour Lemon has changed a lot in the last few years," Travis mumbled under his breath to Elena as they walked across the street.

"Yeah. It's better at lunchtime, I think. The after-dinner crowd has gotten a little raucous, although you have to admit it's good cover."

"That's true."

As they got to Travis's truck, he pressed the key fob, hearing the alarm system chirp and the doors unlock. He stayed on the passenger side, helping Elena into the car. To anyone watching them, they would look like they were on a date and he was taking her home. A perfectly gentlemanly maneuver. Slamming the door, Travis checked over his shoulder, looking in both directions. The two drunk guys had disappeared. He didn't see any movement, but the tingle running up and down his spine made him wonder what he was missing. He pushed the thought away, trying to convince himself he was being paranoid.

Walking around the back of the truck, Travis ran a single finger through the layer of dust and grime on the paint from going to the crash site earlier that day. As soon as things calmed down, he'd have to get it cleaned up again. If they calmed down again. And something told him that was a big if. The truck had been a present to himself after Kira died. A concession he purchased using money that he'd set aside for a breeding program that Kira desperately wanted to start. In the five years she'd been gone, it still hadn't begun. He worried the idea of equine mamas and babies running around in the fields in front of the ranch would be a constant reminder of the life that he'd lost with Kira.

Sliding into the driver's side, Travis locked the doors and started the engines, checking the mirrors. He caught Elena's eye as he did, "See something?" she frowned.

"No. Not exactly."

He saw Elena check the mirrors, her body moving a little stiffly, "Not really? What does that mean?"

Travis pressed his lips together and shook his head, suddenly feeling unsure. "I'm sure it's nothing. Maybe I'm being paranoid. The last twenty-four hours have been...

surprising," he said, searching for the word that would describe it the best.

"Care to talk about it?" Elena pushed a few strands of short blonde hair behind her ear.

"Probably not until we get back to the ranch."

Elena nodded but didn't say anything. It wasn't as though Travis didn't want to talk. That was the entire purpose for dragging his wayward former colleague back to Bishop Ranch. But he didn't want to do it in the truck, and although part of the reason was because he was afraid of eavesdropping devices, the other part of it was that he really wanted to be able to see Elena's reactions. He hadn't seen her in a long time, but if he had to bet his life on it, he knew he would be able to tell by looking at Elena whether she was telling him the truth about what was going on or not. And given what had gone on in the last twenty-four hours, he was out of patience with half-truths. It was time to get down to the nitty-gritty. The best way for him to do that would be by staring Elena in her pretty Russian face and looking for any telltale signs of deceit.

Driving back to the ranch house, the two of them lulled themselves into a casual conversation about Travis's horses. "I still don't understand exactly what this sport is that you do. What is it called?"

"Reining."

"Like the weather?" Elena scowled.

"No," Travis shook his head, "like the leather reins on a bridle."

"Ah, I get it. Now, what exactly do you do?"

Travis sighed, "Reining is a cowboy sport developed to test horses and riders on their ranch skills, you know, the stuff that ranch hands need to do on an everyday basis. And cowboys, being as competitive as they are, turned it into a sport. The riders follow a pattern to show off their skills. Everybody does the same one depending on what the judges want to see. It simulates the maneuvers you'd use herding cattle – things like turning around quickly, that's called a rollback, spinning, that simulates if you had to change directions, and the slide stop which is..." Travis stopped for a second, blinking. "I have no idea what that's for. It's just fun."

"And you go to competitions for these?"

"Oh, yeah. There are competitions all over the country. Actually, some of the best trainers are from Italy."

"No kidding?" Elena cocked her head to the side. "An Italian cowboy. I like the sound of that."

"Cute, very cute." Travis shifted his grip on the steering wheel. "One of the biggest shows in the country isn't far from here. It's called 'Run for a Million' and it's in Las Vegas. I haven't qualified for that yet, but I'm trying."

"A million of what?"

"Dollars."

"Whoa. That's a lot of money for a horse show."

Travis nodded but didn't say anything else. As the words came out of Elena's mouth, the truck passed onto the mile-long stretch that led up to the house. Travis felt his mind start to focus, his stomach tightening. He hoped bringing Elena to the ranch wasn't a mistake. He was betting on his memory of her, and not on the information Gus had given him the day before. He glanced over at her and then focused his eyes back on the road again. His gut told him Elena was the same person that he'd known five years before, but a little voice inside of him that sounded an awful lot like Gus kept chattering away, suggesting otherwise. He sighed. Only time would tell. And they were running out of that in short order.

As he pulled up in front of the house, he let Elena out before pulling into the garage, "What's going on with your shoulder?"

Elena jumped out of the truck with her normal, almost Olympic-level athleticism, reaching behind her and dragging the backpack out of the cab of the truck. "Just got it banged up a little bit. Rough landing." She raised her eyebrows but didn't say any more.

As Travis pulled the truck into the garage and got out, he glanced over his shoulder, "That wouldn't have been from a bumpy plane landing, would it?"

Elena grinned, "I'll never tell. You know how spies are."

The banter between the two of them made Travis feel a bit more comfortable as they walked into the house. He slid his boots off and pointed for Elena to do the same. She didn't say anything as she did, just leaving them sitting next to his on the mat near the back door, her shoe size half the length of his boots. "Can I get you something to drink?" Travis said, walking into the kitchen.

"If you have water, that would be great. I feel like my mouth is filled with sand."

Travis reached into the refrigerator and pulled out a couple of bottles of water and handed one to her. "Thanks. I'm glad you found me. There are some things I need to tell you."

Travis put his finger up to his mouth and shook his head. A slight sensation of nausea ran through his body. Gus had been in his house. There was no telling if he had managed to plant any listening devices while he was inside. And if he did, even though he was dead, certainly someone would be listening. Who that someone was, Travis wasn't exactly sure.

A cloud passed behind Elena's eyes; as if a door had slammed suddenly shut, the clear blue irises darkening by half a shade. She glanced down at the ground and then back at him, the square of her jaw set, "Well, maybe you can take me out to see the horses before you take me back to my hotel. I'd love to see them."

A suggestion and a misdirection. Elena was on her game. Travis pressed his lips together. "Sure. We can do that." Travis met her eyes. He wagged his finger, beckoning for her to follow him.

Carrying the backpack in her left hand, Elena followed as Travis walked into the family room and touched the switch for the bookcase. He started talking as he keyed in the code for the locked door and swiped his thumb on the fingerprint reader, "Yeah, I've really enjoyed living out here for the last five years. It's quiet and peaceful. No one to bother me." He nodded, ushering Elena inside the war room. The lights flickered on automatically, the monitors of the security feeds humming to life. Travis closed the door behind them, waiting for a second until he heard the bookshelf click into place in the family room hiding the entrance to the war room. He walked over to a built-in cabinet above the computers and opened it. Inside, there was a black box with a bank of knobs and switches. He powered it on, using a red switch on the left side of the box and then turning the dial. He pulled his cell phone out of his pocket. No signal. The jammer was working.

"Okay, you can talk now. I'm blocking any signals."

Elena shrugged off her backpack, her face grimacing, "What is this place?"

"It's my war room."

42

"For what kind of war, Travis? You aren't an agent anymore." Elena spun to look at him, her eyes wide, after taking in Travis's secret room. "Or are you?"

"I'm not. I'm a skip tracer. That's why I have this room. It's where I do my work."

Elena walked slowly around the room, taking it in. Travis knew she was cataloging everything that was inside, from the security monitors to the locked cabinets, to the jamming equipment. "Don't you think this is overkill for a skip tracer?" Elena said, frowning.

"Actually, no. Not with what's been going on since yesterday. It comes in handy. Besides, it's a write-off. I have surveillance footage of the horses. Some of them are worth nearly a hundred thousand dollars. Business expense."

Travis sat down on one of the stools and pointed for Elena to do the same. "Okay, now that we can talk freely, how about if you tell me what the heck is going on."

Elena whistled under her breath, "Wow. Not much for a warm-up, are you?"

"I'm not in the mood to waste any more time on this." Travis narrowed his eyes, "Spit it out. Whatever it is, just tell me straight."

Elena sighed, her red lips hanging open for a second, her eyes narrowing, "Okay, but how about if you start?"

"Not a chance. Let's go, Lobranova. I'm up to my eyeballs in a hot mess and the only thing that connects everything is you."

"Me?" Elena pointed to her chest, her eyes wide. "How's that possible?"

Travis crossed his arms in front of his chest. He felt the tension building in his body. Elena was going to have to give him something soon, something that he could believe. At the moment, all she was doing was playing games. "That's what I'm asking you. Up until Gus showed up at the ranch yesterday, everything was fine."

Elena slumped down on the stool again, a wave of concern crossing her face. "Gus? Like Gus Norman? What was he doing here?"

"Yes, that Gus. I've given you something. Pony up some details. Now." Travis knew the words coming out of his mouth sounded stern and impatient, but that's exactly how he was feeling. He was overtired and frustrated by all the running around. He hadn't realized until that very moment how much calm he'd had in his life over the past five years since he'd left the Agency. He didn't miss the chaos of the spy business, that was for sure.

Elena got up off of the stool again and walked to the other end of the room, stopping in front of the security monitors. Travis observed her as she watched the screens change every few seconds, rotating from the inside of the arena to the camera angles above each of the stalls, to the cameras placed along the driveway and on the perimeter of the cabin. She spun around, staring at him. "I'm in trouble." The words came out in a tumble.

Travis gave a single nod. "I kind of figured that part out. What's going on?"

Elena walked back to the stool and turned the cap on the water with a little bit of difficulty, wincing as she did. She took a drink and then set it down on the worktable looking at Travis. "This all started a few months ago. I got an assignment to track some Russian activity that didn't seem legit. It came from the director himself."

"Director Stewart?"

Elena nodded, "Yeah. He's still there. He's still running the Russia desk, although they've expanded it by giving him a good chunk of the Eastern Bloc. So now, our team covers all of those countries and all the nonsense the Kremlin is constantly putting out."

Travis nodded to himself. It made sense that the director would be given more geography to cover. While Russia was a lot to manage, all of the countries that surrounded it, including places like Belarus and Ukraine, although they were not part of the Soviet Union, were still considered sympathizers to some extent. In other words, if the United States had to decide whether a country like Belarus was going to side with their Russian patrons or NATO, they'd bet on Russia. That's why the Agency clumped all of those countries together. And, it made sense for the people that worked on the team to run free in all those countries, at least the ones that Travis still knew about. Elena was fluent in multiple languages, many of which were covered in that territory.

"What kind of activity was Stewart worried about?"

Elena looked away for a second. "You remember I have a cousin who's linked to the Russian government?"

"Yeah. Wasn't his name Grigori or something like that?"

"Yeah. Exactly. His name's Grigori Stefankovich. I don't know him well. I haven't been back to Russia on a social trip, if you will, since I left when I was a teenager. But he and I stay in contact through channels. He sent me some information that looks like Russia is moving troops toward the Georgian border."

Travis frowned for a second, thinking through the geography of that part of the world. Russia took up a large chunk of the Asian continent but was bordered by states that extended southward toward the Middle East. Georgia was one of them. "Georgia? Aren't they already in the back pocket of the President of Russia? They're pretty much a Russian proxy already, aren't they?"

The one thing that Travis remembered from his time with the CIA was how fast alliances could change. On Monday a country could be a favorable ally to someone and by Tuesday the entire scope of geopolitical strategy could have changed. The first few times it happened while he was with the Agency, he'd watched in horror as agents scrambled around the office, recalling spies and deploying them to other regions around the world. The shifts had seemed quite strange, as though gravity had tilted and instead of walking on the floor, he was now walking on a side wall or ceiling. But, after a few months of the twisting and turning of geopolitical negotiations, by the time it happened to him, Travis was used to it.

"They are, although they've become much more friendly with the West in the last few years. That's something that is annoying the Russian President to no end, according to what Grigori told me. So, the President's way of dealing with it is by running so-called military exercises on the Georgian border."

"That's fairly common, though, isn't it?" Travis asked.

"It is, except when it's a false flag operation."

"A FALSE FLAG OPERATION? Travis scowled.

False flag operations were a technique used by virtually every country around the globe. He remembered hearing about it when he was in training with Delta Force. The instructor had stood up in front of the classroom and said to the soldiers, "The easiest way to explain a false flag operation is it's a bait and switch. Bottom line — it's a distraction from the real agenda."

False flag operations had been used in one way or another for centuries. One of the most famous examples was the original Trojan horse, a wooden horse sculpture filled with soldiers proffered as a gift to the leaders of Troy. The moment the statue was wheeled inside the city walls, soldiers tumbled out, nullifying Troy's walled defenses to help them capture the city.

Now, countries had become more sophisticated and were willing to take bigger risks. Military exercises, or so they were frequently called, were used to distract from other agendas that countries might have. Travis remembered reading an article online about how the Chinese were busily flying unnerving surveillance missions over Taiwan, all the time they were quickly scooping up land in the Southeast Pacific and claiming it as their own. The Western allies were so concerned about their interests in Taiwan that they didn't pick up on the fact that China had taken over a whole series of islands as new territory until it was too late. All the screaming and negotiation at the UN after the fact had done absolutely nothing to remedy the situation. The Chinese had simply outmaneuvered the Western allies with a simple sleight-of-hand.

"So, what's the real agenda?"

"That's what I've been trying to figure out," Elena said; her jaw set.

43

Travis noticed that simply talking about the false flag operation put Elena on edge. She eyed her backpack as if it might squirm away when she wasn't watching. Laying her hand on it, he saw her pinch the canvas with her fingers. She was prepared for Travis to lunge for it and rip it away from her.

Travis had no interest in anything of the sort. He cleared his throat. "By definition, a false flag operation is a deception. You said you don't have any idea what the Russians are really after, but you must have a theory, at least, right?" Travis stood up from where he'd been sitting on the stool watching Elena. He started walking the length of the room at a plodding pace toward the surveillance monitors and then turning in the other direction towards the computers. He waited, listening.

"All I can say is that the evidence I found pointed to someone in our division being compromised. I'm not exactly sure who. We've grown since you were there. There are literally hundreds of operatives. I've had a couple of theories, but every time I turn around, those prove to be false."

"Like who?"

Elena pressed her lips together, "I'd prefer not to say, at least not until I'm sure. We're talking about people's lives and careers here, Travis. This isn't a game."

The words stung. He knew the risks involved. He'd been out in the field with Elena and lost Kira. She should know that. "I'm aware," he growled. "And yet, you seem to have people chasing you who would like to see you dead."

Elena locked eyes with him as he paced, her gaze level and calm. "That's part of the business. What is unsettling is that it's not just the Russians who want to see me wiped off the face of the planet."

"You think the CIA wants you dead too? They don't just want to talk?" Travis tried to keep his face relaxed. Gus had mentioned he thought Elena was a traitor. It was probably better if Travis pretended he didn't have that information, at least for the moment. He needed to hear the facts from Elena.

Elena nodded, "Yes. I think that's the case. I mean, from the military's perspective, I get it. I just broke into Camp Swift, strolled my way into their intelligence hub, and stole a pack of highly sensitive intelligence files. If I were them, I'd be irritated too."

She'd managed to kick a hornet's nest if half of what she said was true. Travis glanced down and then at her again, "What was in those files, Elena?"

"A variety of things." She picked at a cuticle and then looked at him. "Some of them have satellite views of troop movement on the Russian border, detailed photographs of their so-called exercises happening near Georgia."

"The intelligence hub at Camp Swift is focused on Moscow?"

It was a question that slipped out of Travis's mouth before he had a chance to really think about it. The United States had a platoon of very expensive, highly sensitive satellites skimming through the skies at all hours of the night and day, crisscrossing the globe. Travis remembered when he was in high school, his football coach had used a video camera to capture their games. If someone messed up and tried to lie about it, the coach would whip out the video footage and stare them down with the comment, "The eye in the sky doesn't lie."

And it was the same now.

Although the Soviet Union as an entity had folded, the Russian propaganda machine had never been sharper, carrying no shame about their blatant lies. They would quickly say one thing and maneuver in a completely different direction. Satellite images were one of the only ways to prove whether what the diplomats and the press core from Moscow were screaming about were true or not. And most of the time it fell under the heading of not.

"Other than the satellite footage, what else did you manage to find?" Travis stopped his pacing, propping his palms on the worktable, watching Elena. Her face was relaxed. There was no unnecessary movement or fidgeting. As best Travis could tell, she was telling the truth.

She raised her eyebrows and then tilted her head to the side, "I haven't had a chance to sit down and look at the files. At this point, I'm just hoping they survived the trip here." Pressing her lips together, she said, "I found some additional evidence of the mole in our division."

Travis narrowed his eyes. Two things she had mentioned were interesting — her trip to get to his ranch and additional intelligence on the breach in his old division. "What kind of evidence?"

Elena stood up, "Apparently DCS, you remember, the Defense Counterintelligence and Security Agency, intercepted some communications going back and forth to the KGB. They flagged them as being suspect, but no one has responded to the issues presented, at least not yet."

Travis frowned, "You're saying DCS picked up some sort of

a conversation that's been going on, all the while there are thousands of troops massing on the Georgian border? No one has followed up yet?"

"Yep, that's about the size of it. So then, the question becomes, which one of the operations is the false flag? Is it the communications or is it the troop movements?"

Travis slumped down on the stool in front of him, propping his chin in his hands, thinking. After a minute, he glanced at Elena, "What are you not telling me, Elena? A conversation is nothing to get all that excited about. If I remember correctly, we all had our contacts within the Russian government, people like your cousin Grigori, even. What makes this conversation all that different?"

Elena blinked and then licked her lips, "Because it's about toppling the US government."

44

"What are you talking about? Like a coup?" Travis stammered. His relaxed posture had become ramrod straight.

Elena nodded, "It looks that way. Between the information I've gotten from Grigori and these other intercepts — like I said, I haven't had a chance to dig through them. I only gave it a glance as I copied them over onto my laptop, but based on what I saw it looks that way. The Russian president isn't that excited about having Robert Mosley in office for another three years."

President Mosely was one of the most aggressive presidents the United States had had in a long time. He wasn't afraid to make waves in Washington or around the world. Travis shrugged, "No Russian president ever likes their American counterpart, not unless they completely change their policy towards them."

"Apparently, President Mosley has been firmer with President Yanovich than he would have liked. There have been some not-so-subtle threats about increasing our wheat, oil, and natural gas production and shipping them to Europe."

"Enough that the United States and Europe wouldn't need Russian exports anymore?"

Elena nodded. "That's exactly the case. True open market competition. Pair that with a memo I found where one of Mosley's policy advisers suggested it might be time to scale back on aid and subsidies going to the Russians and you might be able to see how President Yanovich might get his drawers in a twist."

Travis shook his head. Why the United States sent any aid to enemy countries, Travis could never understand. From a humanitarian level, it was understandable. Sending food and first aid supplies to countries that couldn't afford it was one thing, but sending aid to Russia – billions of dollars in cash every year – had never made any sense to him. Russia always prided itself on having the biggest and the best of everything. They had piles of cash to build expansive government buildings filled with marble floors and gold faucets but couldn't bother to feed or get medical supplies for their own people. None of it made sense to him. And the same policy applied around the world. The US had given aid for generations as a way to keep a thin semblance of leverage over countries like China and Iran in addition to Russia. The subtle threat was if they didn't play nice, the US would pull the additional funding. But did those countries really need American funding in the first place? With the American deficit running in the trillions of dollars with growing needs at home, Travis had concerns of his own about supplying the Russians with anything extra. And apparently, President Mosley did too.

"President Yanovich's way of dealing with this is through saber rattling at the Georgian border and at least launching the hint of a coup against Mosley? Two unsettling fronts to decipher at one time, not to mention everything else that's going on in the world." Travis shrugged, "I know our intelligence services are good, but that's a lot."

Elena chewed her lip, "If the threat to Georgia is real and the Russian troops try to reintegrate the territory and install a favorable government to Moscow, then you're looking at additional problems. Georgia is just a hop, skip, and a jump from the Middle East. You know as well as I do that Russia and Israel have a tenuous peace at best. They certainly aren't friendly. If Russia managed to control the Georgian territory, they could easily launch military operations into Israel. It wouldn't take long for Israel to see Russian jets in their airspace."

Travis sighed. "If the Russians are really going into Georgia, it could throw the entire Middle East into a high alert status."

"Exactly."

Travis had spent a considerable amount of time while he was in the agency traveling through Israel. It hadn't been one of his primary mission locations, but rather a convenient launching pad. Their division, the one he worked in with Kira, Gus, and Elena, focused on Russia and the associated countries, but with Israel being relatively close and one of America's best allies, the CIA frequently shuttled agents through Tel Aviv, using one of the many safe houses they had set up with the support of Israel's Mossad for briefings, among other things.

Travis tapped a single finger on the worktable. If the Russians made the kind of move Elena was talking about into Georgia, the relationship between the United States and Israel would force the US to respond. No matter how opposed an American leader was to protecting Israel, every American president had done exactly that, no matter how irritated their constituencies became. The long-standing friendship between America and Israel demanded the highest level of cooperation, not to mention the strategic value of being able to access intelligence, weapons, and bases centered just off the Mediterranean Sea. The relationship between America and Israel had to stay unbroken. The Russians invading Georgia would force the US to run a proxy war against the Russians to protect Israel. Travis shuddered. "I get the ramifications of what's going on in Georgia. But you haven't said much about this potential coup. Is there a reason for that?"

"It's because I simply don't know, and to be honest, it's hard to think clearly when you have two governments trying to kill you."

45

Elena's honesty hit Travis full force, like a baseball bat between the eyes. She had hinted the Russians wanted her dead and, at best, the Americans were unhappy with her, but to say that they were both out to get her, was a completely different assertion, especially given the fact that she was an American agent in good standing. Even though she was working on American soil, which technically, she shouldn't have been, it still should have afforded her not only protection but also the benefit of the doubt. Apparently, innocent until proven guilty was no longer in fashion.

"You're sure you're a target of both governments?"

Elena narrowed her eyes, staring at Travis. She balled her fists, "Travis, I'm having a hard time believing you just asked me that question. I mean, if Gus has been here, then you must have some idea of what's going on. I'm sure he told you the Russians and people at the Agency are after me. And you have to know about the plane crash. It was all over the local news."

Travis looked down, feeling the heat gather in his cheeks. His stomach clenched. He owed Elena more than doubt-filled leading questions. "You're right, I'm sorry. Tell me what's going on and how I can help."

Elena reached up and absentmindedly massaged her right shoulder, her face softening, "Here's what I can tell you — after I broke into the intelligence hub at Camp Swift, which I know I shouldn't have done, I took off and ended up grabbing a plane. The MPs were hot on my tail. I needed to get out of there. Then I got shot out of the sky."

Travis nodded, "I saw the wreckage."

Elena's mouth fell open. "You did? How?"

Travis pulled Kira's bracelet out of a drawer in the work-table, laying it on the surface. "The NTSB investigator working the scene found this."

Elena stared at the table. "You found it."

Travis raises eyebrows, "More accurately, the bracelet found me. The NTSB investigator found the coordinates on the back of the bracelet and drove here yesterday." Travis's heart was pounding in his chest so hard he felt like he could hardly breathe. Maybe he wasn't breathing at all. The next words came out as a whisper, "That bracelet was Kira's, Elena. How did you get it?"

Elena glanced away from Travis for a second. An uneasy silence settled between the two of them, the conversation stalling to a chilly silence, as though an iceberg had entered the room and they were both watching it float by.

Travis searched Elena's face, waiting for her to answer. He couldn't read anything from her expression. Her cheeks weren't flushed, her porcelain skin was exactly the same color as it had been a second before. Her red lips had a slight pout to them as though she was about to say something but the words hadn't formed yet. She stared at the floor, absentmindedly pushing a clump of clipped blonde hair behind her ear. "How I got the bracelet is a pretty easy question. After you left the Agency, it had to be about a year and a half later, the lead agent in Quito sent a box of things they'd retrieved from the operation in Ecuador. The bracelet was in it. I told Director Stewart I would get it back to you, but I kept thinking about how you'd lost Kira, how despondent you were at the funeral, and I was worried the bracelet would..."

"Bring up bad memories?" Travis finished her sentence for her.

Elena nodded, closing her eyes for a second. "I'm sorry, Travis. I know I should have come here and given it to you myself as soon as I got it. It was too painful. I know how much you loved her."

Travis looked away, acid eating at the inside of his stomach. By the time he looked back, Elena was staring at him, "Did they find anything else?" He hoped that Elena knew what he meant because trying to choke the words out past the lump in his throat seemed nearly impossible.

Elena shook her head, "No, Travis. Honestly, I'm not even sure how they got the bracelet. It came back with no explanation."

Travis pushed at the sterling silver and turquoise links absentmindedly with his finger, straightening them, like maybe it would straighten the knots out in his own life. Agents didn't travel with personal items on their bodies. It was a way of protecting their identities. But maybe Kira had been so excited it was her last mission that she'd forgotten, or maybe she'd been so thrilled to have the bracelet she couldn't bear to leave it home or at the office. Travis closed his eyes, thinking back to that day. He tried to remember whether he saw the bracelet on her wrist when she'd left the ranch that morning for the airport, but the images he had in his mind of her were fragmented, as though someone had taken a beautiful portrait and smashed it into a million fragments with a sledgehammer. His mind could only surface shards of memories from their time together, the tilt of Kira's head, the way she held her hand, a smile pulling at her lips. Nothing he could do could make the entire image pull back together. His arms drooped at his sides. He didn't say anything, but he knew he didn't have to.

Elena filled the silence between the two of them, "The best I can figure is either she left it in her desk drawer at the office in Quito and somebody tossed it into a box after she passed away and forgot to go through her things until later, or maybe she left it in the safe house? Honestly, Travis, I wish I had more information for you, but I don't."

Travis sighed, "Let's skip ahead. What prompted you to bring it with you?"

"I knew you used to live in Texas. Wasn't exactly sure where, but when I headed this direction, I grabbed it, figuring I could at least mail it to you or drop it off here at the ranch, depending on how things went." Elena glanced at the ceiling, "And then things went kinda off the rails. I had it in my backpack and then, the MPs were chasing me, and the plane —"

"And then you got shot out of the sky."

Elena nodded. "You saw the damage... That missile came out of nowhere. It had to be the Russians."

"You think the Kremlin seriously sent a kill squad after you?"

"Who else would it be, Travis?"

Travis shook his head, his stomach tightening, a wave of nausea pressing on his guts. "Elena, a kill squad from Moscow is no joke. Looks like you really kicked the bees' nest."

"You're telling me."

Before Elena could say anything else about the plane crash, a shrill beep emitted from the surveillance system, a red box blinking around one of the images. Travis got up, striding toward the monitor. He narrowed his eyes. A van was approaching faster than Travis would have liked. "We've got company."

Elena joined him, her tiny frame almost a foot shorter than him. "You aren't expecting a delivery?"

"Nope."

Travis didn't take the time to explain. He turned on his heel and took two steps toward the locked cabinets in the center of the room, quickly keying in the code and running his thumbprint across the scanner. The locks popped open, revealing his weapons cache. He tossed Elena a pistol and then handed her an AR-15 with a tactical scope already zeroed in, while grabbing the same for himself. Elena grabbed her backpack, strapping it over her shoulders, pulling the straps down tight before hanging the rifle over her shoulder. He saw her wince. From where he was standing there was nothing obviously wrong. If they had company, he hoped he was right. He needed all the help he could get. "You going to be okay?"

"Always. You got ammo?"

"Always," Travis grinned, reaching into the cabinet and tossing Elena four loaded fifteen round magazines for the nine-millimeter pistol he handed her and four loaded thirty round magazines for the rifle. That was nearly two hundred rounds for each of them. If they couldn't stop who approached the ranch with that amount of firepower, they didn't deserve to survive.

46

"It's possible this is someone randomly stopping by the ranch, right?" Elena stared at Travis.

Travis cocked his head to the side as he watched the monitors. "Possible, sure. Likely? Probably not."

"What are we gonna do?"

"We're going to stay here for a minute and then we'll see."

"So you're saying you don't really have a plan."

Travis smiled at Elena, "Not yet. It'll come to me."

Elena groaned.

The next thirty seconds seemed to stretch on and on as the two of them stood shoulder-to-shoulder in front of the security monitors. The van surging toward the house was picked up by a few of the other night-vision enabled cameras scattered on the property – one attached to the trunk of a nearby myrtle tree, one on the roof of the log cabin, and one on a fence post about fifty yards from the house. Travis wondered for a moment if whoever was driving had any idea they were being watched. Probably not. If they had, they certainly wouldn't have come barreling down the driveway at such a breakneck speed, hitting every single pothole, sending the van shuddering and lurching as it bounced its way toward them. Just watching the way the van was pitching over the rough road made Travis's back hurt thinking about how the people inside were getting banged around. Served them right for trespassing.

People.

Was there a single driver? A team? If Travis had to guess, it was more than one. Who exactly was inside and how they'd found him, he wasn't sure, although if anyone knew his name, finding his location wouldn't be all that difficult. His horse business was public knowledge, after all.

Hiding in plain sight wasn't all it was cracked up to be, Travis thought to himself, shifting his weight to a single hip as he waited for the van to stop at the house. He could feel the tension building in his chest. He normally didn't greet visitors wearing a rifle and carrying a pistol, but if these visitors are who he thought they were, they would deserve a very special welcome, one he and Elena hadn't faced since they were stationed in Croatia.

The dust cloud almost had overcome the van by the time the vehicle slammed to a stop in front of the house. Travis took a half step closer to the monitor, watching as he saw three people get out of the van. All men. The driver was of average height, with thick dark hair, a strong jaw, and almond-shaped eyes. One of the other men was tall and gangly with blond hair, all arms and legs. The third man looked like a copycat version of the first, only larger and taller.

Travis swallowed. "Is that –?"

Elena nodded slowly, "That looks like Uri Bazarov." She squinted at the screen, "Is that really him?"

Travis didn't answer. He turned back to the doorway of the war room, opened it, and popped out into the family room. Looking behind him, he hissed, "Stay here. Close the doors behind me. I'm gonna handle this outside."

Travis pushed the bookcase back into place and listened as

the heavy metal door to the war room clicked closed. He was grateful Elena didn't argue. It was one less person to be responsible for.

Moving quickly, Travis went through the kitchen and slipped his boots on, leaving the house through the back door. The war room was safe, but if someone broke into the house, they'd be cornered. That wouldn't do. He circled the garage, his hand on his rifle, lifting it into position, rolling his feet heel to toe, moving silently in the darkness.

Uri Bazarov was a name he hadn't heard in years. High ranking in the FSB, Uri had a reputation for his brutality and completing assignments that no one else had the stomach for. He'd earned the respect of the Kremlin by decapitating the head of one of the most prestigious Russian mafia organizations working on the outskirts of Moscow, one that had corrupted an entire directorate within the KGB, literally sending the rotting heads to his bosses. They were delighted. The remaining directorate members, who stood in the way of Russian expansion, were summarily shipped off in vans far out into the city, led blindfolded to the edge of a deep hole, and shot once in the forehead. The Kremlin had determined they weren't worth more than one round of ammunition per person. The bodies only added to the piles left behind all over the frozen Russian countryside — the result of Stalin's internal genocide against people who didn't agree with his ideas, claiming the lives of anywhere from six to nine million people, depending on who was asked. Eliminating the tainted directorate was nothing more than a continuation of that policy.

After his successful elimination of the corrupted directorate, Uri Bazarov went on to higher, and lower escapades, traveling all over Eastern Europe, eliminating saints and sinners alike, whomever the Kremlin determined was in the way of their new policy to re-establish the Soviet Union. He'd left the body of an oil magnate behind in northern Russia for the coyotes to eat, buried a group of dissidents in Croatia in barrels filled with acid, and taken out an arms dealer in Chechnya with nothing more than a simple car bomb. And those were the ones Travis could remember off the top of his head after not bothering to think about Uri for the last five years.

Travis rounded the back corner of his house as Uri pounded on the front door. Travis led with the long barrel of his rifle extended in front of him, his eye already up to the scope. "This is a new tactic for you, Uri. You're actually using some manners and knocking on the door?"

Uri's two men whipped around, their bodies jerking as though they'd had a spasm, pulling their guns out and pointing them at Travis. Uri wasn't that easily spooked. He turned slowly, as though he was a model on some sort of spinning platform waiting to be seen by an adoring crowd, a sneer on his face. "Agent Bishop, what a pleasure."

"I'm not in the business anymore, Uri. What do you want?"

"Oh, I thought I would stop by to see your lovely ranch," Uri said in a thick Russian accent. "I always knew you were a cowboy, Travis."

Travis felt the back of his neck prickle, "What do you want, Uri?"

He took two steps forward, his men flanking him on each side. "I'm looking for the person and the package that was on the plane that crashed last night."

"I don't know anything about that, Uri. It's time for you to go."

"Oh, but Agent Bishop, I know you do. You see, the people that were shooting at you from the hillside, that was us," Uri said, his voice lifting at the end of the sentence as if he'd given Travis the most wonderful gift ever. "I needed a little time to take a look at that plane, more time than I'd had after I shot the missile at it, but the efficiency of your American NTSB caused me some problems. As I said, I'm only looking to recover the person and the package that was on that plane."

Travis shook his head, "I don't have anything for you, Uri. You need to get off my property."

Uri took two steps closer to Travis, narrowing the distance, "You don't mind if I have a look inside first, do you? I'd hate to think that you are hiding something in your house that belongs to me."

Russians were all the same, Travis thought to himself. They thought that if you were born in Russia there was absolutely no way you could live in another country and not still be Russian. "Are you talking about Elena? She's more American than I am."

Uri bristled, "We have a saying in Europe, 'the heart of the Motherland beats forever.' It doesn't matter where a Russian moves to, Agent Bishop, Elena will always be Russian. Always." He glanced toward the front door, "Now, if you don't mind, I'm going to head inside and see if I can recover my property."

"I do mind," Travis said, lining up the sights on his rifle on the gun the blond man was holding. Travis pulled the trigger, the round erupting and covering the distance in a millisecond, knocking the barrel of the gun out of the man's hand. Uri turned with a furious yell and drew his own weapon, firing at Travis who had darted back behind the corner of the cabin. He had to do what he could to keep them away from the inside of the house and away from Elena. Waiting for a moment, he stuck his head out around the corner of the cabin as the blond man, now without his pistol, charged at him.

The lanky blond man rushing Travis had closed the distance too fast. Travis couldn't get a shot off. He dropped his rifle and stepped forward, ready to pull his pistol, when the first punch connected with his face. The blond man was all arms and legs, tall and gangly. The punch wasn't particularly strong, but he had a long reach, Travis realized as his head snapped back, the fist landed on the side of his jaw. Pain shot through his face and his neck as he lowered his stance and gave the man a good uppercut in the gut. Travis glanced up just long enough to see Uri's bodyguard pulling him away from the tussle. As he did, shots rang out from behind him. They weren't his.

Travis glanced over his shoulder, seeing Elena's diminutive figure swamped by the rifle, her tiny face pressed to the scope. "I told you to stay inside!" he grunted, still wrestling with the blond man.

"You looked like you needed some help."

Travis glanced up, seeing Uri's bodyguard grabbing the outside of his right arm, groaning in pain. Elena had managed to put a shot across the flesh. She was an expert marksman. It was a warning. One that wouldn't come again.

Travis continued to wrestle with the blond man. He wasn't giving up. Travis caught a glimpse of his face. He was in a blind rage, as if everything he'd never been able to accomplish in his life was coming down to one moment. Having spotted Elena, Uri and his bodyguard were now circling the side of the house. Elena sent another shot flying towards the bodyguard, clipping him on the outside of his knee. He immediately fell to the ground, yelping. Travis, focusing on the blond man who wouldn't back off, wedged his way up underneath the man's chest and with a shove, managed to push him away. Travis could feel the tension in his chest, his breath coming in raspy waves. The blond man stood for a second, holding his fists up as if he was in a boxing ring. "Elena! Get back in the house!" Travis yelled, pulling his pistol.

As the words came out of his mouth, the man reached forward with an arcing kick, managing to dislodge the pistol out of Travis's hands. It rattled away and landed in the dirt out of reach. From the corner of his eye, he saw Uri's bodyguard slumped in the dirt, scooting back towards the van as quickly as he could, then crawling to a half-standing position, yelling for Uri and dragging his injured leg behind him. The man fired a couple of shots as he did. Travis ducked, the rounds chipping away at the hand-hewn logs over his head. Out of the corner of his eye, Travis saw Elena advance. She lined up the rifle and aimed it at the man she'd already shot twice. Instead of staying where he was, the man charged at her, his chin down, his eyes narrowed. Travis glanced at him and then yelled for Elena, "Take the shot!" Just as he did, Travis heard the crack of her rifle, a single red dot emerging between the man's eyebrows. His body slumped to the ground. Seeing his comrade down, the blond man attacking Travis redoubled his efforts, his face bright red, an animalistic groan coming from inside of him as he charged. Travis looked to his left. He'd lost his pistol and his rifle. Reaching to his left, Travis ripped a set of deer antlers off the wall as the man charged at him, raising them high above his head and bringing them crashing down on top of the man's body. The man looked at him, surprised as the hardened bones from the antlers penetrated his skull and his chest. His eyes widened and then rolled back in his head as his body collapsed in a heap on the ground.

Travis staggered backward, landing next to Elena. By the time he looked up, the van's headlights showed it careening halfway down the driveway. Uri was escaping. Elena started running after it, the rifle still up to her face. "Come on! He's getting away!"

Travis sat on the porch for a second, calling after her. "We're not gonna catch him, Elena. He's gone."

47

For the next hour, Travis set about his business after having a brief discussion with Elena about what to do with the bodies of the two Russian kill squad members that were now laying in the darkness of his driveway. Elena suggested she disappear and that he call Langley and let them know. They had cleaners that took care of these problems, she rationalized. Travis gave her a firm no, "If you call Langley, they'll know exactly where you are even if you get a head start. And if you're trying to get them off your back, this isn't the way to do it." Travis shook his head, "No. I'll take care of it."

Shaking off the soreness from the brawl he'd had with the dead blond man on his front porch, Travis walked down to the barn and got the tractor, driving it back up to the house. Elena, still wearing the backpack with her laptop in it, helped him to roll the bodies into the bucket. He drove it out to the far reaches of his property, the headlights quivering over the rough ground. He drove about fifty yards over the line onto his neighbor's property and dug a hole, dropping the bloody bodies inside and using the bucket from the tractor to make short work of covering them up. Traveling back to the cabin, only the sounds of the tractor engine humming in his ears, he at least had the satisfaction of knowing that if the bodies were discovered they wouldn't be on his property. Part of him wanted to feel bad for dragging his neighbor into what could become an international scandal, but they were large landowners that had ten thousand acres amassed in the parcel next to his and never even used it. He'd only met them one time when he and Kira had first bought the property and hadn't seen them since. From what he'd heard in town, they only came to their house once a year or so. The odds of them being able to find the bodies were tiny, and if someone did find them, they'd have to go through the rigmarole of trying to locate the landowners and figure out the situation. If nothing else, it would buy him some time to deal with the rest of the information Elena had.

When he got back to the log cabin, the lights of the front porch were on, making it nearly as bright as daylight. He found Elena, on her hands and knees, still wearing the backpack, scrubbing spots of blood off of the front porch. "I found a scrub brush and some soap in the garage. I figured I'd clean this up before it stained," she said, splashing a bucket of water across the wood decking, her face set and determined as if getting the porch clean would solve all of their problems. They both knew it wouldn't.

Travis stayed on the tractor, cutting the engine, hearing something in the distance. The alarm on his phone beeped. Looking at the night vision images from the camera, he could see another pillar of dust coming from the driveway. He glanced at Elena and watched as her body trembled. He held up his hand, "It's not Uri. I know who it is. You can relax."

Elena stood up, staring, her lips parted, a few drops of water dripping from her fingertips. Travis rested his forearm on the steering wheel of the tractor and watched the blue SUV make its way to the house.

Patrick stepped out of the SUV, narrowing his eyes, "Hey! I

know it's late, but I thought I'd stop by and give you an update. Seems like you're in the middle of something, though."

Travis nodded, staying on the tractor, "Kinda. NTSB Investigator Patrick Mills, meet your pilot, Elena Lobranova."

Travis watched Patrick's expression change from confusion to recognition as though a lightbulb had turned on inside of his head. He pointed at the tiny blonde woman, "You flew the plane? The one that got hit by the missile?"

Elena shifted her eyes to Travis who gave her an almost imperceptible nod, "Yes, that was me," she said, her English only slightly tinged with a hint of Russian.

Patrick threw his hands up in the air, "Where have you been? Are you all right? Listen, I have a lot of questions for you."

Travis shook his head, "Patrick, now is not the time."

Patrick glanced down at the trail of water that was running toward him off the porch. It was tinged pink, carrying a few flecks of bone and brain matter. Patrick stepped off to the side as the rivulet approached him. He jumped as though someone hit him with a hot coal, "Is that blood?"

"Uh-huh…"

48

Patrick nearly tripped over his own feet trying to get away from the rivulet of blood, brain matter and bone Elena was busily scrubbing off of the front porch of Travis's house. His face had gone pale as he jumped onto the front porch on the other side of where Elena was working. "What the heck happened?"

Travis raised his eyebrows, "I'm not sure you want to know."

Patrick glared at him, his eyes wide, "I most certainly want to know. I want to know everything."

Travis got down off of the tractor and motioned Patrick over to a set of chairs that were at the other end of the front porch, leaving Elena to do the work she had assigned herself. Travis knew it would be better if he gave her a little space. She'd been through a lot. She would join them when she was ready. "Have a seat before you pass out."

"I'm not going to pass out," Patrick groused. He slumped down in the seat and looked at the ground, "At least I don't think I'm going to. I've seen blood and stuff before at crashes. You caught me off guard." He lifted his chin, "I wasn't prepared."

Travis tried not to smile, "Right. You weren't prepared. I get it."

Patrick placed his hands together in his lap and looked down for a second and then glanced over at Travis, "Okay, I'm ready now. What happened here? And how did the pilot get to your ranch house?"

Travis glanced over his shoulder at Elena. She had stood up from where she'd been scrubbing the decking and was now hosing the surface again, her posture ramrod straight. He guessed she'd be at it for the next few minutes, at least long enough for him to tell Patrick what was going on. "That woman over there," Travis said tilting his head to the side, "Is the pilot that flew the plane that you found. She's also a CIA agent. I used to work with her."

Patrick started to get up out of his chair, "I've got questions for her that I need to get answers to."

Travis laid a hand on Patrick's forearm with enough pressure that Patrick sat down again, "Easy there, Patrick. She's been through a lot. She's not the kind that appreciates being pressured."

Patrick scowled, "Copy that. Can you please give me some background here? I thought I heard a tinge of an accent in her voice."

Travis nodded, "That would be correct. Elena was born in Russia. Lived there till she was a teenager. Came over here with her parents and became an American citizen. After she went to college, she joined the Agency. She's a darn good agent, Patrick. No matter what happens, remember that." Travis knew the words sounded cryptic, but someone besides him needed to believe in Elena. And on the off chance that Uri came back, Patrick would be his only line of defense, and maybe the only one left to tell the story.

"And somehow, she survived that missile strike on her

plane..." Patrick said absentmindedly; as if he was thinking out loud. He glanced up at Travis, "What about the blood I saw?"

Travis stared off in the darkness, wondering how much he should say. If he'd still been part of the Agency, the line would have been clear. He would tell Patrick only enough to manipulate him into doing what was best for the mission. But Travis wasn't part of the Agency anymore and based on what he'd seen over the last day or so, he was glad he got out when he could. The Agency had been known to take twists and turns in terms of their decision-making at other junctures in the past, blurring the line between right and wrong, sliding precipitously off the moral high ground to something that resembled moral quicksand. It seemed Director Stewart had allowed at least the Russian division to veer south of that line in a pretty significant way. But in reality, Travis wasn't Agent Bishop anymore. He was Travis Bishop, skip tracer, ranch owner, and performance horse trainer. He didn't have to live by the rules the Agency set out anymore unless he wanted to.

"Elena and I know each other from work. We were partnered up on a bunch of different missions. Our language skills are complementary, so the division we worked for would frequently send us out together. If she didn't know the language, I usually did."

"That still doesn't explain the blood, Travis." Patrick stared at the ground where the pink-tinged water had soaked into the dirt, his face pale.

"Right. A couple of hours ago, Elena and I were in the war room. We met up at a restaurant in town and we needed to talk privately. The surveillance system went off. A van carrying three Russian operatives showed up here. They were coming after Elena and the laptop she has with her."

Patrick glanced over at Elena, "I'm assuming the laptop is in the backpack she hasn't taken off since I got here."

Travis looked toward Elena. She was back on her hands and knees, scrubbing the deck again. If he counted right, it was her fourth or fifth round of scrubbing. The backpack slid back and forth on her small frame as she moved her arms. Travis noticed that every few seconds, she'd sit up, taking pressure off of her right shoulder. Clearly, something happened to it in her travels to get to him. "That's correct. She has information on that laptop that will clear her name and also illuminate a couple of false flag operations, or at least one, that is going on right now with potentially devastating impacts to the United States."

"Clear her name? What are you talking about?"

Travis spent the next couple of minutes filling Patrick in as best he could on what he and Elena had talked about, the information she'd gotten from her cousin Grigori at the Kremlin, the troops massing at the Georgian border, and the coup that was being planned. "The problem is, not only is the Agency concerned that Elena is a traitor, and she's got a Russian kill squad after her, but trying to decipher the intelligence that will lead us to the real move Russia's making is nearly impossible."

Patrick leaned his head closer to Travis, his voice barely above a whisper, "Somebody thinks she's a double agent?"

At that moment, Travis wanted to slap Patrick across the face. Whatever he'd done in the military apparently didn't have much to do with subtlety. Patrick was about as delicate as a Mack truck. In some ways, it was refreshing. Travis didn't have to worry about what was going on in Patrick's head. Patrick simply blurted it out. Travis shook his head, "Yes, but it's not true. Elena is a patriot. An American. She's saved my life more than once."

"Do you believe her?" Patrick whispered.

Travis nodded as Elena walked over to them, the bright lights from the porch casting a sharp shadow of her form on the wood deck. "All cleaned up. What do we do now?"

Travis was just about to respond when his phone rang. It was a number he didn't recognize. He frowned, staring at the display for a moment before answering it. "Hello?"

"Hello, Agent Bishop."

"Hello, Uri."

49

"I'm sorry we didn't have more of a chance for a friendly chat when I visited your lovely ranch earlier," Uri said in broken English.

Travis stood up from the chair where he was sitting on the front porch, leaving Elena and Patrick to stare at his back as he walked into the darkness. "I'm not much one for trespassers, Uri. What do you want?"

"Travis?" A female voice came on the line.

Travis stopped dead in his tracks, frozen. He swallowed, unable to move. His hand started to shake.

"Travis, are you there? It's me, Kira. Can you hear me?"

Travis felt like he'd been hit in the chest with a ton of bricks, his lungs unable to inflate. "Kira?"

He heard Uri chuckle on the other end of the line, "Yes, Travis. That was Kira. And she's with me. How do you like that? If you had bothered to offer me a proper greeting when I'd come to your ranch earlier, perhaps even poured me a shot of vodka as part of a warm welcome, then maybe I would have been able to share this most interesting information with you at the time. I have to say I didn't realize you had such a hot temper on you, Agent Bishop. Working in the wild, wild west of Texas has brought out your animalistic side if you ask me."

Travis walked further into the darkness away from Elena and Patrick, silently praying they would leave him alone. He headed toward the paddock fence on the other side of the driveway, propping his arms on the fence post in the dark, using the sturdy structure to steady himself. "I'm not exactly used to a Russian kill squad showing up on my property and attacking me."

"And all we wanted to do was talk!"

"I highly doubt that. Your boys had their guns drawn. That's not the way to start a conversation."

"And you did quite a job on Alexander. Did you bury him and Sergey already?"

Travis didn't bother to answer the question. He knew Uri was baiting him. "You have Kira."

"I do."

"Put her back on the line, Uri."

"You know I'm not going to do that, Agent Bishop. You've heard her voice. You know she's alive."

"What do you want?"

"Now we get to the fun part!" Uri said, with the sound of fake glee in his voice. The next words came out in a growl, "I'll make you a trade, Agent Bishop. You hand over Elena Lobranova and her laptop and I will give you back the love of your life. How does that sound?"

"You know I can't do that, Uri. Elena isn't mine to give. I don't work for the Agency anymore."

Uri sniffed, "That's disappointing, but you've heard my terms, Agent Bishop. We can make the trade as the sun comes up. I'd even be happy to come to your ranch again and bring Kira to you. Maybe you can give me the courtesy of showing me what you did with Sergey and Alexander's bodies. I'd be happy to take them off your hands and send them back to Russia for a proper hero's burial."

Travis paused, looking over his shoulder. Elena and Patrick were sitting next to each other under the lights of the porch, the two of them talking. Elena had taken the backpack off and balanced it between her knees. Uri had put him in an impossible situation — he'd asked him to betray his country and a fellow agent on the slim hope that he could get the woman he loved back. It was an impossible decision. Uri had him over a barrel.

"I'm not hearing an answer, Agent Bishop. In my mind, this should be an easy trade. You get back the woman you love, I get back Elena and her information. You could even go ahead and have kids and build the breeding program that you and Kira had talked about for so long."

Uri was still playing with him. Part of him couldn't believe the voice he'd heard on the phone was actually Kira. He shook his head, trying to get the cobwebs out of his mind.

"Still nothing, Agent Bishop?" Uri clucked on the other end of the line, "That's a shame. I thought you were more decisive than that. Listen, I understand what a challenging proposition I have put in front of you and that you might need a moment to gather yourself. After all, you've assumed that your beloved Kira has been dead for the last five years when she's been quite well, in fact. It has to be shocking to your system. I will text you a number where you can reach me. Don't bother trying to track it. It's a burner phone, using only the finest Russian technology that we've acquired from our friends, the Chinese. You will undoubtedly find it impossible to track. Sunup is what time around here? Six a.m.? That sounds like a good round number to me. Text me your decision in the next two hours and we will make the trade, or not. If not, then I'll eliminate Kira. It's that easy."

The call ended without Travis saying anything more.

Travis walked back toward the porch where Patrick and Elena were sitting, his shoulders slumped, his face turned toward the ground. As he approached the porch, he looked up at Patrick and Elena. Elena narrowed her eyes, "Who was that?"

"It was Uri. He's got Kira."

50

"Kira?" Elena exploded, "How's that possible? I thought she was dead!"

Travis leaned against one of the posts of the porch and scratched the side of his face, lifting his chin slowly, "So did I."

Elena narrowed his eyes at him, "Wait. He wants to make a trade, doesn't he?"

Travis nodded slowly.

Patrick jumped into the middle of the conversation, stammering, holding his hands up as if begging everyone to stop because they were moving too fast, "Slow down. What exactly is going on here?"

Elena looked at Travis and then at Patrick, "I'm guessing Uri told Travis that he would give back Kira in return for me and my laptop. Is that about the size of it?"

Travis nodded, still not saying anything.

Patrick whistled, "Are you kidding me? This is like something out of a spy novel."

Travis shook his head, "No, Patrick, this is real. Very real."

Elena got up and started to pace, "How did you know it was Kira?"

"I heard her voice. Then Uri mentioned that we could have a family and start the breeding program with the horses if she came back. That's something Kira wanted to do."

Elena shrugged, "Travis, he could've duped her voice. She might not even be alive. The information he gave you isn't recent, is it?"

Travis stood up, feeling himself straighten. Elena was right. Technology had evolved to such a level that Uri could have recorded Kira's voice or pulled it off of recordings the KGB had of her and had it altered. Elena was also right about the fact that the information Uri had offered was old. Their plan to have kids and start the breeding program was prior to them getting married, and that hadn't happened. There was nothing new or timely about what Uri had offered him. It wasn't like in the old days when a kidnapper would send you a picture or a video with someone holding up a newspaper from that same day. Technology had blurred the lines between past, present, and future in a way that made discerning the truth nearly impossible.

"No, it isn't. You're right."

"What do we do now?" Patrick said.

"We?" Travis said, looking at Patrick. "There is no we in this, Patrick. Elena and I are going to have to sort this out."

Patrick shot up out of his chair as though someone had hit a launch button. He held his hands up near his head, "No way! I finally tracked down the pilot from my plane crash and you want me to skedaddle. That's not happening. Whatever you've got going on, I'm following you until the end. I need Elena for my reports. A missile strike isn't something I can ignore."

Travis glanced at Elena. She raised her eyebrows. He knew that look. She was going to let him decide. "Okay, you can stay for now," Travis muttered.

Elena shifted her gaze to the side and then stood up, "I think I'd better go. Patrick, I know you need to talk to me, but me being here has put Travis in a bind."

Travis took two steps toward Elena and laid his hand on her shoulder, "I don't want you to go anywhere, Elena. At this moment, I can't even be sure that Kira's alive. Now that I've killed a couple of Uri's guys, I'm gonna be on a kill list myself by the time the sun's up. Uri won't take it kindly that we offed his team. Either way, we have to figure out what's going on. If there's a coup to take down the US government, like your cousin said, we've gotta get the information to someone who can take care of it. I can't leave you out on your own, not with Uri and his goons running around after you."

Elena's lips parted and she blinked under the front porch lights, "But what about Kira?"

Travis shook his head, "I don't know. We'll figure it out when we get there."

51

A chill had come over the Texas night air as Travis, Elena and Patrick sat together on the front porch. After a couple of minutes of silence, Travis looked at the two of them. "Let's go in the house. We've got work to do."

Travis walked around the back of the house, picking up the rifles as he went. Back inside, he headed straight for the war room, opening the bookshelf and the steel door. Glancing at the interior, which was untouched despite the carnage that happened just a few hours earlier on the front porch, part of him was grateful. People always said that a man's home was his castle. In Travis's case, it was more like his fortress. And now, people had come for him, threatening the things that he held near and dear to his heart. He couldn't stand aside and do nothing. That's not who he was. And it was definitely not who he had been trained to be.

As the lights flickered on automatically in the war room, Travis set the rifles down on the counter and walked to the security system, resetting the bright red alarms that were still flashing on the screen. He unlocked the firearms cabinets and quickly reloaded the magazines he and Elena had used to deal with Uri's people, leaving the guns out on the counter. Elena and Patrick took up positions at the worktable. Elena unzipped her backpack and pulled out the laptop. "I didn't have a chance to check this earlier. I'm hoping there's another message from Grigori."

"Did you have that on the plane?" Patrick asked, pointing to the laptop.

Elena nodded, "Yeah. It ended up sliding the entire way back under the tail section during the crash. Luckily, the strap got caught on one of the metal supports. Otherwise, it would've ended up in the middle of some cow pasture somewhere."

Travis could hear the computer whirr to life. Elena uncoiled a black cable and pushed it into the side of the machine, handing Travis the other end. He plugged it into the bank of outlets at the end of the worktable.

As Elena cracked open the laptop, Travis noticed it wasn't a standard laptop someone could purchase at a big box store on any given afternoon. It was a Toughbook, military-grade, the kind used out in the field and almost impossible to destroy – the best kind to have if it had to survive a plane crash. The last time Travis had used one was with the CIA. He'd taken it to Belarus to use while questioning a terrorist the military had captured.

A heavy silence hung over the war room for a minute as Elena worked on her computer. "I only had a little time to look at the files I pulled from Camp Swift," she said, in a voice that was barely above a whisper. "I was in the safe house when I did that, but a lot has happened since then."

Patrick glanced at Travis, "Is that the same safe house —?"

"Yes." Travis nodded.

"How did you two...?"

Travis interrupted again, "Remember that pen we found at the loft?"

"The one from the restaurant?"

Travis gave a curt nod, "That's the one. I found it there. Elena lost it in the couch cushions."

From across the table, Travis could hear the keys of the laptop being tapped. Elena was staring intently at the screen, her eyes scanning back and forth, her lips slightly parted. "I think I have another message from Grigori. Hold on..."

Travis's heart tightened in his chest. He felt like he was only really with Patrick and Elena in body and mind. The other part of him, his heart, was searching for Kira. Had what Uri said been true? Had Kira been Uri's prisoner for the last five years? He pressed his lips together and shook his head. Something about it didn't make sense. The Russians were known to keep prisoners for decades, only offering them up when they became valuable. It was much like how people stored away money or food for a rainy day or a disaster. It seemed like all of Russia ran on that premise, waiting to see what they could leverage to get what they wanted out of their enemies, and even their allies.

And now Russia wanted one of their own back — Elena.

Travis looked at her. She was still typing frantically on the computer. He tried to imagine in his mind a scenario where the same van came barreling down the driveway again, this time containing Uri and Kira, Travis boldly shoving Elena and her laptop toward Uri as Uri dragged a beaten and worn Kira to him, dropping her body at his feet.

That was even if Kira was still alive. Questions flooded his mind. Questions about what had happened in Ecuador and where she had gone. If she hadn't been killed in a car bomb, then what exactly had happened? Had Uri and his goons dragged her away as it was about to explode, and she was so grateful she immediately agreed to work for him? That theory simply didn't seem plausible. It wasn't the Kira he knew. Still, hearing her voice, or Uri's facsimile of it, had dredged up a wound in his gut that he thought was already healed.

Travis stood up from the stool and started pacing back and forth, his fingers interlaced behind the back of his head, alternately glancing at the floor and the surveillance monitors at the other end of the room. All it would take would be a single text to Uri agreeing to his conditions to get Kira back.

Just one little text.

Travis whipped around, looking at Elena and Patrick, the room suddenly seemed small, the breath catching in his chest. "You two keep working. I'm gonna walk down and check the horses."

Letting himself out of the war room, feeling Patrick and Elena's eyes boring into his back, Travis went to the back door, slid his boots on, and walked out into the cool night air. The mockingbirds were still calling out with their incessant night song from a stand of trees in the middle of one of the paddocks. The war room had become claustrophobic, as though the walls were getting closer and closer to him. He wasn't used to having company in there. He wasn't used to having company at all.

Reaching the barn, Travis slid open the door, stepping inside. He flipped on a light switch, one that illuminated a single bank of bulbs near the doors. As much as he needed to get out of the war room, he didn't want to disturb the horses too much while they were sleeping.

With the light cascading through the stable, he heard some rustling from inside a few of the stalls, a brief nicker coming from about halfway down as if one of the horses was alerting the rest that Travis had shown up unexpectedly. Travis walked past the first set of stalls, crisscrossing the aisles, checking to make sure the horses had water. The horses looked at him with curiosity and sleepy eyes. Travis didn't break them out of their schedule very often, only if they had to leave for a show in the dead of the night to avoid traffic on the freeways while they hauled the heavy gooseneck trailer, or if he had a sick horse and was waiting for the vet. Thankfully, neither of those situations happened very often.

Crisscrossing the aisle again, he stopped at Scarlett's stall and slid the door open. The mare was laying on her side, her muzzle resting on the curl of fresh shavings Ellie had layered in each of the stalls. She lifted her muzzle slightly, extending it towards Travis in greeting, but didn't bother to get up. Travis squatted down near the mare's head, rubbing his hand down Scarlett's face and then scratching behind her jowls. Part of him wanted to tell her all about Kira, about how he'd heard her voice and ask if the mare remembered Kira spending the night with her in her stall when she was a baby. But part of Travis didn't want to break the silence with something that could be so far from the truth. Sitting in the stall that night, he knew that was the biggest problem he was having — ferreting out the truth. The reality was he knew Elena was alive sitting in his war room. That he could be sure about. Whether Kira was alive or not, he had absolutely no idea. He'd heard something that sounded like her voice but what the truth of the situation was he didn't know. He swallowed, realizing there was a distinct possibility that Kira had never given up her allegiance to Russia, unlike Elena. Maybe her so-called death in Ecuador had been nothing but the KGB's way of getting her off of the Agency's books. He shook his head, knowing he was knee-deep in the muddy waters of half-truths that spanned the history between the CIA and the KGB or whatever they were calling themselves at that moment.

Travis put the palm of his hand on the side of Scarlett's face as she rested her muzzle on the fluff of shavings again. Without making a noise, Travis stood up and backed his way out of the stall, closing the door to the questions in his mind.

52

"How are the horses?" Patrick mumbled through a mouthful of chips as Travis walked back into the war room.

"Fine. What's going on here?"

Elena glanced up at him but didn't say anything. She was still typing on her laptop, an instant messaging box open on the screen. She sucked in a breath as though she was going to say something when Patrick interrupted, "I realized I was starved so I went and found these chips in your cupboard. Hope you don't mind," he said, chewing.

Travis could see little flecks of salt and crumbs on his worktable. He tried to ignore it. "That's fine. You're welcome to anything in the house." Travis walked over to the desk and pulled off a paper towel, handing it to Patrick. "Here. Try one of these."

Patrick held up a single hand, "Thanks," he said brightly.

Elena licked her lips. "I was able to open an encrypted chat with Grigori. The Kremlin is abuzz. They've got something going. He's still not one hundred percent sure what's going on except that the coup is moving forward. President Yanovich is running it personally. There's not a lot of time left."

If Travis remembered anything about his Russian political background, President Yanovich was a former KGB agent, from a long line of agents, much like Uri was. In Russia, being part of the secret services was almost a family business, the same way that being a butcher, or a baker might be. Generations of families were brought up around the dinner table eating bowls of thick borscht and slabs of black bread discussing the ins and outs of how to rid the world of the threats from the west; the children were indoctrinated to hate everything American almost as soon as they started wearing a diaper. Despising America was a way of life in Russia, at least for the spy families.

"Tell me what's going on," Travis said.

"Grigori said there's a team in Washington. It looks like they are supposed to be at a briefing tomorrow on the situation on the Georgian border. Apparently, an operative from the FSB is going to be involved in that briefing. That's all Grigori knew."

"Any idea when or where?"

"The when is sometime tomorrow. The where? The White House. Other than that, I don't know." Elena stared at Travis, her fingers gripping the side of his worktable. "I gotta ask, Travis. What are you going to do about Uri?"

Travis looked at Elena and then Patrick and then glanced back in her direction, "I'm not trading you for Kira. There's nothing I can do about Georgia, but we can't let the government go down. I'll deal with the Kira issue — if there is one, after that. I'm guessing it's another deception from Uri. Let's get to work."

Elena nodded, then spent the next few minutes going through the rest of the details she got from Grigori and the ones that she was able to piece through on her own. She went back over the false flag operation that was running in Georgia, pulling up a map for Patrick so he could understand the ramifications. All in all, her briefing took about twenty-five minutes. Travis sat silently on one of the stools, watching her work, patiently answering Patrick's questions.

"You think this is the real deal?" Patrick drummed his fingers on the table.

Elena nodded, "I do."

Travis looked at the ground, sighing, running the edge of his fingernail against the side seam of his jeans, "The problem is, we can't just waltz into the White House. We have to get the information to someone who's connected with DC, someone who can introduce us to a person who has the power to make decisions."

Elena shrugged, "I can call the Secret Service office and see what they say."

Travis shook his head, "You know as well as I do the minute they hear that CIA Agent Elena Lobranova has called the office, whoever's on the desk is gonna alert Langley. They'll track the call and come after you and probably ignore the message. No. That's not going to work."

Travis scoured his memory, trying to think of anyone he might know who had the contacts that could help them. He drew a blank, both from his time with Delta Force and with the Agency. The White House wasn't his area of purview.

Patrick shoved the last chip in his mouth, crumpled the bag into a ball and tossed it into the wastebasket, "I think I might know somebody who could help."

"Who's that?" Travis scowled, immediately remembering Patrick's weaselly little boss, Doug Parsons, with his ruby red lips. If it was someone like that, his answer would be a big fat no.

"How about the Governor of Texas?"

Travis frowned, "The Governor? Like, the actual Governor of Texas?" He knew the words coming out of his mouth sounded like he didn't believe Patrick, but he didn't.

Patrick nodded, using the paper towel Travis had given him to wipe the salt off his lips, "Yeah. James Torres. We were college roommates at the University of Texas. Still keep in touch."

Elena rubbed her chin. As Travis looked at her, he realized she was having the same problem he was. Neither of them believed Patrick. "Are you serious?" Elena asked.

Patrick shrugged, seemingly offended, "Yeah, you two. We were college roommates. I studied Avionics, he was in Political Science. And, like I said, we still keep in touch a couple of times a year. I have his number on my cell phone. And there's something a lot of people don't know about him that might help our case."

Travis raised his eyebrows, "Like what?" Travis was fully prepared for Patrick to launch into some discussion about how the current Governor of Texas folded his socks or only ate peanut butter and jelly sandwiches on white bread with the crust trimmed off. His gut told him it would be some sort of nonsense like that, something that didn't pertain to their case at all.

"He's former DIA."

"DIA?" Elena sputtered. "You're kidding me?"

"Yeah. After I got out of the Marines, he and I spent a weekend up at his family's cabin. We went hunting, drank a bunch of beer, you know, that kind of stuff. It was before he decided to get into politics. He told me he'd done some stuff, stuff he wasn't proud of. We were trading war stories about the time I was deployed. Turns out, he was DIA and ran a bunch of missions overseas. Thought about making a career over it, but he was losing too much sleep."

Travis shook his head, a wash of relief covering him. Knowing one of Patrick's friends was not only the Governor of Texas but a former Defense Intelligence Agency member changed the calculus significantly in their favor. The question was, would Patrick be willing to leverage his friendship with James Torres to help them? Travis felt his palms start to sweat a little bit and his pulse pick up. "Are you willing to reach out to him? Set up a meet?"

Patrick whipped his phone out of his back pocket, "Sure. I can text him right now. What do I tell him?"

Elena held up her hands as Patrick's thumbs were poised over the cell phone, ready to type. "Hold on a second, Patrick. We need to talk this through. You're going to be texting him on an unsecured line. We have to be careful what we say."

Patrick's shoulders slumped, but he nodded. "Okay. Tell me when you're ready."

Travis and Elena spent the next couple of minutes walking through possible things they could say to the Governor of Texas to get him to meet them in person. After negotiating a few of the finer points, Elena cleared her throat and looked at Patrick, "Here's what I want you to tell him — 'I have interesting information about the plane crash near Camp Swift. It reminded me of the time we spent at the cabin. Can we meet privately ASAP?'"

Patrick sent the text a second later. Now all they could do was wait.

53

Only a few minutes had gone by before Patrick's phone chirped. Travis had spent it pacing back-and-forth in front of the worktable and obsessively cleaning the spot where Patrick had eaten an entire bag of chips. "Wait! Here it is!" Patrick said excitedly. "He sent me a message back."

"What does it say?" Elena said, the words coming out of her mouth slowly.

"It's a list of coordinates and it says one hour."

"Read them to me," Elena said. She stared at the computer screen, both of the men watching her. "Looks like it's a dirt road about ten miles from here." She pivoted the laptop towards Travis. "You know where this is?"

"I have no idea, but we'll find it. Let's get packed up. We're out of here in ten minutes."

Exactly eight and a half minutes later, a minute and a half ahead of Travis's schedule, the three of them walked out to Patrick's NTSB vehicle. They had decided collectively it made more sense to take Patrick's SUV since the governor was likely to be traveling with a security team, even though it was nearing the middle of the night. Seeing one of their own government vehicles at the location would likely give the governor and his security people a bit more comfort than if they rolled up in one of Travis's unknown trucks.

There was very little chitter-chatter in the SUV as Patrick wound his way down the driveway and back out onto the main road. Elena sat in the back seat, serving as the navigator. Travis rode shotgun. Scenarios played their way through his head as they went. It was one thing for them to get a meeting with the governor. It was something completely different to have the governor agree to help them. And if they were hoping to act on the information Grigori and Elena had found, they would have to take action.

Travis scanned the area as they got close, every muscle in his body feeling like it had been shortened incrementally, nervous energy flooding through his system. The area where Governor Torres asked them to meet was nothing more than a dirt road in the middle of nowhere. There were no lights, no structures, and no homes nearby. The road Governor Torres had chosen was empty, barely more than a single lane cut through the middle of a couple of fields. The only unnatural thing about it was a broken-down barn they had passed about a half mile before, the side of it crumbling like a deck of cards, the shape of it illuminated by the moonlight.

According to Travis's watch, they had arrived at the meet twenty minutes early. He got out of Patrick's truck and stood near the back bumper, leaning against it. As he got out of the car, he told Patrick to leave the headlights on. "Don't you want me to turn them off so nobody sees us?" Patrick asked.

Travis shook his head, "No. I'm sure your friend the governor will be traveling with a security detail. They'll be far less jumpy if they can see us. The best way for them to see us is to leave those headlights on."

Patrick gave a nod, glancing at Elena, who gave a brief smile.

After standing outside in the dark by himself for a minute, Elena slipped out of the SUV. "You doing okay? This is a lot for somebody who hasn't been working in the field for a while."

"I can handle it."

"I know you can handle it, but the idea of your dead fiancée suddenly coming back to life has to be unnerving."

"It is; if that was really her." Travis looked away. He stared at the ground, avoiding her gaze.

Elena raised her eyebrows, "You're thinking it wasn't?"

Travis shrugged, "I have no idea what to think anymore, Elena. All I know is if there's a way we can protect the American people, then I'm still all in for that. Doesn't matter whether I'm in the Army, the CIA, or I'm retired."

Elena grunted. "You didn't retire, you quit."

The words stung. Elena was, technically, correct. Like any other job, Travis had given his two weeks' notice to the CIA, gone through two days of debriefing, and handed in his badge and received a stern warning not to speak of anything he had seen or done during his time with the Agency.

It had been easy to do that until now.

"You know I had my reasons."

Elena looked at the ground kicking at the dirt with the toe of her boot. "I know. But you left me behind."

Travis furrowed his eyebrows, "Not exactly behind. I left you where you were. I'm the one that stayed behind."

Elena shrugged, "Yeah, you're probably right." She glanced down the road. "I think our guest is arriving."

Travis turned in time to see the faint glimmer of headlights from a single vehicle glowing in the distance. He stood and watched for a second as it drew closer. From the height of the headlights, he could tell it was an SUV — presumably one of the many matching black four-door executive transportation vehicles the government purchased every year. Travis and Elena weren't the only ones that saw the headlights coming. Patrick popped out of the driver's side and walked to the front of the vehicle, waving to Travis and Elena like a kid who had spotted a long-lost love, "Come on, guys. He's here."

Travis glanced at Elena. She cocked her head to the side and then walked around the front of Patrick's SUV, joining him in the glow of the headlights. Everything in Travis wanted to hang back, take up a position off the side of the road in some cover and watch for a minute before he walked out into what could easily be a kill zone. Patrick's puppy-dog eager attitude was unnerving, but Travis realized Patrick hadn't had the same experiences Travis had. In Patrick's mind, he was simply meeting his friend and former college roommate, the guy he'd shared beers and late-night studying with. Travis shook his head and stared at the ground, wishing that he had the same happy-go-lucky innocence around him.

To anyone watching and not knowing the story, seeing Governor James Torres hop out of the front seat of the SUV might have seemed like something highly suspect, maybe even a drug deal. That was about as far from the truth as could be. The governor had been elected two years before mostly on his policy, but his dark good looks didn't hurt. Travis stood off to the side, waiting as Patrick met him between the two vehicles. Governor Torres strode toward them wearing black track pants, black and white running shoes, and a zip-up black jacket. Elena leaned toward Travis as they watched Patrick and James Torres greet each other between the two vehicles, "He definitely looks more gangster than governor, don't you think?"

Travis looked down at the ground shaking his head. Elena always had a quip that would lighten the situation. "Let's just hope he's got some governor in him too. We need a break."

From the driver's side of the vehicle, a single man wearing black pants and a white shirt with no tie and a black windbreaker got out of the vehicle and walked toward the front bumper. He didn't approach Travis and Elena, nor did he interfere with the conversation Governor Torres and Patrick were having. Travis watched as Patrick and the governor hugged each other, broad smiles across both of their faces. Patrick waved the governor forward, walking toward Patrick's NTSB vehicle where Travis and Elena were waiting.

"Hey guys, this is Jim," Patrick stuttered, "I mean Governor Torres."

"You're welcome to call me Jim," Governor Torres said, extending his hand to both Travis and Elena, his voice low, but friendly. "Anybody who's a friend of Patrick's is a friend of mine." He glanced back at Patrick, "Not to be rude, but what's going on here? I don't frequently get to run around in the middle of the night like I used to. I'm assuming this is a critical issue? You said something about a plane crash?"

Patrick glanced at Travis and Elena. Travis gave him a nod, encouraging him to start the conversation. What they had to tell the governor needed to come from someone that Jim trusted. That would be Patrick. "Jim, we had a plane crash about twenty-four hours ago. Highly suspect. A missile strike took down her plane." Patrick pointed to Elena.

In the area between the two vehicles lit by the headlights, Travis could see the look of concern flash across Jim's face, "Oh my God, are you all right? Patrick? A missile? What are you talking about? We get planes down all the time, but a missile? I haven't heard anything about this." The words came out in a tumble, his concern ranging from Elena's health to the lack of communication in his office.

"Yes, sir. I'm fine. And yes, it was a missile. Likely a shoulder-fired version. Caught the top of the fuselage. I was lucky. I saw it right before impact and had enough time to attempt to bank underneath it."

Patrick put his hand on Elena's shoulder, "It was a rough

landing, Jim. I'm sure NTSB is trying to get their ducks in a row before they notify you. The good news is Elena made it."

Jim held up his hand, "Sorry, I'm still stuck on the fact that we're talking about a missile here. Are you sure?"

Travis cleared his voice, "Sir, I served with Delta Force. I can confirm that what I saw was consistent with missile damage. Patrick felt the same. The charring around the edges is conclusive."

Jim narrowed his eyes and lifted his chin looking at Travis, meeting his eyes, "Thank you for your service. Delta Force is no joke."

"No sir, it isn't."

Jim looked at Elena, "Any idea who shot the missile at your plane?"

Elena sighed and looked to the ground for a second and then at the Governor, "Sir, I'm with the CIA. I believe that a Russian kill squad was sent after me and that's who launched the missile at my plane.

"A kill squad? On American soil?" Jim held up his hands, "Okay guys, give me the full picture here."

Over the next couple of minutes the three of them briefed Governor Torres, stopping periodically to answer his questions, starting with Elena's assignment to follow up on the false flag operations that Russia was running and ending with the cryptic messages she'd been getting from Grigori. "Sir, we are running out of time. It's the middle of the night, and whatever is going to happen is going to happen sometime today at the White House," Elena said and then stopped, "I can get myself to Washington DC, but I have to be able to get into the White House, or at least talk to somebody in the Secret Service."

Jim nodded; as if the pieces were coming together in his mind. "And you need someone you can trust, someone who's going to listen to what you have to say. Is that what you're telling me?"

"Yes sir. That's exactly the case. If I call and explain who I am..."

"They're immediately going to call Langley and hold you for questioning instead of taking action. I get it." Jim chuckled, "Unfortunately, when I say 'I get it,' I mean I really do. I'm not sure if Patrick told you, but I'm former DIA." He narrowed his eyes, "How good is your intel, Elena?"

"It's highly credible, sir. My cousin works in the Kremlin and has been a reliable source for years. We're running out of time. This briefing that's planned, it's going to happen at some point today. Someone is in position to try to take down the US government at the highest levels."

"Any idea exactly how that's going to happen?" Jim said, crossing his arms across his chest.

"No, sir. I wish I did. If we can get to DC and get someone at the White House to listen to us, at least they'd have the fore-warning to know that something is going on. We might even be able to help them stop it. But..."

Jim held up his hands, "You need somebody to pull some strings for you." He glanced over at Patrick, "I think you found a big string-puller. And I'm willing to help. I don't normally do this, but I've known Patrick for years and if he's going to vouch for you, then I'm willing to walk out on a very thin limb and get you some help. How does that sound?"

"Good, sir," Elena said. "Thank you."

Jim waved his security man over to him from where he was standing in front of the Governor's SUV, "Can you call the airport and have them fuel up the jet? Tell them to be ready within the hour and file a flight plan for three headed to DC. See if you can get landing permission at Andrews so that they are close to the White House." The security guy turned to walk away but Jim stopped him, "And let's make sure we have a car and driver meet them at the airport."

Governor Torres's security man nodded, putting his phone

up to his ear. A minute later, Jim turned back and looked at him. The man gave a single nod. "Okay, you guys are all set. Listen, if half of what you have told me is true, then you might be just about to stop one of the biggest terrorist attacks on our country in decades. If you need anything else, Patrick's got my number. Don't hesitate to call. I'll do what I can. In the meantime, I'm gonna look into that missile strike and tell the White House to expect you."

As the group split apart, walking to their respective vehicles, Elena looked over her shoulder, "And Governor?"

"Yes?"

"If you talk to anyone at Camp Swift, they might be a little irritated with me. I not only stole the plane, but I grabbed a couple of intelligence files while I was at it."

Jim looked at the ground shaking his head, a smile on his face, "Man, that takes me back to the old days. I'll keep that in mind and tell them to not get their panties in a twist." He turned to face them one more time before getting into his SUV, "All of you, be careful. I'd like to see all three of you come back from this in one piece."

Travis called behind him, "So would we…"

54

With Governor Torres's order to have the jet fueled and ready to go to DC, there wasn't time for the team to do anything other than head directly to the airstrip. After being given directions to where they were headed from Jim's security man, the three of them piled back into Patrick's SUV, heading directly for the airport. It was a forty-minute drive. The pilot had been told to stay and wait for them, but given what was going on, they were all anxious to get in the air and get moving.

There wasn't much chatter in the SUV as they drove, Patrick navigating down the road where they'd met Governor Torres and then onto more well-developed roads and finally the freeway.

Pulling up to the gate for the private airfield, Patrick slowed his SUV to a stop, seeing the guard step out with his hand up. "Can I help you, sir?" the uniformed man at the gate said.

"NTSB. Investigator Mills. We should have a jet waiting on us?" he said loudly.

The young man nodded, "Yes, sir. The Governor's office, correct?"

Patrick nodded, "Yes."

The young man used his hand like a directional sign, pointing toward the center of the airfield, his fingers glued together flat as a pancake. "If you'll head directly over toward the middle hangar, sir, you'll see a white jet has been pulled out on the tarmac. You can park next to the hangar. I believe the pilot is ready and waiting for you."

"Thanks."

The guard nodded, going inside and pressing the button to remove the concrete barriers. As they slid down below the surface of the road, Patrick inched the SUV forward, the vehicle giving a little shudder and then a lurch as it rolled over the barricades.

Just as described, the jet was waiting for the three of them. As soon as the car approached, Travis could see someone get off the plane and stand by the steps. Patrick parked the NTSB's SUV exactly where the guard had told him to. The three of them jumped out, jogging to the plane. Travis could hear the thrum of the engines warming up, the smell of jet fuel exhaust hovering in an acrid cloud around the back of the plane. The pilot, a man with a shiny bald head and a thick mustache with wide brown eyes, looked at them, "You're from the Governor's office? Heading to Washington, DC?"

Patrick nodded. "That's us."

The pilot pointed up the steps, "Welcome aboard. We can get in the air as soon as you get yourselves settled. Do you have luggage?"

The three of them shook their heads. There hadn't been time. The only one who brought anything with them of significance was Elena, who was still toting her black backpack with the laptop inside.

As the three of them climbed the narrow steps onto the Gulfstream, they found themselves inside of a modern, leather-clad interior. The pilot followed Patrick up the steps, securing the ladder behind him. He stopped for a second looking at them, "We didn't have time to get a cabin attendant, so if you don't mind, you'll have to help yourselves while we are in the air. There are drinks and snacks on the plane. Our flight will take a little under three hours. It should be a smooth ride except for our takeoff." The words sounded surprisingly cryptic for a pilot of a top-of-the-line corporate jet.

Travis frowned, "What do you mean?"

The pilot cleared his throat, "I've been advised there was a missile attack in the area about twenty-four hours ago. Because of that, we will be using a combat lift-off. That was the only way I could get the tower to approve our departure. In layman's terms, make sure you're buckled up. It's going to feel like we're going straight up, which is pretty much what we're going to be doing. The goal is to get out of range of anything in the sky that shouldn't be there as fast as possible."

Travis glanced at Patrick. He'd gone suddenly pale. Patrick mumbled under his breath, "I hate flying."

Travis tried not to smile, "Patrick, you're an NTSB investigator."

"Yeah, I find them when they're on the ground already, not up in the air."

As promised, the pilot disappeared, locking the cockpit door behind him. A second later, the jet moved smoothly down the tarmac, picking up speed. Travis gave an extra tug to his seatbelt as the nose of the plane edged up in the air. It was a wild ride. The G-forces from their rapid ascent pushed Travis deep into the leather upholstery on his seat, his back plastered to the leather for the first twenty seconds of the flight.

Travis rolled his head to the side, glancing at Elena and Patrick who had taken up seats on the other side of the aisle, trying to determine how they were doing. He'd been in his fair share of rough takeoffs and landings while he was with Delta Force. Based on his experience, the one on the Gulfstream wasn't too bad. Elena had her eyes closed, her hands folded in her lap. He'd seen her do that many times. She told him once that it was her way of escaping from an uncomfortable situation. She'd go deep inside of her head and try to remember something from when she was in Russia, or the last meal she'd eaten, or the way the sand felt between her toes on a beach. Anything to not face reality.

For as calm as Elena seemed, Patrick was exactly the opposite. His eyes were wide open, his mouth a gaping hole. His hands gripped the side of the seat, his head thrust back at an unnatural angle as though it was about to snap off his body. Travis frowned and called to him, "Patrick, relax. It will be over in just a second."

Patrick did not respond, only letting out a wheeze.

A moment later, the plane leveled off, the pilot coming on the intercom system, "Okay, folks. That's as rough as it should be for the rest of the flight into DC. Feel free to get some rest and grab snacks. There's an intercom next to the door to the cockpit if you need anything. If not, see you on the ground in a few hours. Enjoy the flight."

Travis glanced at Elena and Patrick. They'd made it up into the air without a missile being shot at them. At least that was one good thing. Now it was time for some sleep.

TWO AND A HALF HOURS LATER, Travis awoke, feeling the plane starting to descend beneath him. He glanced at Patrick and Elena. Elena had pulled her knees up into her chest and was sound asleep, curled up like a kitten basking in the sunshine, her thick black eyelashes so long they nearly touched her cheeks. Patrick, on the other hand, was wide awake. He had an array of crumpled empty chip bags around him. He shrugged at Travis, "I was bored and hungry. You guys were sleeping. The snacks are good," he said, shoving another handful of chips in his mouth.

Just as Travis was about to say something sarcastic to Patrick, the pilot came on the intercom system again, "I hope you guys were able to get some rest. We've started our descent into Washington, DC. We've been cleared to land at Andrews Air Force Base. Based on what I am told, there should be a car waiting for you when you get there. Make sure your seatbelts are fastened. We should be on the ground in the next eighteen minutes. Enjoy the remainder of the flight."

Travis shook his head. He wondered if there was a class in pilot school that taught them to talk through the same conciliatory, bland script on every flight. Their voices sounded much like a person on a meditation track saying to take a deep breath and blow out all of the worries in life. Travis shook his head. Commercial pilots were nothing like the guys he'd met in the military. The guys that flew the birds and planes over hostile territory had ice cold water running through their veins, willing to take off in any type of weather or any threat situation if it meant fulfilling the mission or saving lives. Travis frowned, wondering if the bald guy flying the luxury jet had any idea what was supposed to happen in Washington DC. Travis stared out the window. He knew time was ticking. If they weren't successful, by the next day, things could look very different in the American government, and likely not in a good way. Travis swallowed. Governor Torres had gotten them an open door. The question was if it would be enough for them to stop whatever the Russians were planning.

55

The jet touched down light as a feather at Andrews Air Force Base exactly sixteen and a half minutes later by Travis's watch, at which point the pilot directed the pointy nose of the Gulfstream toward a hangar that had bright lights on, a single ground crew member waving glowing tangerine orange sticks in what was left of the darkness, directing them where to park.

Stepping off of the plane, Travis drew in a deep breath, the bright pink-orange dawn just cresting over the horizon. Off in the distance, he could hear the thump of chopper blades as the first crews from Andrews headed out on maneuvers that morning. He gave a nod to the pilot who gave him a wave and pointed toward a blue sedan parked nearby. The three of them took off at a brisk walk angling for the car.

As they approached, a young man with bright red hair jumped out of the vehicle. Everything about him reminded Travis of an overgrown leprechaun, overly excited and enthusiastic. Travis gauged him to be right around six feet tall with pale, freckled skin and facial features that somehow looked smashed onto his face, as though he'd been in one too many bar fights. He glanced at the three of them as they approached. "You from Governor Torres's office?"

Patrick glanced at Travis and yelled over the din of a passing helicopter, "Yes."

"I'm John O'Brien, Secret Service." He shook each of their hands. "Let's get in and I'll run you over to the White House."

Travis leaned over to Elena as they got in the car, "Torres wasn't playing around, was he?"

"No, he wasn't."

During the thirty-five-minute drive between Joint Base Andrews in Maryland and the White House, O'Brien chattered about Washington DC, asking them if they'd ever been there before and what tourist places they'd been to. Based on the way he avoided any serious topics, Travis had the distinct feeling that O'Brien had been told to escort guests to the White House without asking too many questions. At least his conversation filled the empty space. It was a welcome distraction from the thoughts of Kira running in his head. He felt tension in every inch of his body. There were too many variables he couldn't account for.

Not surprisingly, Patrick did most of the talking. He'd plopped himself down in the seat next to O'Brien while Travis and Elena rode in the back. That was fine with Travis. That gave him time to think, time to consider what they were up against.

The problem was that for all of his thinking and considering, he had no real idea what was going on. He glanced at Elena, who seemed to be staring off at the homes and buildings and traffic they passed as they drove, lost in her own thoughts. It had been years since Travis had been to DC, five to be exact, from when he'd handed in his badge and driven off the Langley campus for the last time. Technically, Langley was in Virginia, but as far as he was concerned, the whole geographical area was Washington

DC. Most people treated it that way. Travis glanced at Elena again. She still hadn't moved, her face tilted towards the window outside, the backpack sitting on her lap. She was hugging it as though it was threatening to get up and walk away. Travis studied her hands. Her knuckles were white. Trouble was brewing, and she knew it. At least he wasn't the only one that felt that way.

As they pulled up in front of the White House gates, O'Brien handed his credentials to the Marines stationed at the barricades. The rest of them had to hand over their driver's licenses before they could go onto the property. All in all, the process was smooth, the Marine in charge efficiently handing the cards back to the correct people within a minute of their arrival, the others glowering at them from behind rifles resting on their hips.

Pulling through the multiple gates and barricades, O'Brien angled the sedan around the side of the building, parking not anywhere near the picturesque venues that most people stopped to see from the fence a half-mile away as they walked down Pennsylvania Avenue, or even the back of the White House, where television crews loved to capture the president as he ran out to jump onto his helicopter or chase kids around during the annual Easter egg hunt. O'Brien drove the car to a nondescript side entrance, parking between another sedan and an oversized black SUV with tinted windows. He waved each of them out of the car, "Come on. I'm supposed to take you directly to the Secret Service office. We'll get you some credentials while you're in there."

Travis raised his eyebrows. He knew the governor had arranged to get them into the White House, but taking them directly to the Secret Service office might be helpful, or it might get them kicked right out on the street depending on who heard their story. The only one among them who had any credibility was Elena, and even that was suspect with the rumors going around about her intentions toward the American government.

O'Brien kept up his chitter-chatter as they wove their way through a tangle of identical white hallways and then down two flights of steps. "A lot of people don't realize what a complicated building the White House is. When I started working here, I think I spent the first two weeks getting lost nearly every single day." He pushed open the door to the second subterranean level below the White House's main level. "Lots of people know about the bunker below the White House, but they don't realize there are tons of offices between that and the ground level. That's where we have our security hub."

Travis followed O'Brien, Patrick, and Elena as they wove their way through a couple more hallways, ending up in front of a door that was simply marked S210. O'Brien pushed it open and Travis was immediately confronted with a hubbub of people moving in and out of the offices, all of them wearing dark navy blue, gray, or black suits and white shirts with ties. "This is home sweet home," O'Brien said. I'm supposed to take you directly to Agent Spector's office. Right this way.

Elena leaned over toward Travis, "Governor Torres did us a solid. John Spector is the Head of Secret Service White House Operations. I met him one time a long time ago. Heard him speak at a conference. He's got his head screwed straight on his shoulders."

Travis didn't say anything. He just nodded, watching the agents move in small groups toward the door, whispering politely into their radios. Part of him felt like he was back in the CIA and had slid down another hole into a world where things were upside down. It was another Alice in Wonderland moment, one of about a million, if he could remember that many.

O'Brien ushered them right into John Spector's office. As Travis walked in, John Spector was seated behind his desk, his head bent down over a stack of papers, his pen moving in a methodical fashion as he checked each line on the sheet of paper in front of him and then signed at the bottom. The three of them stood with O'Brien for a minute, Spector still scanning his papers, not looking up. Completing his signature at the bottom of one of them, he set down the pen and looked up at them, "You're from Governor Torres's office?"

"That's correct."

Spector looked at O'Brien, "Thanks for picking them up, O'Brien. That's all. Close the door on your way out."

As the door clicked closed behind O'Brien, the three of them were left in the office with John Spector. He stood up, reaching over his desk and offering each of them a handshake and then pointing to the chairs in front of his desk. They were littered all over the room. "Sorry, this office usually looks like a furniture factory. It's one of the only quiet spaces we have to meet. Wish it was different, but the White House division is always running at a fever pitch." He glanced at each of them, as if mentally scanning their features, "How can I help? Governor Torres said that you had information that was time-sensitive and critical to the White House."

Travis swallowed. What happened in the next minute or two would determine whether or not they would get the Secret Service to cooperate with them or whether they would end up standing outside, on the other side of the metal fences, barricades, and Marine protection. He sized up Spector. Like O'Brien, he seemed to be a little over six feet tall but had a narrow build, a dusting of black curly hair on his head, and matching ebony skin. He was neatly dressed in a charcoal gray suit, white shirt, and a gray tie. The lump under the right side of his suit coat told Travis that he was armed, as he should be. He was Secret Service.

Travis cleared his throat, "Sir, we appreciate you seeing us on such short notice. I'm going to give you a brief overview and then I will let NTSB Investigator Mills and CIA Agent Elena Lobranova bring you up to speed on the details." Travis stared at the ground for a second and then back at Spector, who was staring at him, "Two days ago I was approached by one of my former colleagues at the CIA, who had contacted me to track down Agent Lobranova."

Spector raised his eyebrows, staring at Elena, "Were you missing?"

"I didn't think so, sir," she said sarcastically.

"Agent Lobranova had gone dark to protect herself and her mission. Since my time with the Agency, I've been working as a skip tracer. Agent Gus Norman came to my ranch unannounced and asked for help to find Agent Lobranova. He was killed later on that evening."

Spector frowned, "Killed?"

"Shot by a sniper, sir."

"A sniper? Are you sure?"

"I am, sir."

Patrick stammered, pointing his finger at Travis and raising his eyebrows, "Travis was Delta Force."

Spector gave a single nod, "Continue."

Over the next couple of minutes, Travis gave John Spector the highlights of what had happened during the last forty-eight hours including Gus's death, Elena getting shot out of the sky by a missile, their conversation with Grigori, and their concerns about the false flag operation.

"President Yanovich has been on thin ice with some of the old guard at the Kremlin recently, sir," Elena said after opening her laptop and showing him some of her documentation. "Many in Russia would like to see the country resume its former structure as the Soviet Union. But President Mosley's pro-America stance has placed President Yanovich in a dim light, one the Russians don't like; as if Russia is second-rate."

"They still want to see themselves as a superpower, huh?" Spector said, tapping the end of his pen on his desk.

Elena continued, "To cut to the chase, sir, sometime today, President Mosely is scheduled to have a briefing about the troop movements near the Georgian border. We believe that during that briefing an attempt will be made on the government of the United States."

"Like a direct threat to the life of the President?"

Elena nodded, "It's very likely, sir."

Spector pressed his lips together, his face hardening. He turned toward his computer, typing furiously. "Agent Lobranova, I just checked the agenda for today. That briefing is about to start."

56

Agent Spector clicked on his computer, standing up, leaning over his desk. "The delegation to meet with President Mosely is on their way to the Oval Office now. The Joint Chiefs are already there."

Travis looked at Spector, "Can I see the video feed?"

Spector spun the monitor toward Travis. He could see a group of dignitaries headed down the hallway, briefing books in their hands. Two men with square heads and dark hair that matched their dark suits walked in front, then a woman with long dark hair, and finally a man with scraggly hair, wearing a charcoal gray suit. Just before the group went out of sight, the last man in the group turned. Travis's eyes widened, his heart pounding in his chest, "Gus! That's Gus!"

Elena shot up out of her seat and stared at the screen. "That's him! What is he doing here?"

Travis pointed at the video feed, "That's the man that was killed the other night."

A gray pall covered John Spector's face. He pressed a button on his phone and held it up to his ear. "We need to move, now!"

O'Brien came bursting through the door, "What's going on?"

"The delegation that's briefing the president – where are they?"

"Their security just peeled off. The briefers are in the Oval Office."

Spector pointed at Elena, "O'Brien, take her to the hub and get her connected with all the intelligence that we have. See if she can fill in the pieces for us." O'Brien waved furiously at Elena, who scooped up her laptop and ran out of the room after him.

Patrick stood up, his phone to his ear, slumping down in his chair. "I need to call the NTSB and issue an alert in case there are more missile strikes planned."

Spector looked at Travis and growled, "You're with me."

The two men took off running down the hallway, hitting the doorway for the stairs without breaking stride. Travis followed Spector as he took the steps two at a time, running up to the main floor of the White House. They emerged in a red-carpeted hallway. Travis charged down the hallway behind Spector, making his way between groups of aides and interns and congresspeople on their way to and from meetings. He could see Spector up ahead of him speaking into his radio on his wrist as he ran. The two men broke down to a walk just outside the Oval Office.

A team of four agents stood outside of the Oval Office door, each of them with their guns drawn. He looked at Travis, taking the gun from one of the agent's hands. It was a Glock 17, a full-sized nine-millimeter model. "You know how to use one of these?" Spector said, staring at him.

Travis pulled the slide back checking to make sure it was loaded and then looked back at Spector, his jaw set, his grip on the gun firm. "You bet I do."

Spector looked at the agents that were waiting, "Stay out

here and set up a perimeter. Notify Walter Reed of incoming and get the FBI here."

Spector shook his head, "You're coming with me. You can identify this guy. I'm gonna tell you right now, the President isn't gonna like this. He doesn't like drama and he doesn't like to have his meetings interrupted. That's why only the two of us are going in at the moment. Understood?"

"Understood."

Travis and Spector strode the few feet left to the door to the Oval Office as one of the Secret Service agents hustled the President's private secretary down the hallway and away from the scene. Spector turned the knob to the door slowly. Travis listened, only hearing muffled voices and a few grunts. Giving it a gentle push, Spector disappeared inside, Travis on his heels. The instant Travis pushed the door closed behind him, he heard a voice behind him, "You found me, Travis," Gus snorted.

Travis turned in time to see Gus hiding behind the door. He had a gun leveled at Spector's head and pulled the trigger. Spector's body dropped to the floor before John had a chance to defend himself. Without thinking, Travis pivoted on the balls of his feet, keeping his back to the wall, his gun up and ready to fire, his finger on the trigger. His heart was pounding in his chest. He could feel the sweat gathering at the back of his neck.

"You came a long way to ruin my fun," Gus declared, lowering the gun near his side.

Scanning the room, bile rose in the back of Travis's throat. Six members of the Joint Chiefs in full dress uniform were seated on two pale yellow couches that faced each other. Between them was a Queen Anne's style oval coffee table. Four of the six of them had their heads lolled off to the side, foam gathering at their lips. Two already had a pallor to their skin, blood dripping from their eyes. At the head of the grotesque gathering was President Mosley, still seated in his chair, the woman who'd been with the delegation holding a gun to his head. "Hello, Travis," she said sweetly.

Travis's eyes focused on the woman. A wave of nausea covered Travis. Thoughts pounded the inside of his mind. He felt like he couldn't catch his breath. "Kira?"

"I've missed you," she said while poking President Mosley's head with the barrel of her gun. President Mosley sat stock still, his eyes locked on Travis. Travis gave him a brief nod, hoping he would see by the look on Travis's face that he needed to stay calm. The Secret Service trained for hostage situations like this. They would know what to do. Travis just had to buy them some time.

"That was your voice on the phone last night, wasn't it?" Travis said, scanning the room. He was looking for anything he could use to his advantage. He could see Gus out of the corner of his eye, pacing back and forth in long strides muttering to himself, staring at the bodies of the Joint Chiefs as they lay dead and dying.

"It was." Kira shifted to stand right behind the President, using his body to block hers. President Mosely's hands were gripping the arms of his wooden chair, his knuckles white. His mouth was hanging open, his suit coat rumpled slightly.

"What happened in Ecuador?"

"Clearly nothing, you idiot!" Gus erupted, moving over to stand near Kira. "You thought she died. That was part of the plan to get her away from the Agency."

"I thought you died, too."

"No, I was trying to smoke out Elena. Uri helped me with that. I heard you ended up finding her."

"She found me."

"That's a shame. If you had done what I asked you to do and given her back to me, all of this could've been avoided."

"Not sure I believe you. Kinda looks like this was the point." Travis glanced over his shoulder toward the Oval Office door. It hadn't moved, Agent Spector's body blocking the entrance. Outside of the windows of the Oval Office, Travis thought he could see shadows of people moving. He hoped that the other Secret Service agents were getting in position to breach, but with the gun to the President's head, the odds weren't good that he'd survive if they did. The President still hadn't said anything, his eyes locked on Travis.

Kira yanked on the back collar of the president, "Stand up," she hissed, keeping the barrel of the gun to his face. President Mosley wasn't terribly tall, maybe only five feet seven inches. Kira, wearing heels that matched her burgundy skirt and jacket, had a good two inches on him. She wrapped her arm around the President's throat, his eyes wide and his lips pressed together in a grimace, as Kira kept the gun to his head. "I wore some special jewelry today, Travis." She opened the hand that was around President Mosley's throat exposing the inside of her ring, a short needle protruding from the inside of it. "I loaded this with one of Russia's finest nerve agents, Novichok. Have you heard of it? That's what got to all of these other fine men. Gus and I have been inoculated. You could dump us in a barrel of it and nothing would happen to us."

Travis didn't say anything, ignoring Kira's commentary. He kept the gun trained on Kira and watched Gus from his peripheral vision. Protecting the President was the priority. As he watched them, Travis was calculating. Something had to break soon. They couldn't stay like this for much longer.

Travis glanced at Kira. Even if he was able to get a shot off on her, Gus would still have the upper hand. It was two on one. Two Russians against one American. The odds weren't in his favor. His mouth felt dry. His hands started to shake. No more waiting. It was time to push. He kept his voice steady, leveling his gaze at Kira. "So, what are you gonna do? You gonna shoot him or poison him?"

"I haven't decided yet." As she answered, the sleeve from

her jacket slid down her arm as she readjusted it around President Mosley's neck. Travis could see a silver and turquoise bracelet glisten in the Oval Office's media-friendly lighting. Travis's eyes locked on the bracelet. Kira must have seen the shift in his eyes. She glanced at her wrist and then chided, "Oh, do you like my bracelet? Gus gave it to me."

Travis licked his lips, "It looks almost identical to the one I gave you."

"It is. It's always nice to have a special piece of jewelry from the man I love."

At that second, Kira turned to look at Gus, a smile spreading across Gus's face. Kira was baiting him. The reality of what happened landed on Travis like a ton of bricks. Kira and Gus had both been turned. They were both double agents, working for the Russians. Worse yet, Gus had stolen Kira from him. His own feelings about Kira choosing Gus and Russia over him didn't matter. His duty to the United States did. Something cracked inside of Travis. With a yell, he charged toward Kira, pulling off a shot that hit her right in the side of the temple as she stared lovingly at Gus. Before her body hit the ground, Travis threw his body over top of President Mosley, knocking the man to the ground underneath him with a thud and a groan. Lifting the gun, Travis aimed for Gus and caught him in the back as he turned to run.

Still in motion, Travis jumped up, standing over Gus and firing two more shots — one in his chest and one between his eyes, kicking the gun away from him and then away from Kira.

Leaning down, Travis offered President Mosley his hand and got him seated in the chair again before opening the door and yelling, "All clear! We need medics in here right now!"

EPILOGUE

The chaos that ensued after the attack in the Oval Office took days to unravel. The immediate consequences were that two of the six Joint Chiefs died on the scene, all of their bodies testing positive for the popular Russian poison Novichok. The hazmat teams from the CDC determined that the chemical agent, one of Russia's most favorite methods for taking out dissidents and people that didn't agree with their politics, had been rubbed on the briefing books that Gus and Kira had provided to the team. The other two men that were with Gus and Kira had disappeared before the meeting, slipping out a side door. The Secret Service caught them a block away as the attack ended, waiting in a van for Kira and Gus to return to make their escape. Before they ever left the scene, one of the men admitted Gus's code name was Stinger. Later on, it was discovered that a jet was fueled and waiting in a private airstrip less than an hour away from the White House with a short-term flight plan filed to Atlanta and then a jaunt overseas to land in Moscow the next day. That flight never happened.

The four remaining Joint Chiefs were treated on the scene

with an antidote and then airlifted to Walter Reed Medical Center where doctors predicted they would have a long-term recovery after time in the ICU, but would survive, likely with symptoms they'd never be able to recover from.

The President, the resilient man he was, shrugged off all but the most cursory medical examination, only agreeing to be ushered out of the Oval long enough for the hazmat teams to clean the poison and the dead bodies out of his office. There were five in total — two of the Joint Chiefs, Gus, Kira, and John Spector.

A phalanx of black-suited Secret Service agents ushered President Mosely down the hallway into a secure conference room. Travis, Patrick, and Elena joined him a second later. President Mosley loosened his tie and pulled off his jacket, laying it across the back of a chair. He started pacing at the head of the room while the three of them stood at the other end, two agents on either side of the President blocking their access to him. After a minute of pacing, President Mosley stared at the agents, "For God's sake, go make yourself useful and get these poor people something to eat and some water."

One of the Secret Service agents eyed up the three of them and then glanced back at the President, "Sir? We were told to stay with you."

"These people just saved my life. If they were gonna take me out, they had plenty of time to do it. I'm safe, now get outta here and go be helpful."

President Mosley shook his head, "These guys are well-intentioned but sometimes they really miss the point, if you know what I mean." He flopped down into the chair where he'd hung his jacket. He waved at the three of them, "Please, sit."

After a brief conversation about what had happened and how Travis, Patrick, and Elena had gotten to the White House, the President stood up and walked to the door of the room. "I've got some cleanup to do, including sending a hearty thanks to

Governor Torres. I hope you'll excuse me." He looked over his shoulder, "And by the way, thank you."

Travis, Patrick, and Elena spent the next three days in Washington DC, guests of the President. They were given a suite at the Continental Hotel downtown and a car and driver to use at their discretion. It was O'Brien, who had become like their personal tour guide, except the only places they were seeing were the inside of debriefing rooms after they'd talked to the Secret Service, the FBI, the CIA, the DIA, and a handful of other alphabet agencies that Travis started to get confused about after the first twelve hours.

Once the myriad of debriefings was over, the White House's travel agency scheduled Patrick and Travis for first-class flights back to Austin. Doug Parsons had been calling Patrick incessantly, needing him back at the office to deal with the fallout from Elena's plane crash. Patrick had to break the news to Doug that he'd found the pilot, but she wouldn't be able to help them. Elena had slipped away somehow in the middle of one of the debriefings. O'Brien mentioned later that she'd gotten recalled to Langley. Travis blinked when he heard the news. She hadn't bothered to say goodbye, but that was very Elena.

O'Brien dropped Travis and Patrick off at Reagan National, giving them a wave and a salute as he pulled away from the curb in front of the departures doors. Neither of them had any luggage, just the information given to them by the travel office for their flights. As they walked inside, Travis stopped, staring at Patrick. "You go on ahead."

Patrick shrugged, "What do you mean?"

"I've had my fill of planes." Travis turned on his heel and walked away.

AFTER RENTING a car at the airport, telling the young lady behind the counter wearing a nose ring and green streaks in her hair that it would be a one-way trip to Austin, she looked at him and chirped, "That's a long way to drive. You should fly."

Travis didn't bother answering her. He grabbed the keys out of her hand and stomped away. Everyone had an opinion.

Two days later after eating more fast food than he could stomach and taking brief naps at truck stops along the way, Travis pulled into the ranch, leaving the sedan parked outside with the keys in it. When he was an hour out, he called the rental agency in the area and told them to come pick up their car. They said they'd be there sometime that afternoon. He'd left the keys in it so he wouldn't be bothered when they showed up.

Travis got out of the car, taking a deep breath. He didn't go directly into the house. Instead, he walked down to the barn to check on the horses. It was early, the sun barely up over the horizon. They were due for their feeding, but Ellie hadn't arrived yet, though Travis would bet she was on her way. Travis walked halfway down the aisle going to the third stall on the left, the one where Kira's mare, Scarlett, had her home. Travis slid the door open, stepping into the stall, breathing in the woody scent of the pine shavings, the sweet smell of the hay left from the night before and the earthy scent of the animal in front of him. He put his hand up slowly, not wanting to spook the young mare, rubbing his hand on Scarlett's smooth neck. He stood there for a long time, soaking the warmth of her body into his hand. Scarlett was the only connection he had with Kira, and now she was gone. Really gone. And Travis had been the one who killed her.

As he walked out of the stall and closed the door, he noticed a new halter with a brass nameplate attached to the leather. He squinted, staring at the scrolled engraving. It read, "Scarlett – Owned by Kira Pozreva." A note hung from the halter on a thin thread with black block printing on it. The note said, "For Scarlett. Never forget the Motherland. Love, Uncle Uri."

Travis yanked the gift tag off the halter and stared in the distance. Kira and Gus might be finally gone, but somehow the life he had tried to leave behind wasn't ready to leave him.

A body disappears right from under the nose of law enforcement. What it contains is a threat unlike one Travis has ever seen before. Can he solve the mystery in time? Get Threat Rising now!

If you'd like to join my mailing list and be the first to get updates on new books and exclusive sales, giveaways and releases, click here!
I'll send you a prequel to the next series FREE!

THANKS FOR READING!

Thanks so much for taking the time to read *The Moscow Brief!* I hope you've been able to enjoy a little escape from your everyday life while joining Travis on his latest adventure.

If you have a moment, would you leave a review? They mean the world to authors like me!

If you'd like to join my mailing list and be the first to get updates on new books and exclusive sales, giveaways and releases, click here! I'll send you a prequel to the next series FREE!

Enjoy, and thanks for reading,
KJ

MORE FROM KJ KALIS...

Ready for another adventure? Check out these series!

Investigative journalist, Kat Beckman, faces the secrets of her past and tries to protect her family despite debilitating PTSD.
Visit the series page here!

Disgraced Chicago PD Detective, Emily Tizzano, searches for a new life by solving cold cases no one in law enforcement will touch.
Visit the series page here!

Intelligence analyst, Jess Montgomery, risks everything she has — including her own life — to save her family.
Visit the series page here!

Made in the USA
Middletown, DE
02 November 2023

41828045R00195